LEFT TO CRAVE

(An Adele Sharp Mystery—Book Thirteen)

BLAKE PIERCE

Blake Pierce

Blake Pierce is the USA Today bestselling author of the RILEY PAGE mystery series, which includes seventeen books. Blake Pierce is also the author of the MACKENZIE WHITE mystery series, comprising fourteen books; of the AVERY BLACK mystery series, comprising six books; of the KERI LOCKE mystery series, comprising five books; of the MAKING OF RILEY PAIGE mystery series, comprising six books; of the KATE WISE mystery series, comprising seven books; of the CHLOE FINE psychological suspense mystery, comprising six books; of the JESSE HUNT psychological suspense thriller series, comprising twenty one books; of the AU PAIR psychological suspense thriller series, comprising three books; of the ZOE PRIME mystery series, comprising six books; of the ADELE SHARP mystery series, comprising fifteen books, of the EUROPEAN VOYAGE cozy mystery series, comprising four books; of the new LAURA FROST FBI suspense thriller, comprising six books (and counting); of the new ELLA DARK FBI suspense thriller, comprising eleven books (and counting); of the A YEAR IN EUROPE cozy mystery series, comprising nine books, of the AVA GOLD mystery series, comprising six books (and counting); and of the RACHEL GIFT mystery series, comprising six books (and counting).

An avid reader and lifelong fan of the mystery and thriller genres, Blake loves to hear from you, so please feel free to visit www.blakepierceauthor.com to learn more and stay in touch.

ISBN: 978-1-0943-7610-3

BOOKS BY BLAKE PIERCE

RACHEL GIFT MYSTERY SERIES
HER LAST WISH (Book #1)
HER LAST CHANCE (Book #2)
HER LAST HOPE (Book #3)
HER LAST FEAR (Book #4)
HER LAST CHOICE (Book #5)
HER LAST BREATH (Book #6)

AVA GOLD MYSTERY SERIES
CITY OF PREY (Book #1)
CITY OF FEAR (Book #2)
CITY OF BONES (Book #3)
CITY OF GHOSTS (Book #4)
CITY OF DEATH (Book #5)
CITY OF VICE (Book #6)

A YEAR IN EUROPE
A MURDER IN PARIS (Book #1)
DEATH IN FLORENCE (Book #2)
VENGEANCE IN VIENNA (Book #3)
A FATALITY IN SPAIN (Book #4)

ELLA DARK FBI SUSPENSE THRILLER
GIRL, ALONE (Book #1)
GIRL, TAKEN (Book #2)
GIRL, HUNTED (Book #3)
GIRL, SILENCED (Book #4)
GIRL, VANISHED (Book 5)
GIRL ERASED (Book #6)
GIRL, FORSAKEN (Book #7)
GIRL, TRAPPED (Book #8)
GIRL, EXPENDABLE (Book #9)
GIRL, ESCAPED (Book #10)
GIRL, HIS (Book #11)

LAURA FROST FBI SUSPENSE THRILLER
ALREADY GONE (Book #1)
ALREADY SEEN (Book #2)
ALREADY TRAPPED (Book #3)
ALREADY MISSING (Book #4)
ALREADY DEAD (Book #5)
ALREADY TAKEN (Book #6)

EUROPEAN VOYAGE COZY MYSTERY SERIES
MURDER (AND BAKLAVA) (Book #1)
DEATH (AND APPLE STRUDEL) (Book #2)
CRIME (AND LAGER) (Book #3)
MISFORTUNE (AND GOUDA) (Book #4)
CALAMITY (AND A DANISH) (Book #5)
MAYHEM (AND HERRING) (Book #6)

ADELE SHARP MYSTERY SERIES
LEFT TO DIE (Book #1)
LEFT TO RUN (Book #2)
LEFT TO HIDE (Book #3)
LEFT TO KILL (Book #4)
LEFT TO MURDER (Book #5)
LEFT TO ENVY (Book #6)
LEFT TO LAPSE (Book #7)
LEFT TO VANISH (Book #8)
LEFT TO HUNT (Book #9)
LEFT TO FEAR (Book #10)
LEFT TO PREY (Book #11)
LEFT TO LURE (Book #12)
LEFT TO CRAVE (Book #13)
LEFT TO LOATHE (Book #14)
LEFT TO HARM (Book #15)

THE AU PAIR SERIES
ALMOST GONE (Book#1)
ALMOST LOST (Book #2)
ALMOST DEAD (Book #3)

ZOE PRIME MYSTERY SERIES

FACE OF DEATH (Book#1)
FACE OF MURDER (Book #2)
FACE OF FEAR (Book #3)
FACE OF MADNESS (Book #4)
FACE OF FURY (Book #5)
FACE OF DARKNESS (Book #6)

A JESSIE HUNT PSYCHOLOGICAL SUSPENSE SERIES
THE PERFECT WIFE (Book #1)
THE PERFECT BLOCK (Book #2)
THE PERFECT HOUSE (Book #3)
THE PERFECT SMILE (Book #4)
THE PERFECT LIE (Book #5)
THE PERFECT LOOK (Book #6)
THE PERFECT AFFAIR (Book #7)
THE PERFECT ALIBI (Book #8)
THE PERFECT NEIGHBOR (Book #9)
THE PERFECT DISGUISE (Book #10)
THE PERFECT SECRET (Book #11)
THE PERFECT FAÇADE (Book #12)
THE PERFECT IMPRESSION (Book #13)
THE PERFECT DECEIT (Book #14)
THE PERFECT MISTRESS (Book #15)
THE PERFECT IMAGE (Book #16)
THE PERFECT VEIL (Book #17)
THE PERFECT INDISCRETION (Book #18)
THE PERFECT RUMOR (Book #19)
THE PERFECT COUPLE (Book #20)
THE PERFECT MURDER (Book #21)

CHLOE FINE PSYCHOLOGICAL SUSPENSE SERIES
NEXT DOOR (Book #1)
A NEIGHBOR'S LIE (Book #2)
CUL DE SAC (Book #3)
SILENT NEIGHBOR (Book #4)
HOMECOMING (Book #5)
TINTED WINDOWS (Book #6)

KATE WISE MYSTERY SERIES
IF SHE KNEW (Book #1)

IF SHE SAW (Book #2)
IF SHE RAN (Book #3)
IF SHE HID (Book #4)
IF SHE FLED (Book #5)
IF SHE FEARED (Book #6)
IF SHE HEARD (Book #7)

THE MAKING OF RILEY PAIGE SERIES
WATCHING (Book #1)
WAITING (Book #2)
LURING (Book #3)
TAKING (Book #4)
STALKING (Book #5)
KILLING (Book #6)

RILEY PAIGE MYSTERY SERIES
ONCE GONE (Book #1)
ONCE TAKEN (Book #2)
ONCE CRAVED (Book #3)
ONCE LURED (Book #4)
ONCE HUNTED (Book #5)
ONCE PINED (Book #6)
ONCE FORSAKEN (Book #7)
ONCE COLD (Book #8)
ONCE STALKED (Book #9)
ONCE LOST (Book #10)
ONCE BURIED (Book #11)
ONCE BOUND (Book #12)
ONCE TRAPPED (Book #13)
ONCE DORMANT (Book #14)
ONCE SHUNNED (Book #15)
ONCE MISSED (Book #16)
ONCE CHOSEN (Book #17)

MACKENZIE WHITE MYSTERY SERIES
BEFORE HE KILLS (Book #1)
BEFORE HE SEES (Book #2)
BEFORE HE COVETS (Book #3)
BEFORE HE TAKES (Book #4)
BEFORE HE NEEDS (Book #5)

BEFORE HE FEELS (Book #6)
BEFORE HE SINS (Book #7)
BEFORE HE HUNTS (Book #8)
BEFORE HE PREYS (Book #9)
BEFORE HE LONGS (Book #10)
BEFORE HE LAPSES (Book #11)
BEFORE HE ENVIES (Book #12)
BEFORE HE STALKS (Book #13)
BEFORE HE HARMS (Book #14)

AVERY BLACK MYSTERY SERIES
CAUSE TO KILL (Book #1)
CAUSE TO RUN (Book #2)
CAUSE TO HIDE (Book #3)
CAUSE TO FEAR (Book #4)
CAUSE TO SAVE (Book #5)
CAUSE TO DREAD (Book #6)

KERI LOCKE MYSTERY SERIES
A TRACE OF DEATH (Book #1)
A TRACE OF MURDER (Book #2)
A TRACE OF VICE (Book #3)
A TRACE OF CRIME (Book #4)
A TRACE OF HOPE (Book #5)

CHAPTER ONE

In the quiet, in the mist, beneath the rustling branches of old, regimented trees, Adele Sharp stood over the body. Her breath plumed on the chill air, mingling with the swirl of opaque moisture. The trickling stream whispered at her feet. An accusatory sound, a burbling, murmuring hum of gossip as the water fled, carrying rumors through the rest of the park.

Adele's hands trembled at her side... With soft motions, she wiped the mud from her sidearm, placing it back in her holster, then buttoning it. Part of her wanted to fling the weapon as far away as she could, hiding it in the woods on the edge of the park.

But even now, she could hear the sound of sirens. Could hear the sound of rapidly approaching feet.

"Adele!" Agent Renee's voice was easy to pick out among the others shouts and calls. "Claudia! Hello!"

She didn't have the strength to respond. Behind her, Agent Renee's young daughter still clutched her backpack like a shield, sheltered under the bridge above. Her small shoes were stained in mud, and she kept shooting Adele looks of fear, as if wondering if she dared respond to the shouts in the woods.

Adele felt a lance of shame. "It's going to be fine," she murmured over her shoulder, not quite looking at the terrified ten-year-old.

She looked back towards the water. At least he was face-down. This way, in death, he could no longer watch her.

The Painter... a man with many names, none of them his original. She only knew him as the monster who'd tortured her mother to death.

And now Adele, and the rest of Paris, would only know him as a corpse.

Thin trails of red from the gunshots to his legs were still staining the stream, carried away by the churning liquid. His hand still clutched the knife he'd been reaching for, desperately.

He simply hadn't been able to let go of that stupid knife.

And so he'd drowned. His legs too weak from the wounds to rise.

And she'd watched him...

She could've helped—Adele knew that much. She could have

pulled him from the stream. But she'd shot him, watched him bleed in dark satisfaction, then watched him drown. She could still envision those little bubbles escaping from his horrible little mouth. The way they'd burst on the stream, a few feet further from where he'd submerged, thanks to the current.

It wasn't so much that she'd watched...

Wasn't even so much that she'd shot him.

More so... it was because she was glad that she'd done it.

Glad she hadn't helped. Glad she'd let him die.

Of course, according to DGSI training, refusal to render aid to a subdued suspect was akin to homicide. She'd killed the man who'd murdered her mother. Who'd tortured Robert Henry. Who'd hunted her ex-boyfriend.

"Adele!" a sudden, yelping shout from on top of the embankment. She heard footsteps, cursing. The sound of sirens still in the distance.

More murmured voices as figures followed Agent Renee's lead down the muddy embankment towards the bridge.

"Adele, where is—are you—"

The large Frenchman was shouting, but she could barely even hear him. She began to point under the bridge, her fingers still trembling horribly. So this was what shock felt like—she'd experienced it before, but never so potent. Her mind was misfiring. She couldn't quite make sense...

Ten years of her life... Ten years of motivation had all led to this.

Who was she now? What was she?

"Adele—Adele are you—Claudia! Holy Christ—Claudia! Come here... It's fine darling, come, come to me. No—no, don't be scared. Come here, dear please. Officer get away from her! Get back. Claudia, are you okay?"

Adele was still staring at the water, still staring at the corpse beneath the stream. One of the pale hands was fluttering now, loose, jounced about by the turbid churn. She didn't want to look back. Didn't want to meet John Renee's eyes. How many officers were with him?

Vaguely she heard more voices, the sound of more footsteps on the muddy hill. She heard the slap of booted feet against the bridge over the water. Then a shout from an unfamiliar tone. "A body—captain, there! See it?"

"Shit—go get an EMT. Agent Sharp!" another voice she didn't recognize barked. "Sharp, is he dead?"

More cursing, hurried footsteps. She was still standing over the corpse, still shivering. But she managed a single nod.

Dead? Was he?

Practically impossible to believe. How could he be dead? After all these years... was the bogeyman in the closet finally gone? Was she finally free?

Christ... It seemed unbelievable.

She thought of Robert Henry. Thought, even, of offering up a little prayer of gratitude like he so often had. But the words didn't fit her lips the same way they had his. She thought of closing her eyes, picturing her mother's smile. The truest love she'd ever experienced.

But this, too, seemed only a figment, a flyaway thought.

"What happened?" a voice demanded at her side. She felt a rough hand tugging at her arm. "Agent Sharp—what happened?"

"I'll make my report," Adele said softly.

Instead of one of Robert's prayers, instead of her mother's kiss, now all she could think of was the sound of her gun. The faint recoil on her hand. The grunt of pain. The mocking, malicious voice of the agonized serial killer. The way he'd dragged himself to grab his knife...

The churning, the thrashing...

Then the eventual silence.

"Self-defense," she said simply. "It will all be in my report."

And only then did she risk a glance back, under the bridge. Five officers in blue uniforms and thick jackets were moving about the scene. One of them, a woman, was trying to pry Claudia from John's grip, but Agent Renee kept snarling at her like some Doberman, flashing his teeth, eyes furious. Claudia was crying, her head pressed into her father's shoulder where she hugged him fiercely, holding onto the only familiar face.

Renee wasn't a fixture in the young girl's life, but he'd been making an effort in recent days. He'd been trying.

And now, he had a haunted look. The scar under his chin stretched down the side of his throat, towards his chest. It stood out pale in the mist.

"It's going to be alright," Renee murmured in his daughter's ears. And Adele was stunned to see him crying. "I won't leave you. I swear it. I won't." He stroked his daughter's hair. The backpack was now discarded on the ground at Renee's feet.

How often had John Renee said the same things to her. *It's going to be alright.*

And he'd been right. It was alright.

But to make it so, she'd killed a man. She'd watched him die when she could have helped. She'd been forced to pull the trigger before, but only when confronted with danger herself. This... this was different.

Self-defense?

He'd been disarmed... Desperate. Drowning. She'd stood only a pace away, refusing to lift even a finger. She'd seen enough cases prosecuted against cops who overstepped the bounds to know that if there'd been a camera on her, this one would be a slam dunk for the prosecution.

She was a murderer.

Just like the painter had wanted...

It's not the same thing... A small voice in her mind protested. *Not the same thing at all.* She wanted to believe this. Wanted more than anything to believe she'd won. He hadn't.

She felt the hand still tugging insistently at her sleeve, trying to pull her away from the stream. She stumbled, feet pressing into slick mud and pulling again with a faint sucking sound. She didn't want to leave. Didn't want to move.

She wanted to keep an eye on the monster. Just to make sure.

Another little shiver trembled down her spine. John and his daughter were beneath the bridge, but Claudia's tear-filled eyes were open again. They glanced around, blinking. When they settled on Adele, though, Claudia just stared.

Adele looked back, shivering again.

No one had been here to witness the shooting. No one had seen him drown.

No one except for John Renee's ten-year-old daughter.

Would she tell what happened? Would she even be able to piece it together? She'd been so frightened. Adele had saved her, in a fashion. The killer had wanted to do horrible things. But would Claudia understand any of it?

"Please—come with me. I need you to answer a few questions, agent. Would you like a jacket?"

The voice in her ear seemed a disembodied thing. She was only staring at Claudia now.

The girl looked away again, burying her face in her father's shoulder.

Another jolt of panic.

What if Claudia told *John*? Would she be able to face him?

Renee had offered to get his hands dirty on her behalf in the past... But he cared for her because she was better than that. At least, that's what he'd said. A fat lot of good it would do to preserve their relationship to embark on the next stage behind bars.

The same niggling voice in her mind returned. *You did what you had to...*

"Shut up," she snarled beneath her breath, beginning to move, allowing herself to be guided away by the officer at her hip.

No amount of trying to convince herself she'd done the right thing—done what she *had* to do—would change the fact that she'd killed a man in cold blood. She could remember countless other times where she'd rushed to the aid of a suspect after they'd been contained. Only months ago, in Venice, she'd shot a killer, then hurried to his side to stop the bleeding.

But this time... no.

She'd watched him die. She'd let him drown.

And she'd meant to do it.

"Come this way," the voice said at her side. "Please, Agent Sharp. Just a few questions. You can speak with your partner later."

Questions indeed. The first of many questions, interviews, maybe even interrogations.

CHAPTER TWO

Their luxurious mountain home stood against the backdrop of the Swiss Alps. Snow-tipped peaks and gray flanks cradling prickling firs caressed a descending horizon of wispy clouds stippled with starlight.

Anita Vosloo's turn signals blinked behind her as she locked her Mercedes' doors. She strode around the car, briefcase in one hand, her high heels clicking against the smooth asphalt of the driveway.

She heard the quiet whir of the metal gate behind her, up the driveway, slowly closing. Ahead, their home overlooked the mountains, with a hot tub in the backyard, visible just around the edge of the brickwork.

A light was on in the garage, and she paused, peering through the window.

"Henry?" she called, frowning. She could see the edge of his BMW mirror through the garage's window. His car was here...

"Henry?" she called, louder, frowning.

But where was he?

She sighed, glancing towards her keys then back at her sedan. Her husband had made a habit out of parking the cars for her. At least, that's what he said. *For her.* Really, it was for him. He was worried she'd accidentally scrape the paint of his beloved BMW.

"Just the one time," she muttered beneath her breath. She glanced at her watch, and then her cell phone. No messages.

Normally, when the gate up the driveway triggered, it would alert her husband's phone. He had ample time to reach the driveway and pull her car into the garage. She couldn't remember the last time he'd been late.

Briefly, she wondered if she ought to just do it herself. But she remembered the last time someone had scraped his car, and how Henry hadn't left his study for a week. She sighed, muttering beneath her breath about men and their toys before deciding it was perhaps best to just find her husband.

She moved up the mansion's steps and towards the two, large oak doors. A sizable cardboard box, with multiple strands of plastic binding, rested on the top step. The box had been ripped open, packing foam visible where it had been returned to the container once the desired contents had been removed.

She paused long enough to glance towards the label on the front of the large, empty box. *Leon Antiques.*

"Ah, it arrived," she murmured to herself. At least this would put her husband in a good mood. "Henry! Where are you? I'm home, dear!"

But again, no response. She pushed open the door to their home—they rarely locked it--and stepped into the main atrium. Two curling staircases met at the top of an overhead walkway. But the lights downstairs were off... Strange. She glanced off down a side hall, towards her husband's study.

The door was closed, but there was no light beneath the doorway either.

Strange...

She frowned but then spotted an item in the middle of the atrium, beneath the walkway.

A large grandfather clock. The same item they'd bid on at the auction only days ago. The packing material outside had been clue enough but now here was the actual prize.

Even in the dark, the antique clock, with its brass face and etched Koa wood sides was something to admire. A sinker redwood frame for the misty glass up top only helped seal the abalone trim.

Another one of her husband's little toys.

It was quite a nice piece, though. Henry had insisted they win it at the auction—and when her husband wanted something, he often got it.

She reached out, flicking on the lights.

But they didn't work.

She frowned, glancing towards the switch and trying it again. The lights remained off. "Henry?" she said, a bit quieter now, speaking into the enormous, old home. A slow shiver trembled up her spine.

She lowered her briefcase slowly, and took a hesitant step further into the house, towards her husband's study. He normally kept the door closed when he was working on a day-trade, but why were the lights off?

Her fingers trembled in front of her now. She frowned at this subconscious reaction. Normally, she didn't consider herself a particularly timid person.

Why weren't the lights working, though?

Where was her husband?

She reached the door to her husband's study, feeling a cold dread flooding through her. Her fingers gripped the handle, and she wet her lower lip with a dab from her tongue.

Then, as cold as the snow-capped mountains, she tried the handle.

The door swung smoothly open, revealing a large study, with an enormous oak and mahogany desk and a model ship on top of an aquarium in one corner. Her husband's computer was still on—flashing lights and fast-moving scroll as the computer tracked the changes in the market. Binders and binders of information, printed, rested against the side of her husband's desk.

But no sign of the man himself.

She stared towards the aquarium, watching the piranhas in the tank swirl about. She hated those fish, but her husband was quite fond of the little, prickly-toothed devils.

She tried the light switch by the door...

This one didn't work either.

Had the breaker switched? Perhaps Henry was dealing with the lights.

She glanced through the room a final time, looking for any sign of—

Ding...

She nearly leapt from her skin, whirling around at the sudden, muted noise. Eyes wide, heart hammering, she winced, readjusting her foot where she'd nearly twisted her ankle in those stupid high heels.

Where was that sound coming fr—

Ding!

A faint, pathetic noise... Coming from the grandfather clock.

She stared at the old antique, and the glassy face stared back. Another faint *Ding!*

Cold shivers still maneuvered up her back, but as she stared at the clock, her heart raced... Something was off with that sound. She remembered the deep, bass boom of the clock striking the hour back at the auction house. It was one of the things that had drawn her husband to it.

Another, pathetic little *Ding!*

She approached the old antique, suddenly very conscious of how much larger it was than her. The top was nearly a foot taller, and it was wider than two of her standing side by side.

Ding!

Now, the shivers up her back came with a churning stomach. She reached out the same shaking hand, wishing desperately the damn lights had been on.

"Henry?" she called again, louder.

Ding!

She gripped the brass latch on the side of the antique clock, pried it open with relative ease. And then, feeling quite silly for being spooked by a stupid clock in a big house, she opened the grandfather clock. *Ding!*

Darkness met her gaze. The shadow of the stairs above, the interior shadows of the clock, the lack of lights—it all made it difficult to see.

Nothing… Nothing in the clock at all. 'he'd been acting silly.

This was all...

What was that?

A pale *something* suspended in the shadows. She reached out, hesitantly, prodding the pale thing.

Cold skin.

A hand.

A scream caught in her throat. The motion of her push suddenly knocked loose a false, wooden panel.

A body spilled out, tumbling towards her and crashing to the ground in front of the old clock.

Now, the scream ripped from her lungs. Anita stumbled back, screeching at the ceiling, hands in front of her to protect her face.

But the body w'sn't moving... a corpse.

Dead.

'he'd stumbled back so far, her shoulder blades pressed to the door of her husb'nd's study now. Her ankle ached—this time, in her haste, she *had* sprained it.

Still gasping, wide-eyed, staring in horror, her vision adjusted in the dim dark.

She recognized that combover, reddish hair streaked with white. Recognized those eyes—normally so warm, so friendly. Now empty and cold.

"Henry...," she murmured, horror in her chest, hyperventilating now. "H—henry..."

Her dead husband just stared back at her, his one hand laying ahead of him, flat on the tiled floor as if he were reaching towards her, pleading for help.

Dead.

"Henry!" she screamed again.

But this time, the sound was drowned out by a deep, bass, *DONG!* as the grandfather clock rang again.

CHAPTER THREE

In Adele's assessment, “paid leave” might as well have been called “incentivized exile.” She lay on the couch, her arm over her eyes, blocking out the sunlight streaming through her apartment window. In the kitchen, she could hear her father—who'd extended his stay—moving about the unit. By the sound of clinking glasses and swishing water, he was tidying up.

Seven days had passed since the incident in the park.

Seven days of lounging around her apartment, waiting for one of two results. The all clear from Foucault himself, allowing her back into the field, or—the far more horrible option—a knock on the door, followed by a raid of cops with cuffs, looking to drag her downtown.

Every ring of the doorbell, every thump of her neighbors' closing doors, or the rustle of the postman just outside her unit—it all roused a sense of dread.

Would they believe her report? So far, it didn't seem like John's daughter had contradicted anything. At least, not that Adele was aware of. Claudia had simply told the police that she'd been kidnapped, and Adele had saved her. For now, that's all they knew. But stories could often change...

“Gaaaah!” she moaned at the ceiling, her eyes still hidden behind her raised arm. “This is the worst!”

Her father turned off the faucet in the kitchen. She heard the faint sound of swishing cloth as he dried his hands. Then, the Sergeant's gruff voice echoed into the living room. “Haven't heard back yet?”

“No.”

“They said it would take a few days, yes?”

“It's been seven, Dad!” she moaned.

Adele wasn't particularly proud of her tone. She felt like a child, kicking and groaning on the way to the dentist. But part of her liked this space.

Children couldn't be blamed... not really.

Not the way an adult could be.

Children, by and large, didn't murder.

The same sense of anxiety she'd familiarized with swirled through her stomach. Adele hunched now, wincing on the couch and wishing with all her might she could just be swallowed by the cushions.

She could still hear his sneering voice. Could still feel the recoil of her weapon as she shot him. Could still hear the faint burble of bursting air as he drowned in the stream. And more than any of it, could feel the way her mind had reeled. Her legs had anchored to the muddy shore beneath the bridge.

She'd watched him die. She'd wanted him to die.

Was it really murder?

Yes. A small voice blurted back just as quickly. A voice she'd been contending with for the last seven days. A voice she didn't much like at all.

He'd been hurting Claudia—he'd been threatening Adele.

But he was unarmed. Injured.

He'd been reaching for a knife.

But then he'd let it go. He was drowning. You could've helped him. You were duty bound to render aid.

Adele felt another burst of anxiety in her stomach. There were no two ways about it. She'd killed a man. Her finger had been on the trigger. Her indifferent gaze had glared down like a spotlight on his drowning form.

Of course, he'd deserved it. He'd deserved far worse.

That wasn't the point.

"Deserved" had nothing to do with legal. Justice didn't always have anything to do with it either. The Spade killer, the Painter as he called himself, had skated in Paris on a technicality—statute of limitations. They didn't have evidence for his most recent murders. So the police had let him loose. Claudia had been captured because the justice system hadn't done its job.

How was that right?

She shivered again, pressing her head against the stuffed arm of the cushioned couch. No matter how she justified it, or what way she looked at it, Adele knew the truth. Evil people did evil things—it was her job to stop them without becoming like them.

And she'd failed.

She was... a... a...

Murderer. The same voice whispered.

"Merde!" she spat at the ceiling.

"Language!" her father snapped in English.

Adele wrinkled her nose, lowering her arm and blinking against the sunlight stinging the back of her eyelids. "This is my place, isn't it?" she said petulantly.

"Well, you should have a no-swearing policy wherever you are," her father returned, standing near the kitchen still.

"I have a swearing policy," she said. "At least two curses per day or you're fined. Let's hear it Dad. Give me your best cuss."

She heard a resigned sigh, followed by thumping footsteps as her father's sturdy frame moved from the kitchen towards the couch beneath the sun. She heard a faint creak as he sat on the opposite arm of the couch.

She blinked, wincing against the sun and shifting her head a bit so her father's outline blocked most of the glare. He wore a familiar white t-shirt and his sailor-strong arms, hairy as ever, were flecked with soap bubbles from the sink. His thick, drooping mustache hadn't been combed yet this morning and jutted wildly every direction.

"This isn't like you," her father said simply, staring at her. "Get off the couch. Go *do* something."

She looked back at him. For a moment, she felt irritated, but then the tone of his voice penetrated her cloudy thoughts. Not angry, not judgmental... *concerned.* Odd this. Her father was concerned for her? He rarely showed it.

She sighed, waving the same hand she'd shielded her eyes with. "I'm not supposed to go anywhere. Not until I'm cleared."

"You're not supposed to leave Paris. That's not the same thing as going for a jog or a swim. You used to love swimming."

"Yeah. Like two decades ago."

"That long? You're getting old, Adele."

It took her a second to realize he was joking. She snorted, rolling her eyes. "Not all of us can stay young forever like you." She propped up on the couch, blinking and allowing her vision to adjust to the light through the window.

Her father had been staying with her during the incident. He'd extended his stay after he'd heard what had happened. What she'd done.

He was...

Happier now.

It seemed strange to say it. But his gruff edges, his harsher mannerisms—they were still there, but *less* somehow. He smiled more. She'd even caught him whistling the other day.

"You know, Adele...," he said carefully, his hand moving from the couch towards her foot. For a moment, it looked like he wanted to pat it out of affection, but instead he lost his nerve and patted the cushion. Still, his eyes were gentle. "I want you to know something..."

"We're not out of soap, are we?"

“Funny. No, I'm being serious. Listen to me.”

Adele remained propped on her elbow, watching her father. If anything, he looked nervous all of a sudden: uncomfortable. His cheeks were turning an odd rosy hue.

“What is it? Are you alright?” she said suddenly, pushing up a bit further until she was sitting straight postured, her arms dangling over her knees towards her feet.

“I’m fine—I’m… Yes. T’at's what I wanted to say... Just...,” his voice grew hoarse and he looked away now, scowling towards the ground as he so often did when he got even a whiff of an emotion. But he summoned some hidden courage and looked back at her. “You did good, kid.”

“I... I'm not sure what you mean.” Of course, she knew exactly what he was talking about.

“You did what I never could. For years I tried. Years. But you did it. You put that evil little runt in the ground. You buried the bastard.”

“Language,” she reminded him, half out of humor but also to deflect. She didn't want to talk about this with him. Not again.

“No, Adele, I mean it.” This time, he did place his hand on her foot, patting it like one might a puppy's head. Still, for him, this was the same as a deep hug and tears. “I'm proud of you,” he said, his voice hoarse. He bobbed his head, his wiry mustache shifting. “Very proud.”

He couldn't quite bring himself to look her in the eyes, and his cheeks were still tinged red. The sunlight behind him illuminated his form, washing them both in a warm glow.

He'd been acting odd ever since she'd told him. Ever since he'd drowned. As if he wanted to reconcile... Cleaning her dishes, even something as stupid as patting her foot. And now this... *proud.* She could count on half the knuckles of one finger the number of times her father had said anything like this. Did her father want to reconcile? To turn over a new leaf?

How often had she hoped for this very thing? How often had she desperately wanted reconciliation with her dad?

But now... like this?

She forced a smile, allowing it to twist her lips. But it was painful. Inwards, she only felt horror. She hadn't told him the truth. Hadn't told anyone.

“Dad,” she said hesitantly, her own voice also hoarse. “Look—I... It's not what you think.”

He wasn't listening though, still frowning at the ground as if lost in thought, his hand pressed against her shin, his skin warm.

She went quiet, still. Did it even matter to tell him? Would he care at all? Self-defense. That's what she'd said. That's what she'd told everyone.

Would her father care that she'd let him drown? Would he care that his baby girl was now a killer, too?

Was she just being too hard on herself?

That wasn't how the courts would see it. Certainly not in the present climate. No. If it ever leaked, what had actually transpired in the park—if Claudia told someone, Adele would spend the next couple of decades behind prison bars.

No... She couldn't do that to him. He'd lost his wife already. She wouldn't plant the seed that he might lose her too.

So she kept her smile fixed, reaching out to pat her father's hand where it rested. "Thanks, Dad. I'm proud of you too. I'm glad it's...," she swallowed, feeling a surge of anxiety. "Glad it's over."

The Sergeant was still lost in thought, but as she retracted her hand, her phone began to buzz.

Adele's heart jolted. Seven days had passed. She was expecting the all-clear any day now. If the news was coming by phone, rather than a battering ram at her door, then it most likely was good news.

She pried her phone from her pocket, swiveling until her feet hit the cold ground and the sunlight caught her silhouette.

When she saw who was calling, though, she felt a jolt of nerves.

Not Foucault. Not work.

John wanted to video chat.

She hesitated, thumb hovering over the screen. Did she want to see him? Want him to see her?

"Who is it?" her dad said. "Not Jim, is it?"

"John, Dad. You know his name."

The Sergeant grunted. "Whatever. You gonna answer—that beep is annoying."

"It's my phone, Dad. Look fine—I'm answering."

She sighed, pushing off the couch and moving towards the kitchen as she held the device up towards her face.

It took a second for the phone to connect, but then her screen changed, and she found herself looking at the handsome face of John Renee. His hair was neatly in place, gelled, save a single strand dangling over one eye. His dark gaze seemed to flick around a moment as if trying to decide if he ought to look at the camera or the screen.

At last, he settled on something in between. "Adele," John said, his voice a bit delayed compared to the motion of his pixelated lips.

She waved, nodding. Her stomach still twisted. Was he calling because his daughter had told him? Was this how she was going to find out her fate?

"Hey Adele," John said with a sigh. "Look, I just wanted to call to see how you were do—"

"Fine."

"No, I mean just—"

"Doing great, John. How are you?" Adele's voice softened. "How's Claudia?"

John gave a half-smile at this, nodding. "Good. She's good. Thanks for asking. Scared—with her mother right now. But—yeah, she's tough."

"Renees often are."

He nodded, brushing a hand through his hair. The loose curl lifted but then fell again, hopelessly out of place. "Just wanted to let you know I'm sorry for not contacting you sooner. Things have just been—"

"Busy."

"I was going to say hectic. But yeah. Busy. We've been seeing a counselor with Claudia. Her mother is going to home-school her. My visiting weekends have been extended."

"Good for you."

"Yeah, I guess so." He scratched his jaw, his fingers brushing over the top of his scar. "Never really saw myself as a, well, you know, *dad.* But there's a first time for everything."

Adele glanced towards where her own father was still sitting on the arm of the couch, peering out the window into the streets of Paris.

"I'm happy for you. So you think you're going to take some time off still?"

John bobbed his head. "Leave of absence for another few days at least. Just until Claudia is feeling better. Though, I'm not sure after something like that you ever *truly* feel better. Just... Just thanks Adele. For, you know. Everything."

Adele smiled back, nodding. "I'm glad I got there in time."

"Yeah. Me too." John scratched his chin. "Look, I should probably let you go. But was just thinking it might be nice next week if you wanted to stop by during one of my weekend days. Claudia has been asking about you."

"She has?" Adele's heart skipped a beat.

"Yeah. Think she wants to thank you for saving her. I know I've already said it, but for what it's worth, I'm also super, super—"

"You've done the same for me many times," Adele cut him off, feeling another surge of guilt. “Thanks John. Really. I'd love to spend some time with your daughter. Just tell me when.”

Though she was smiling again, though the sunlight streamed through the window, Adele couldn't shake the strange, dark cloud descending on her... It came like chill wind, like a sudden shiver... A strange sense of sheer...

Isolation.

Her father was proud of her. John wanted to spend time with her and his daughter.

Her relationships were all doing great—for now... So why did she feel so isolated?

Liar... the voice whispered.

She gritted her teeth, but disguised it by forcing another smile. “Thanks John,” she said. “Oh—hey, look, I'm getting another call. I'll hit you up tonight. Alright?”

“Sounds good. Take care, Adele.”

Adele flashed a thumbs up and used the same motion to swipe to the next call, frowning as she did.

This time, as she spotted the name, her heart went still.

Foucault.

On the phone.

Good news?

She glanced towards her door. No shadows in the hall. No sound of police officers preparing to barge in. She answered.

“Yes, sir?” she said, her anxiety heightened.

“Hello, Agent Sharp,” Foucault said. “How are you?”

“Fine sir. Great sir. What's the news?”

“Right—well, I have your clearance form here. Just waiting for a signature. I know it's sort of rushed, but with Agent Renee taking a leave of absence we're a bit short staffed. I was wondering if—”

“Yes! I mean, sorry... Yes, I'd be happy to.”

“Well... Alright then. It's a fresh case, and I already have a primary assigned. You'll be assisting. Is that amenable?”

“Whatever you need sir,” Adele replied reflexively. Part of her wondered if this was the best idea, taking a new case so quickly after what had happened last time. But she couldn't spend the next week trapped in her apartment. Not again. She needed a distraction. Needed something to focus on.

“Look, Adele,” Foucault said, “this is an important one to me. It's...” He cleared his throat and for a moment, Adele frowned. Did the executive sound... *nervous*?

"Is everything alright, sir?"

He sighed on the other end. "Yes, Agent Sharp. It's fine. One of the victims is a close personal—well, my cousin, in fact."

Adele's eyebrows shot up. "I'm—I'm so sorry."

"Me too. But look, I need the best on this, Adele. If you can solve this for me, I'll owe you one. I don't normally—well, you know how I operate—I don't normally pull levers. It's not my style."

"Of course not."

"But if you solve this, I'll owe you a favor as well. Find who killed him."

Adele felt her stomach twist. Again, she wondered what Foucault might think if he knew what had actually happened in that misty park beneath the bridge, amidst the mud and streams of swirling water.

For now, though, he was offering an olive branch.

His own cousin, murdered. Horrible. Truly. Her heart went out to him.

But another part of her, a small, whispering part suggested just how valuable it might prove to have the Executive of the DGSI owe her something. Especially if any *other* news about the death of the Painter came to light.

"I'll do it. Should I come in for details or—"

"Yes. I'll brief you myself. Come quick. Thanks, Adele," he cleared his throat again. "Just—yes, well, thank you. See you shortly."

Then he hung up.

CHAPTER FOUR

Adele glanced out the passing windows as the elevator moved up from the garage. A small, pink café sat outside the DGSI headquarters. The whole place still faintly smelled of paint as the building had only been renovated for federal use fifteen years ago.

And yet to Adele, it felt like only yesterday. All of this seemed new, in a strange way. Foreign. Even as the elevator doors dinged open, revealing the carpeted, third hall's floor.

Adele inhaled shakily, staring down the hall towards the foreboding opaque glass door. Things felt different now, somehow.

As the doors closed behind her, she summoned some inner courage and marched towards the executive's office.

Before she reached the door, though, she pulled up short.

Foucault was sitting in the hall, spinning a cigarette between his fingers. The DGSI executive's pronounced nose beneath dark brows reminded her of an eagle's beak. He wore a neat, pressed blue-pinstripe suit with notched lapels. And currently, spinning the cigarette in one hand, he stared at the glass of his shut office door as if in shock.

Adele approached slowly, clearing her throat as she neared.

He looked up, spotted her and the spinning cigarette suddenly went still.

"Agent Sharp," he said with a nod. "Thank you for your haste."

"Foucault. I thought you quit."

"Wh-oh. Just an old habit. I like holding it is all. Forget about that. Files are there."

Adele glanced towards the seat next to her boss at the two red, plastic folders, each marked with a case number on the front. "Two?" she said.

"Just two for now."

"Which one is..."

"My cousin?" An extended cigarette tapped the top folder. "Hercule Foucault. He was in Belgium at the time." Foucault spoke with stiff, jolting words, his eyes narrowed. His tone was flat, his expression emotionless. But the little white cigarette was spinning rapidly again, between two fingers.

Adele slowly lowered herself on the bench facing the boss's door.

Out of the corner of her eye, she watched the way he scowled above the carpet. Normally, so professional, now Foucault seemed a bundle of nerves.

"Two days before, Herc was the first victim," Foucault said matter-of-factly, his voice tinged with only the faintest of growls. "An antique-collector, my cousin—they found him in an old wardrobe he'd purchased."

Adele picked up the folder and flipped it open, frowning at the crime scene photos. Bright, glossy images beneath the fluorescent lights in the hall stared back at her. A picture of the victim: he looked quite similar to the executive, with the same hooked nose, and thick, bushy eyebrows.

Below, the crime scene photos splayed out as she set the folder on her lap. Pictures of a body found inside an old chestnut wardrobe in a small room. One arm dangled out of the wardrobe where it had been discovered. The face was obscured in the first picture, hidden in shadow.

"Cause of death?" Adele murmured, scanning towards the coroner's report.

"Stab wound," Foucault said simply.

"Ah—yes, here. I see..." Adele leaned in, frowning, tucking her tongue inside her cheek. Now that she had a case file in one hand, sitting next to the executive, she felt a bit more at home. Other thoughts—other, far more distracting thoughts, were now sitting on a back burner.

The hunt always caught her attention. John Renee often called her a bloodhound with a scent, and while she resented the comparison to some animal, the sentiment was accurate.

Plus...

Adele felt a flicker of her own anxiety, her hand trembling where it gripped the top folder. If Claudia told anyone what she'd seen back beneath that bridge, then Adele would need an ally like Foucault. He'd asked her on this case as a personal favor. Being owed one by the head of the DGSI could go a long way in keeping Adele out of prison...

Is that what you want? Adele gritted her teeth, her fingers still shaky. *To get away with it? You're a killer. Just like him.*

She let out a long, shaky breath, pretending to read the coroner's report, but her vision was swimming. Perhaps she was a killer. Perhaps it was too late to take it back.

But for now, avoiding a cell was motivating enough. She knew how Foucault treated his friends. Once, Agent Sophie Paige's husband had been a suspect in a federal case. Foucault had gone to bat for his friend, Sophie, and her family.

It had made all the difference.

"Adele?" the executive was saying. "Did you hear me? What do you think?"

She looked up, startled, hesitant and began to shake her head. "I—I..." She frowned. "Sorry, what did you say?"

"The stab wound. Not a knife. Any guesses?"

Adele turned slowly, flipping the picture again towards the coroner's report and the square photos attached.

There, outlined in cold flesh, she spotted clean puncture wounds. Two of them, both above the heart.

She frowned, leaning in, studying the wounds. They were shaped like diamonds, the wounds about the diameter of a human thumb. But the shape itself was clearly caused by something geometric, with four sides.

"How deep are these—oh, never mind." Adele said, finding the appropriate section in the report. She whistled softly a moment later, looking up, eyes wide. "Pierced straight through the heart? Twice? Not a knife, but it pierced deeper than one."

Foucault, though, was determinedly looking away, down the hall again. Adele winced, realizing she'd shifted the folder, so the coroner's pictures were angled towards the boss. She closed it. "Sorry," she muttered.

He ignored this and said, "We don't know the murder weapon yet. Nothing was found on the premises of either murder. Perhaps a fire poker, maybe some mechanical instrument. Certainly something to pay attention to."

"Right, and the second victim?"

"Swiss. Found in a grandfather clock."

"In? Like inside—the same as the old wardrobe?"

Foucault glanced back and seemed relieved to find Adele had closed the folder. He pushed slowly to his feet, his back arching like a cat in sunlight. "Yes," he murmured. "The same way. The same exact wounds. Two punctures through the heart. Both men," he cleared his throat, "were very wealthy."

"I see." Adele remained sitting. "Alright—well... Perhaps the best starting spot is to retrace—"

"You already have a plane booked for Switzerland, Adele. Remember, I already have a primary for the case."

"Of course, sir. Whatever works." Adele, sensing this meeting was coming to a close, also reached her feet, watching Foucault. A sudden *ding* resounded from the elevators.

"Ah, speaking of... Here she is."

Adele turned, frowning, feeling a slow shiver up her spine.

And then, her teeth pressed tightly together in frustration.

Agent Sophie Paige was marching stiff-legged as ever, towards the two of them, a look on her face like she'd sniffed something smelly.

"Oh," Adele said, trying not to tense too much. "Paige is lead on this one?" she asked innocently.

"The two of you have the best closer rates in the department. Like I mentioned, this one's personal to me, Agent Sharp."

Adele winced, watching as the older DGSI agent approached. Sophie Paige looked like a retired nun. She had dark hair now turning white brushed neatly behind both ears and held in a simple ponytail. She wore no jewelry and her suit looked immaculate. Given the five kids she helped raised, Adele didn't know how the woman always looked so put-together.

As she neared, Adele detected the faintest hint of soap. No perfume—just a clean, soap smell.

For a moment, frowning at Agent Paige, Adele felt an urge to turn to Foucault and make some excuse. More than anything, she wanted to refuse the case.

But if she did that now, everyone would know why.

Things with Paige were rough, but they'd been able to work together in the past. Paige had even kept tabs on the Painter for a few hours the previous week as a favor to Adele. Then again, he'd managed to slip her surveillance. They now, at least, could abide each other's company. To an extent. But years ago, Adele had reported missing evidence to the higher-ups. She thought she'd simply been going by the book. But Paige hadn't seen it the same way when the trail had led back to her husband. Things had worked out in the end, with Foucault intervening on behalf of his friend, but bad blood remained.

The case was personal to her boss. Now, if she refused, it wouldn't just be a slight to Paige, but also to Foucault. Being owed a favor by the executive was a far cry from being resented by him.

She sighed, reaching her conclusion and extending her hand which didn't hold the folders.

"Hello, Agent Paige," she said stiffly.

"Adele," the older agent said. She ignored the extended hand and instead snatched the folders from her grip. "Plane booked yet?"

Foucault nodded. "Yes, Sophie. Do you have everything?"

Agent Paige looked up from the folders, glancing towards Adele. She let out a world-weary sigh, not quite rolling her eyes and yet somehow communicating the sentiment. "I suppose," she muttered. "We should get going, Adele."

And then, the woman turned, marching right back where she'd come from, both folders clutched in her hand, her head bowed as if in prayer as she read the folder while power-walking back to the elevators.

Adele bit back any response, hiding her sudden flare of resentment as best she could.

"Good luck, Agent Sharp," the boss muttered, still spinning his cigarette. His tone hardened suddenly, and his eyes stared off, distant as if seeing something Adele couldn't. "No failure on this one—Adele. I mean it. You and Paige are the best I've got. I expect results." He then growled beneath his breath, twisted his cigarette, tossing it onto the carpeted floor before shoving roughly back through his office door, slamming it behind him.

Adele released a long sigh of resignation, and slowly made the long walk towards the waiting elevator and Agent Paige.

***

Agent Paige had conquered the armrest. The small plane shook and jolted around them as they were carried through a bout of turbulence.

Adele's own arms squished against her as she fidgeted uncomfortably in the airplane seat. She hadn't been allowed the seat by the window or aisle, either. Instead, whoever had booked the tickets, had decided to plop her smack dab in the middle of two economy seats.

Adele shifted again, avoiding the large man sitting in the aisle seat, trying to turn Agent Paige who was by the window, examining the photographs in the folders which she'd displayed on the lowered table. The man on the other side of Adele kept shooting glances past her, towards the photos.

"What?" Paige snapped as the man glanced for a third time.

He pretended he couldn't hear, pushing in his earbuds deeper and staring at the small television screen in front of him, while wiggling his great girth to settle.

Adele tried to avoid the elbow jamming into her forearm, but she was quickly running out of personal space to retreat to. She angled away from the man, trying to examine the folder on Sophie's table.

"Do you mind?" Paige said, scowling as Adele brushed her arm.

"No. Sorry," Adele replied, though it felt like pulling teeth. She wanted to add more but decided this likely wouldn't prove fruitful. "See anything of interest?"

Paige sniffed, glancing back towards the photos. Her perfectly manicured, but unpainted fingernails spread the photos again. She still smelled of soap, and her hair, despite the nozzle of air above, was perfectly in place.

"So... did you volunteer for this?" Paige said curtly, avoiding the spoken question but probing at the unspoken one.

"I—no—Foucault called."

"I see."

"Mhmm."

"Well," Paige said, "I'm sure we'll both behave professionally, yes? When we catch the killer, we're going to *arrest* him. Right?"

Adele felt a jolt of unease. "Wh—what does *that* mean?"

"Nothing."

"No—hang on. What do you mean *arrest* him? Of course, we'll arrest him. What are you implying?"

"Oh don't play thick with me, Adele. You've created somewhat of a reputation for yourself. I'm primary, so we're going to do this by the book. That's all I meant to say."

Adele felt her stomach twist. A couple of things stood out about this, neither of them particularly comforting. For one, she didn't appreciate the inference. What were people at the office saying about the killing of the Painter? Her report had been clear self-defense. But were other rumors circulating?

She glanced sidelong at Paige, but the older woman seemed satisfied with her comments and was now studying the coroner's report.

In addition to this initial unease, Adele couldn't help but notice Paige's use of *"When."*

When they caught the killer. Not "if." When.

A lot of confidence, though the closest they'd come to the crimes at all was this plane ride to Switzerland. Foucault had high expectations. Paige did too.

Adele needed to bring her A game on this one. The two people she least wanted to upset in the French government were now both holding her accountable for the apprehension of this killer. The expectation alone felt like burden resting on her shoulders.

Paige's cold, clipped tone clarified things. Neither of them particularly liked this pairing, but in order to catch the killer of the boss's cousin, they'd have to find—if not the same—a similar wavelength.

“Same MO,” Paige was murmuring. “Two stab wounds to the heart, then both male victims were stuffed into these large, antique items.”

“Any connection between the victims?” Adele murmured.

“Not at first glance. Did you find anything?”

Adele shifted uncomfortably again in her seat. “No. We'll have a better idea when we land and get a look at the crime scene. Apparently it's a mansion in the Alps.”

CHAPTER FIVE

The mountain views, the cotton-white clouds, the steep arches and columns of the old mansion were all lost on Adele.

She marched away from the taxi they'd taken from the airport, grateful to be—finally—free from close confines with Agent Paige. Ahead, in the open double-doors of the enormous home, she spotted Swiss police officers gathered on the threshold, murmuring to each other in conversation.

The three men and one woman perked up, glancing over their blue scarves and black jackets.

"Interpol?" said one of the men, stepping forward and wearing a frown as dark as his overcoat.

"Yes," Adele replied quickly. "Interpol corresponding with DGSI."

"Ah, French," the man replied, nodding once as if he'd heard enough. "Please, come this way," he said in nearly perfect English. He gestured with a hand, and Adele didn't wait for Agent Paige to catch up before entering the mansion.

Instantly, her eyes were drawn to the giant, antique clock set beneath a walkway, framed by a stairwell. The huge, wooden, glass-faced thing was barricaded by police tape and standing in ominous shadow.

Adele blinked in the dark, rubbing her cool hands on her sweater sleeves to warm them. "No lights?" she asked.

The officer who'd followed into the house shook his head. "Someone tampered with the circuit breaker. Electrician is on holiday—going to be another day."

Adele paused, nodding and scanning the room. "Body?"

"At the coroner's," the Swiss officer said. "Crime scene has been photographed as well." He studied Adele out of the corner of his eye, cleared his throat, then said, "Is it usual for Interpol to work through French agencies?"

Adele took a moment to register the question. She kept her gaze on the clock but replied, "It's experimental. I worked in Germany and the USA before this."

"Ah—a marriage of convenience, then?" He grinned.

Adele returned the smile, hers a few notches more reserved. "I suppose so." She glanced back towards the main doors, her eyes flicking to the locks. Then she turned to look at the windows. "Any sign of forced entry?"

"No. Not that we've found."

"Do we know how the killer entered the house? Any open windows?"

"Hard to say. The front door was unlocked, but that was probably due to the wife."

"Ah, yes. And how is our witness?"

The Swiss agent shook his head, his scarf swishing across his jacket. "Not well, I'm afraid. She's still recovering from the initial shock. We got a brief report, but not much. Mostly, she wants us to leave the house."

Adele looked over. "She's here?"

"Yes. Upstairs in the master bedroom. She requested no guests."

Footsteps suddenly joined them, and someone cleared their throat. Then, Agent Paige said, "We will have to disappoint Ms. Vosloo, I'm afraid. Do we know the point of entry?"

Adele looked back towards her partner, wishing Paige had spent more time making her way from the car. Instead, she kept her tone polite. "Already asked—no sign of force."

"I see." Paige looked towards the large clock but seemed disinterested. "Where is Ms. Vosloo? We didn't fly all this way for nothing."

Adele shifted uncomfortably, and the Swiss officer looked similarly unsure of himself. In the doorway, the other officers were all watching, preferring to stand in the threshold where the sunlight could illuminate their gathering, rather than in the dingy dark of the mansion.

The Swiss officer coughed delicately. "I suppose I could ask if Ms. Vosloo would like—"

"Would like what?" This voice came from the stairs, speaking in English with a light accent.

Adele and the others all turned, watching as a small-framed woman, wearing a business suit—which was now wrinkled as if it had been slept in—came down the stairs. Her eyes were framed with red, and her extended hand hovered over the curling rail, not quite touching the surface.

"Ms. Vosloo," the Swiss officer said reflexively, clearing his throat and holding out a mirroring hand as if to keep her at bay. "Apologies. Did we wake you?"

She didn't reply, taking the stairs but then coming to a halt halfway down the steps. She overlooked the entrance, the grandfather clock not visible from her angle, as if this had been intentional.

Agent Paige cleared her throat, beginning to speak, but Adele—quite familiar with Sophie's bedside manner—stepped forward and stood at the bottom of the stairs, looking up at the widow. "I'm very sorry for your loss," she said.

The woman had neat, silver-speckled hair tied back in a bun, and two long, earrings shaped like music notes dangling on either side of her face. Evidence of streaked mascara was visible only in the faintest of trailing shadows, residue of what had been wiped away.

"Is this going to take much longer?" the woman said in an effervescent tone, glancing at the faces below.

"Electrician is delayed," the officer replied, wincing. "We still need more crime scene photos."

The woman on the stairs sighed, her hair flitting and falling with the gust of air. "A crime scene... I never really thought of my home as a crime scene."

Adele cleared her throat. "I'm Agent Sharp with Interpol and DGSI—I don't mean to bother you Mrs. Vosloo. I know how difficult things must be."

"Yes. Difficult. That is one word for it."

"I'm very, very sorry. But you are the one who... who found..."

"My husband? Dead? Yes, dear, I was." Her voice still carried that echoing, airy quality, and Adele realized the woman must have taken something to calm her nerves. Her eyes were dilated, and her motions were trance-like.

"And did you notice anything else?"

The woman waved a hand over the banister. "A body. A body in the clock."

Paige murmured behind Adele. "She's drugged."

Adele just nodded but addressed Ms. Vosloo again. "I couldn't help but notice where the clock was placed. In the middle of the room. Did the killer do that—it would've surely taken more than one person to drag that clock."

"No... No, it was just delivered. My husband won it at an auction recently—it cost us a small fortune."

"An auction?"

"Yes—during a trip to France, in fact. We'd just returned."

Adele frowned, beginning to nod, but now, Ms. Vosloo was leaning over the rail, lifting herself off the ground and kicking her feet like a child imitating an airplane. She wore a dopy grin and seemed, momentarily, to forget everyone there.

"Probably best we return her to her rooms," the Swiss officer said with a significant tilt of his eyebrows.

Paige frowned, but Adele just nodded, turning and moving back through the door without so much as a farewell. A single dot was only a data point. Two, though, formed the threat of a trend. The Belgium crime scene would help narrow in on the pertinent clues.

She was already fishing her phone from her pocket, entering Foucault's number.

His cousin had been killed two days earlier.

As Adele exited the mansion, out into the sunlit mountain view, she heard Agent Paige coming after her. "Adele? Where are you going?"

Adele paused in the driveway, stray gravel crunching underfoot. She ignored the other Swiss officers watching quizzically from the door. She held up her phone in answer, where it was already ringing.

Paige sniffed, glanced at the number, back to the house then to Adele again. "The Belgium scene?"

Adele resisted the urge to smile. Credit where credit was due—Paige knew her way around a case.

"Make it a video call," Paige said firmly. "Foucault can provide the investigator's number—It's Guyenne."

Adele's eyebrows shot up. "From our office?"

Paige snorted. "You think he was going to let the locals trample all over the scene? Guyenne is good at his job. But I want to see his face—make it a video call."

Adele nodded, waiting for the line to connect with the executive in order to get the number for the investigator at the first crime scene.

What dots would connect? Which ones wouldn't?

Adele felt a faint shiver down her spine. No sign of a break-in. No potential witnesses out in such seclusion... What if...

For the first time she considered the horrible proposition...

What if...

What if they *couldn't* catch the killer? What would that mean for her career? Her freedom? Would Foucault be furious?

The phone connected. She heard a faint growl, then a response. "Yes? Did you find anything? Sharp—what is it?"

Adele bit her lip. "Nothing concrete yet, sir. I need Guyenne's number in Belgium, sir—we're going to compare notes."

"You're not *going* to Belgium?" Foucault snapped, but then he paused and huffed a sigh. "Never mind—never mind. No, I get it. Another two days of travel will only allow this murderous scum a bigger lead. Fine—fine..."

"We can go if you'd like...," Adele began.

"No—I hired you because I knew you were the best. What does Paige think?"

Adele glanced towards her reluctant partner. Paige pursed her lips—seemingly a very familiar expression for the lower half of her face—but then she brushed a strand of hair behind her ear. "No," she said simply. "Guyenne's report will be enough for now. We can always head back if nothing comes up. For the moment, I want to see what he's found."

Adele felt her stomach twist, equal parts relieved and stunned that Paige had backed the play. Hopping from country to country would provide more information but also give the killer a greater head start. Especially in the first few days of a new serial case, time was of the essence.

"Sir," she said, "about that number? Please?"

She waited, nerves tingling as Foucault began to text her the number for their colleague in Belgium.

CHAPTER SIX

Adele and Sophie walked side-by-side circling around the garage in search of both privacy and better reception. Adele held her phone up, watching the grainy footage of Agent Guyenne on the other line.

"There... no—wait... yes, I can hear you now—Agent Sharp?" The speaker crackled and Guyenne's round, friendly face flashed across the screen.

Paige leaned in next to Adele, squinting up at the device. "Mati," she snapped, "Stop shaking your arm—you're giving me a headache."

"Oh—Sophie, hello—didn't see you there! Is this better?"

Adele felt a flash of gratitude as she circled around the garage, watching the screen finally settle, displaying the French agent in Belgium standing outside a chateau-style mansion at the edge of a private lake.

Adele whistled softly. "Nice place," she said.

The round-faced agent bobbed his head, moving aside to give a better view of the estate behind him. "Seems like you're in a similar space," he replied, wiggling his fingers towards the camera.

Adele glanced back towards the mountains, her eyes lifting to view the scenic passes beyond. "Both victims came from wealth," she said simply. "We spoke to the wife—she found her husband here."

Guyenne bobbed his head, flashing a thumbs up, over-gesticulating as if worried the pixelation might disguise the motion. "Mr. Foucault was found by a cleaning crew. He was discovered just up there." The phone rotated now, facing the chateau, a pudgy finger gestured towards the second window above the entrance. "Second floor," he said. "In an old antique wardrobe."

"That's what I wanted to speak about," Adele said, moving around the front of the garage again for a second lap. Agent Paige was shorter so had to move quicker to keep up. "Do you have a timeline on that antique wardrobe?"

"When it was purchased?"

"Yes."

"I don't have purchase date. But I did notice packing materials in the dumpsters—so I asked about *delivery* date."

Adele's eyebrows perked. "When?"

"Twenty-four hours before the murder," said Guyenne with a significant nod.

"I see... Did you find any points of entry? Was it a break-in?"

"None. We're still looking into it. How about you?"

Adele shook her head. "The lights were cut—someone tampered with the breaker badly enough to require an electrician."

"Lights were off here, too. Something with one of the main lines. It's up and running again, though."

Adele circled around the garage for a third time, footsteps crunching against gravel and dust. Paige's footsteps tapped staccato as she hurried to keep up.

"Which auction house?" Paige said suddenly.

"I—excuse me?"

"The auction house—where was it? What was it called?"

Guyenne frowned, then lowered his phone. There was the sound of a zipper than crinkling paper followed by muttered grunts and curses. Finally, the man's face moved back into view. "I have the delivery receipt here. Auction house was...," he trailed off and the image on the phone suddenly froze.

Adele cursed, freezing and then taking a step back, holding the phone skyward.

The audio continued, but the picture remained dead. "In France," Guyenne was saying. "Funnily enough. An auction house in France."

Paige suddenly grabbed Adele's arm and began tugging her back towards the house.

"Hang on," Adele said, distracted, allowing Paige to guide her away from the garage. "What was the auction house's name?"

"Umm, one second—just above the—there. Leon Antiques! Get that? Can you hear me? It's Leon Antiques."

Adele frowned, nodding. Now, she glanced towards her wrist, wincing as Paige continued to pull her forward. "What?" she said.

Paige, instead of answering, stomped up the stairs, ignored the Swiss police, but then pulled Adele to a stop around the side column of the entrance. "See that?" Paige said significantly.

Adele felt her stomach twist. She frowned, leaning in, glancing towards a pile of cardboard and Styrofoam that had been pushed nearly out of sight.

"That's what I was looking at before entering the house," Paige said, sounding somewhat smug. "Did you notice it?"

Adele faintly shook her head, distracted now as she leaned in. The phone was chirping at her side as Guyenne tried to speak, but Adele's attention was snared by the printed red letters on the top of the box, near a small logo of an old clock on top of a calligraphy letter "L."

The words simply read: *Leon Antiques.*

Adele stared, then turned sharply to look at Paige, who still looked quite pleased with herself.

"What is it?" Guyenne was saying. "Is everything alright? Paige? Sharp?"

"It's fine," Adele said, her voice numb. "Just—Leon Antiques in France, you're sure? Do you have an address for that?"

Paige was already checking the return address on the box.

Adele for her part had straightened, frowning... The same auction house. Both victims had ordered something recently from the same auction house.

Paige tapped the address with a finger and Guyenne read his off the receipt. Adele's eyebrows shot up. "The same," she murmured. "Both of them ordered from the same place... and then within a couple of days..."

"They were both killed," Paige said with a grim nod. "Well... Switzerland was nice, but I guess we're heading back to France. You set up tickets—I'll get another taxi."

Adele bid farewell to Guyenne in order to do just that, her mind reeling, her heart hammering. Leon Antiques in France. Both victims had ordered from the same auction house, and both had been stabbed to death and stuffed in the items they'd ordered.

It couldn't be a coincidence... But it also came with a level of worry...

Who else had ordered from the auction house? How many other potential victims were out there, even now?

Adele's fingers shook as she dialed the number for a shuttle back to the airport, her shoulder blades facing the beautiful mountains, her head dipped beneath the shadowed entrance of the old house.

CHAPTER SEVEN

The sunlight warmed her skin where Agent Paige stood in the city street outside the auction house, but her heart was cold. Paige *tried* to like the younger woman, but it was a venture in futility. Even now, having exited their second taxi, hours later, walking up the sidewalk outside the old auction house, she couldn't shake her sense of... *indigestion* when around Adele Sharp.

Paige glanced towards Adele where the younger woman pressed her elbow against the crescent glass of the auction house door. A small brass bell tinkled overhead as the door swung in.

For the second time, in the same day, Paige allowed Adele to go first.

She paused, scanning the large, old-fashioned building. It was three stories tall, at the edge of a market street. The glass windows displayed unique, one-of-a-kind items. The store hours were written in peeling paint on the door. Within, furniture, sets of china, silverware, buttons, old-fashioned jewelry, and many other items stacked on tables or counters or draped from hooks.

But Paige was far more concerned with the people. An item was only a threat in a person's hand.

She caught the door before it shut with her foot, holding it in place, still half standing on the sidewalk. She watched Agent Sharp enter the auction house, holding up a hand to catch the attention of a man standing by a podium and gesturing at guests in deeper portions of the auction house. Small placards and printouts of descriptions were placed in plastic dispensers around the items displayed in the front room. Two security guards lingered in the back, keeping an eye on anyone perusing the merchandise. Further inside, through the open door, Agent Paige could hear the barking of an auctioneer echoing down the hall.

The man behind the podium was nodding politely to two older women and gesturing for them to move down the hall. At the same time, he spotted Paige holding the door open and began to frown. Sharp caught his attention though and raised a hand. "Excuse me!"

Even the way she spoke grated at Paige. It wasn't really Adele's fault they had started off on such a bad foot. Paige had tried to process it over the years. And though she understood why the younger woman had reported missing evidence to internal investigations, she still wouldn't forgive that it had led back to her husband. They had tried to work together in the past. Paige had even set up surveillance on the murderer of Adele's mother. But some people simply rubbed each other the wrong way.

Besides, something was going on with Adele Sharp. Paige had been given a copy of the shooting report.

But what had really happened?

It all seemed so convenient. Agent Sharp was more reserved than ever, almost too polite at times. As if she didn't want to rock the boat.

Page sighed slowly, inhaling the faint odor of dust and old wood. No matter. The executive wanted this case solved. She'd been friends with Foucault for a long time. He'd been close to his cousin. The news had come like a sucker punch. If someone at this auction house was behind the murder of her friend's family member, then she would simply have to put her distrust of Adele Sharp on the back burner.

Paige approached where Adele was talking with the fellow behind the podium. The man was shaking his head, brushing a hand through his hair, and gesturing down the hall. As Paige drew nearer, she noted the small golden tag on his chest read *manager.*

"I'm afraid I don't know what you mean," the manager was saying, shaking his head. He was balding, but still used gel to comb his hair aside. A couple of limp strands flopped about as he shook his head. The small man's cheeks were tinged red, flustered. He wore a neat, old-fashioned suit, with a polka-dot bowtie.

Agent Sharp was glancing inside a glass counter at a row of wristwatches covered in diamonds. She regarded the items in the case as she spoke. "I'm not accusing you of anything. I'm sure it's just an unhappy coincidence. But we still need to know who has access to that information."

The manager let out a little sigh, crossing his arms and glancing down the hall where the two older women were still making their way in the direction of another room.

"We're about to start an event," he said. "I've only got a few minutes. Can you come back later?"

"It won't take long on my end," Adele said, looking up.

Agent Paige studied the younger woman's profile, wondering what Adele was thinking. She was good at her job, that much was true. Everything else, she supposed, for the moment, was a distraction

Paige leaned in, tapping a finger against the wooden podium. "What's your name?"

Putting someone on the defensive often yielded better results than Adele's polite approach. By over-asking, and then requesting something simpler, it allowed the subject to think they were being let off easy. Sometimes, people just needed a little encouragement.

"My name?" he stammered.

Paige frowned and nodded, keeping the severe expression affixed.

The man shifted uncomfortably, glancing between the two women as if trying to decide whose query to answer first.

"I... look," the manager said, conspicuously dodging the question. "What did you say? A Mr. Vosloo and Foucault? We have many guests from many countries."

Adele shot Paige a look of gratitude before leaning in as well, causing the wooden podium to creak. She nodded as if in commiseration, but her eyes were like those of a hawk. On one side, Paige still scowling, on the other, Adele with a look of utmost sympathy, and between them, behind the podium, the poor manager looking ready to faint.

His cheeks were flushed, and his thin strands of poorly gelled hair were sticking to the sweat beading across his brow.

"Mr. Vosloo was from Switzerland. He purchased a clock from you. Mr. Foucault was from Belgium—an antique wardrobe."

"I—alright... just... one moment..." Still flustered, and still not wanting to provide his name, the manager ducked behind his podium. There was the sound of a tapping keyboard. A blue screen suddenly glowed, illuminating the fellow's polka-dot bowtie. He was murmuring to himself and shaking his head in frustration.

Behind, the little brass bell tinkled.

"Just a minute!" the man squawked. "The next auction is on the hour! Down the hall!" He continued typing on his keyboard. Then, he looked up, still sweating. "I—look," he said, "I didn't handle these sales. They were both auction room two—alright?"

"So you do have them?" Adele said firmly.

He wagged his head, pushing the edge of a black screen and twisting it. Adele leaned in but Paige remained where she was, watching and frowning.

"Yes, yes—Mr. Vosloo—an antique clock. And there we have Mr. Foucault; a one-of-a-kind wardrobe from the 1800s. A pricey piece. No returns!" he added quickly, scowling.

Adele ignored this last comment. Agent Paige said, still frowning, "Is it common for foreigners to come here and bid?"

The man adjusted his bowtie, clearing his throat importantly and wagging his head. "Very common," he insisted. "We're quite well-known among *certain* clientele."

"Rich people," Paige said.

"I—well, no... Cultured sorts. Look, people come from all around to bid on the unique wares we provide. We often have the items shipped globally. Many hundreds every year."

"I see," said Paige. "And so that means someone on staff here would have the names and addresses of all your clients."

"Yes, yes... But—hang on, what are you getting at? What exactly happened to these items?"

"We're not here about the antiques, sir." Paige frowned. "But about the buyers. We need to speak with anyone on staff who would have access to this." She leaned over the podium tapping the computer. "Who knew the names and addresses of the victims."

"Victims?" he squeaked. "They're—they're not..."

"Staff names," Paige snapped. "Please."

The small man in the bowtie was now white-faced, shaking his head, his fingers trembling as he turned back to the computer, scanning the document for some relevant information.

Paige wasn't looking at him anymore but had turned her attention to Agent Sharp again. Adele had stepped aside to give Sophie lead on the case. This, just as with everything else, struck her as odd. Sharp wasn't normally the submissive type.

Was she holding something back? Hiding something? What was going on with the younger agent?

Before she could consider this much longer, the auction-house manager squeaked. "I have two employees on staff in auction room two, who would have handled both purchases. They're getting ready for a new event, though. Would it be possible for you to come back at a—"

"Not possible," Paige said firmly, her gaze swiveling again. "What are their names? Who had access to the clients' addresses, sir?"

He let out a long, weary sigh, but then began to turn the computer screen again, giving both the agents line-of-sight to employee files now opened on the screen.

CHAPTER EIGHT

Adele found herself in a back room behind an old stage where the event was about to commence. A man in a long, black robe, and a powdered wig was sweating, shaking his head where he paced the wooden floorboards across from her. Agent Paige was busy interviewing another auction-house employee down the hall.

"Look," the large man with a double chin was saying, "I can give you five minutes, but then we have to start. Can you hear them?" he held a pudgy hand to his ear. "They're already getting antsy." One of the gray curls of his fake wig swished as he nodded his head towards a curtain partition across the room, separating this preparation area from the main auction stage.

Adele tilted her head, studying the man. "Why are you dressed like a judge?"

He blinked, then glanced down at his long, black robe. His powdered wig swished as he did, and Adele noticed the oversized gavel looped through a hoop in his belt.

"It's nothing," he said, distractedly, waving a hand. "A gag—a joke. The clients like it." He pulled out the gavel, twirling it. "Look, it's not important. I'm telling you; I didn't have anything to do with delivering those parcels."

"But you know the ones I'm talking about?"

The fake judge sighed. He paused, listening to a murmur of voices beyond the curtain, from the auction floor. "I really have to go."

"You said you had a few minutes."

The large man glared at her, but then nodded with another world-weary sigh. "I know the longcase clock and the mahogany wardrobe. I sold them both in this room. But I don't take note of the clients, and I have nothing to do with shipping. I don't even collect the information; that's the manager's job."

"I see—so who might know the information?"

"Shipping and handling," he said without blinking as if the answer were obvious. The murmur of voices from beyond the curtain was louder now, and the big man in the fake judge's robe twisted from foot to foot like a child needing to pee. Every time the hem of his robe swished across the carpet, it revealed a pair of fancy, suede loafers that didn't quite match the rest of the ensemble.

"Where were you on Tuesday evening?" Adele said.

"Working—I'm always working, dear. I've been overtime four days in a row."

Adele frowned. "Do you have proof of that?"

"The manager will vouch for me. There are cameras in all the auction rooms, too. You'll see me waving this around." He raised his gavel, twirling it again. "Is that all?"

Adele paused, considering this. She would have to double check the claim, but if it was true that the large auctioneer had been working the nights of the murders then that cleared his name. By the sound of things, he didn't interact with the items or addresses either.

"Give me a name—who was working on Monday evening with shipping?"

"Monday? This week?"

"Yes."

The big man paused, huffed a sigh, still twisting about, but then he paused, scratching his chin and frowning. "Ah...," he said, trailing off. "Actually, that would've been Renard Almo."

"Is Mr. Almo here today?"

Here, though, the big man frowned. "Actually, no. He's been off sick for the last couple of days. Tuesday—you mentioned Tuesday? He was sick then, too." The big man tilted his head. "Is that important?"

Adele frowned now, crossing her arms and creasing her own suit. Voices from behind the curtain were calling out questions now, raising their volume. Clearly, upper-crust auction house sorts were used to getting things their way on their timeline.

As if sensing he were going to be let off the hook, at least for the moment, the auctioneer wagged his head. "Mr. Almo was responsible for inspecting and preparing both the clock and the wardrobe for shipping. If you want to speak with someone about those antiques—it's Renard."

"And he's out sick—you're sure?"

The auctioneer bobbed his head. Now, though, he was easing towards the curtain, gavel in hand. "I really have to...," he gestured towards the front of the room.

Adele sighed, considering her options, but then nodded once. It wasn't like the auctioneer was going anywhere—she could check his story and return if he'd been lying.

For now, though, if what he was saying was true, then one of the auction house employees involved with shipping and handling had called in sick on the days of both murders. Was it because he was actually sick?

Or had Mr. Almo been traveling to Switzerland and Belgium on those days?

“Excuse me,” she said, waving towards the auctioneer. “Does Mr. Almo have an address?”

“Yes—yes—the manager will have it. I really have to go—sorry!” The big man dipped behind the curtain. The sound of rising voices from beyond faded and she heard the auctioneer exclaim, “Apologies—apologies! Ladies and gentlemen, we'll start right away, shall we. Normal etiquette, the item list is in your pamphlets in front of you tucked in the seat. We'll be starting with this lovely glass-blown vase... ready?”

Adele turned, the sounds fading as she began to move back down the hall towards the front of the store.

The manager would have Mr. Almo's address.

But would the employee be home? Or was he out on another hunt?

CHAPTER NINE

Adele watched Agent Paige put the rental vehicle in park, coming to a jolting halt outside the single-story home. Paige had insisted on driving, and now Adele was eager to push out of the car first, turning to face the old home on the edge of the street. A quiet neighborhood—with no neighbors or moving vehicles indicating life, besides the faint flicker of a television screen through the window of the house next to their suspect's home.

"This is it?" Paige asked, frowning towards the swirling numbers on the side of the white-painted house.

"Yes," Adele said with a nod, double-checking the GPS on her own phone. "Mr. Renard Almo lives alone."

Paige's expression darkened. Her door slammed shut and the lights clicked as she locked the vehicle and then paced across the sidewalk towards the single-story home. "Guess they don't pay well at auction houses," she muttered. "This place is a dump."

Adele winced at the characterization but was already scanning the windows for movement. No car in the driveway—no garage at all. No movement in the house. No lights.

"I don't think anyone's home," Adele murmured as the two agents took the steps and came to a halt in front of a door with peeling, white paint.

Paige rapped her knuckles against the frame, then waited, listening.

No sound.

Adele leaned in, pressing the doorbell. "DGSI!" she called.

No response. No sound of movement. Nothing. The glow of the television next door continued to paint odd colors across the glass, stretched like the images of some kaleidoscope.

Adele tried the door handle, but it wouldn't turn. "Locked," she murmured. Her feet shuffled, scraping against a dusty stoop. She turned to the nearest window at chest height, her fingers probing towards the frame. No give. "Also locked," she said.

"Move aside," Paige said testily.

Adele complied, watching curiously as the older woman knelt by the lock on the door, examining it. Then, she pulled an oddly shaped hairpin from the base of her ponytail. She pulled a key ring from her pocket, shifting to a long, silver piece of metal.

"Is that a tension rod?" Adele said, leaning in.

"Hush—let me focus."

Adele lowered her hand from the window where she'd been trying to find purchase and instead just watched, half in awe and half in admiration as the woman nearly twice her age began to pick the lock. Another part of her hesitated, though. This wasn't, technically, legal. Adele didn't need more on her plate. But Paige was the lead on this one.

The hairpin and tension rod slipped into the keyhole. Paige grunted a couple of times, holding her breath as she applied proper pressure. Then, tongue inside her cheek, she murmured, "Just one more... There's the pin—there we..."

Click.

Adele's eyebrows shot up. She felt a prickle up her spine and glanced down the street, wondering if any neighbors were watching. "We did call it in, right?" she murmured. "Locals know we're here?"

Paige bobbed her head curtly and then pushed back to her feet. She twisted the doorknob and pushed it open slowly. The old frame creaked, and a few flecks of loose paint fell from the door, flitting down like tumbling leaves.

"Mr. Almo!" Paige shouted. "DGSI! Law enforcement! Is anyone home?"

The house was dark—still no sign of movement. No sounds at all.

Adele swallowed, her lips feeling dry all of a sudden. The auction house employee's own home was sparse. She spotted a small kitchen beyond a living space with a single couch and no television.

"Guess our guy is a minimalist," she said.

Paige was already stepping into the house, though. "Smell the gas leak?" she said. Adele began to shake her head, but Paige cut her off. "Yes, you do. Come on."

It took Adele a moment—at first, she thought Paige was trying to create an excuse for entering the house. But a second later, she did smell something odd in the air. She frowned, following the older agent into the house. The two of them moved slowly, hands on their holsters. The old floors creaked as Paige made a beeline towards the kitchen. "There," she said with a grunt. "He left the burner on."

Adele watched as Paige turned the knob. It had only been left on a fraction of click, but the faint odor of gas still wafted through the room. Paige turned now, pulling open a window, and fanning the air a couple of times. She retreated back in Adele's direction towards a more spacious part of the room. "Keep the door open!" she commanded. "We need a breeze."

Adele complied, leaving the door ajar where she stood, scanning the small, single-story home.

"Mr. Almo!" she called again, not that she expected a response by this point. The cross breeze through the house from the window to the door soon cleared the faint odor of gas.

Paige was now moving down a hall towards the two rooms visible on either side of the short corridor. Adele was busy scanning the walls. No paintings. No television. Nothing luxurious at all.

"Clear!" Paige called, wrinkling her nose in one of the doors. "The man has the grooming habits of an ape," she added. She turned to the next door, pushing it open. "Also clear!" she said after a moment, frowning.

"The bedroom?" Adele called.

Paige nodded. "Empty—just a mat on the ground." As the silver-haired agent rejoined Adele in the hall, the two of them frowned at each other.

"He's not home, then," said Adele. "He called in sick—so why's he not here?"

Paige tilted her head with a significant quirk of a brow.

"Yeah," Adele murmured. "That's what I was thinking, too... Granted, doesn't really look like the guy can afford a plane ticket."

"Unless he has another place," Paige replied. "This might just be a distraction for work. For taxes. For cops..." She shrugged with each guess.

Adele began to turn, but as she did, she spotted an old-fashioned land-line phone set into the wall. She frowned, staring at the device. She hadn't seen one of these in years. And there, above the red phone, she spotted a single sticky-note, taped to the peeling plaster.

"Paige," Adele said, calling over her shoulder. "Look here."

The older woman moved across the room, hastening to Adele's side. The two of them stared at the note, both frowning.

"Is that..."

"Nearby," Adele murmured.

An address, written in bright, red letters, left above the phone. The address was circled twice. And there, above one red ring of ink someone had drawn a small little sketch of...

"Is that..." Paige leaned in.

"Skull and crossbones," Adele murmured. "A death threat?"

Paige, though, was already fishing her keys from her pocket. "Bring the note with the address," she snapped back.

Adele paused, frowning. “You don't think it's his next victim, do you?”

“I'll drive!” Paige barked, hurrying out the door.

***

Adele's stomach churned as they discovered this second address was only a few blocks away. Also a single-story, dilapidated home. This time, though, there was a car in the driveway.

“It's his vehicle!” Adele called hurriedly as she hastened out of their own vehicle and moved up the driveway. Paige came double-time to keep up with the taller woman's strides.

This new house, three blocks away from the suspect's primary address, had a similar white paint job, a similar shoddy door.

The two agents hastened up the steps. This time, through the window, Adele spotted a light on within.

As they neared, Paige reached for the handle.

Suddenly, a cry of pain emanated from within.

“Did you hear—” Adele began, but Paige was already twisting the handle violently and shoving her shoulder against the door. It didn't budge. She began to reach for her key ring again, but Adele shouted, “No time!” She raised her weapon, preparing to slam through the windowsill, but Paige reached it first, pressing her hands flat against the glass and pushing *up.*

The window slid.

Adele's heart skipped a beat and together, with the older agent, the two of them pulled the window open.

Another cry of pain emanated from within.

“Stop!” Adele shouted. “DGSI!”

Both of them, weapons now drawn, pulled through the window. Adele tumbled after Paige, throwing her leg over the sill and then dismounting on the other side. The curtain swished behind them.

They found themselves in another small, sparse home. This time, there were photos on the wall, framed. Mostly of an older man and a younger man. Many of them, judging by the quality, from years ago.

The sounds were coming from the room at the end of an L-shaped hall.

Adele and Paige raced down the corridor, turning towards a doorway.

“Stay still,” a voice was saying firmly. “Don't move—it'll only make it worse.”

“DGSI!” Adele shouted, kicking the door.

Together, Paige in tow, they both burst through the entrance, into the small bedroom beyond. Instantly, they stiffened.

Adele's gun snapped back to her hip, her eyes bugging. Paige similarly lowered her weapon at once.

A young man, who matched the driver's license photo for Renard Almo was kneeling by the bedside of an older man. An IV bag dangled next to the bed, next to a blinking display of lights on a screen. The older man was propped up on a pillow and was wincing as the younger man adjusted a bandage securing the IV drip to his arm.

Both of them were frozen now, looking to the door, wearing identical stunned expressions. And the expressions were *very* similar. The older man had pale hair and wrinkled features but was nearly the spitting image of Mr. Almo.

“I—wha—who are you?” Adele demanded.

“Who are you?” Mr. Almo retorted, his eyes wide, his gaze bouncing from one lowered weapon to the next.

“DGSI,” Paige said, crisply. “Are you Renard Almo?”

“What is it Renny?” the old man murmured. “Who are they? Is this your girlfriend?”

“No, Dad, hush—hang on.” The young man couldn't seem to decide if he should scowl or stare. “Did—what—can I see some ID?”

Paige and Adele both went to their pockets. For her part, Adele was beginning to feel sheepish—a shiver of embarrassment prickling down her spine. Whatever they'd stumbled onto, it clearly wasn't a murder attempt.

Once the man was satisfied with the identifications, he straightened, double checking the comfort of the older man who winced and let out a gasp of pain. “Do you mind?” Mr. Almo demanded after fluffing a pillow and turning on them again. “My father isn't well.”

“This is your father?” Adele said frowning. “You took time off work. You said you were sick.”

Now, for the first time, Mr. Almo looked concerned. He nibbled on the corner of his lip, glancing around for a moment before giving a long sigh and shaking his head. “Is that what this is about? Did Jeanie put you up to this?”

“Why aren't you at work, Mr. Almo?” Paige insisted.

But this time, the old man, in a warbling, strained voice, spoke up. “He's been with me. I hate that fat nurse. She's an ugly slug!”

“Dad!” Mr. Almo retorted. “Please.”

“It's true,” the pained older man said, wagging his head but then wincing and flopping back on his pillow.

Adele felt a jolt of realization. “And was he here on Tuesday as well, sir?” she asked, glancing towards the older man.

He didn't nod this time, trying to remain still but did speak out. “Yes, yes. Most of this week. A new nurse comes Sunday.”

Mr. Almo shifted uncomfortably, looking like he wanted nothing more than for his father to stay silent. At a glance from the two women, though, he massaged the bridge of his nose and muttered. “I just wanted to help my father during the transition. I know I shouldn't have lied to my employers. But... but really? *DGSI?*” He frowned again, shaking his head. “A bit of an overreaction, no?”

Adele slowly holstered her weapon, buttoning it and feeling a bout of guilt. She winced towards Paige who had already sheathed her firearm.

“We're sorry for the inconvenience,” Paige said simply. “Do you have any proof of your whereabouts Tuesday night?”

Mr. Almo hesitated but then wagged his head once. “My dad has a camera out front. I'm sure we can find footage. Why? What is this about?”

“So you're saying you can account for your comings and goings for the last few days?”

“Absolutely. I've mostly been here. Slept on the couch a couple of nights. My dad didn't like the old nurse. What's this about—you're still not answering me.”

“Mr. Almo,” said Paige, “did you see anything unusual on the days you *did* work?”

“Work?”

“Leon Antiques. That's your place of employment, yes?”

“I mean, yes... But—I didn't steal anything. If that's what this is about. I mean look around. I can barely afford to keep the lights on. Most the money goes to pay the nurse. Who said I did? Was it—”

“Please just answer the question, Mr. Almo. Is there anything you can tell us over the last few days? Anything you saw at work out of the ordinary?”

“What? No—nothing. I've been checking out early anyway to come here.”

Now, the man looked sufficiently flustered. Paige shot a glance towards Adele and gave a faint shrug and a nod as if passing the baton. But Adele didn't have anything to add. What more could she say? Mr. Almo wasn't their suspect. He hadn't seen anything.

Paige cleared her throat in an attempt to keep the flow of

conversation, but Adele was already moving, shaking her head in frustration. “I'm sorry for the intrusion, Mr. Almo,” Adele called back. “If you think of anything, please contact the authorities. Anything at all.”

He was no longer facing her, having turned to his father and murmuring towards the old man.

Adele was briefly reminded of Robert Henry, and one of the last times she had seen her old mentor. At the same time, she didn't want to look back. Didn't want to watch the heartbreaking scene. How off could someone be? Hunting down a poor man taking care of his ailing father... The real killer was still out there. Last time, he'd killed on a two-day gap. Which meant they were due for another attack.

She dreaded the next phone call from Foucault.

But even more, she dreaded any report of another body.

CHAPTER TEN

He found the confines of his vehicle quite soothing. The doors locked, windows tinted, an ability to move at fast speeds, not accosted, unmolested... There was freedom in a car. Freedom in the dark, enclosed space. Even idling, now, on the curb, he still had his seatbelt taught, securing him in place.

He liked security. Liked the confines, the closeness, the near space.

His thoughts were on the car, but his eyes were on the large home at the end of the street. He sat behind the tint of his windows, embraced by the shroud of darkness at the end of the street. Everything was so quiet, calm. Even the clouds were pulling across the sky, hiding the final glint of the descending sun as evening made its way into the boudoir of night.

He could see the package already delivered on the porch—could picture, even now, the adulation, the excitement of the auction. The bidding. He'd seen Anders Schitt win the item in the bustle and bluster of the other auction-goers. He'd been in the back of the room, watching from beneath hooded eyes.

He often watched.

He closed his eyes for a moment, savoring the darkness—he'd long familiarized with the dark, with night. And again, tonight, he'd move under the cover of dwindling light.

As he sat there, eyes closed, behind his tinted windows, facing an evening sky, he felt a little chill of arousal.

His lips twisted into a sort of froggy grin, the skin on his face stretching like taffy. He let out a pleasurable little moan, his eyes closed, sealed shut. One eye. Two eyes.

How long he'd wished to just remove them. He'd come so close, once upon a time... the scars around his left eye proved this. But he'd been found before he could complete the operation.

And now, he was glad he hadn't. He couldn't share the darkness with others. He was a willing apostle, a sufferer—facing the light so others didn't have to.

Even with his eyes closed, though, he could see *things.* Memories from his past, flitting thoughts and recollection. He could *hear* things too.

The click of a lock. The sound of his own screaming, as a child, hoarse in his ear.

Now he was crying and could feel the very real tears tracing his scarred face. Both aroused and horrified, he sat there in the front seat of his car, shivering and waiting for night to fall.

It took so long sometimes to bring the bleak black. But other times, it came all at once. Eyes still closed, he groped for the toolbelt on the seat next to him, feeling for the pliers, the wire-strippers... Everything was in order. He would cut the lights the same way he'd done the first two houses.

One eye. Two eyes. A stab wound for one. Another for the second.

Blind, dark, buried.

He smiled and cried, sitting in the seat, and simply waiting for the inevitable release.

CHAPTER ELEVEN

The manager had finally given his name as Mr. Ettiene after another three questions, and more than one attempt at a dodge. Adele still didn't have his first name.

The little man in the polka-dot bowtie back at the auction house was gripping his wooden podium with white knuckles, shaking his head determinedly. The motion was so severe, the glass display cases next to him rattled.

"You're not listening," he insisted, "No one else was here at the time. If you would be specific, perhaps I can help. What, precisely, is our problem?"

But Adele was still frowning, arms crossed, studying the small man and his slicked hair. "What about the other auction floors?"

"They wouldn't have any contact with those two items—it's all streamlined. I can walk you through it once we're closed."

Paige clicked her tongue, shaking her head as she stepped near. She placed a hand on the glass case with the jeweled watches. "Not good enough," she said. "Do you have an accountant? Someone who finalizes sales?"

The man scowled now. "Yes. My mother. She's seventy-five years old. She's good with numbers, but finds it hard to move around due to her *wheelchair...* I can take you upstairs to speak with her if you must," he said, his tone suggesting he wanted to do almost nothing less.

Adele rubbed the bridge of her nose. The small manager and his elderly mother didn't exactly strike her as the sorts to jam large men into furniture. Then again, someone connected to this place was cycling through victims at an alarming rate. Executive Foucault was on tenterhooks, looking over their shoulders.

"Has anyone taken time off in the last few days?" Adele said, feeling her frustration mounting. It felt like they'd been cornered in a dead end, and now she was looking for some glimpse of light, some alternative path.

"No one—except Mr. Almo on sick leave. But you already knew that."

Adele wanted to keep pressing, but she didn't know what to say. She truly had stumbled into a dead end with no way out. She turned in frustration, scanning the front room and display windows of the old, antique auction house. Her gaze skimmed past a cupboard filled with china, landing on a row of porcelain tchotchkes on an ottoman.

Perhaps they were approaching this from the wrong angle...

Her eyes narrowed and she frowned, still staring. It was nearly impossible to shake memories of the Painter—of the dead monster. Thoughts kept coming back, swirling and resting, then flitting away again like birds taking flight.

She could remember tracing the Painter's tracks to a candy-packing factory. She remembered suspecting the truckers... None of it had come to fruition, though.

Why did that matter? What was her subconscious suggesting?

She let out another, longer sigh, then slowly turned frowning at Mr. Ettiene. "Let's say we're not looking at one of your employees." He perked almost instantly. She continued. "Let's say we just want to look into people who were *at* both relevant auctions."

"Yes?" he said, slowly. "I can vouch for everyone who works for me."

She waved away the comment with a flick of her hand, trying to focus. "Could you provide us a list of everyone who attended both auctions?"

The manager still looked relieved. He nodded his head and said, "No."

She blinked. "Come again?"

This time, he paused, corrected the head motion, and said, "No, I cannot. We don't keep that information."

"You don't know who attends your auctions?"

"We don't require registration," he said, a bit of the earlier moan creeping back into his voice. "Please," he insisted, "I don't know what you want from me."

"Something helpful," Paige murmured.

The man in the bowtie ignored this. "Our auctions," he said insistently, rocking back and forth and causing his wooden greeting podium to shift as well, "are open to the public. Anyone can come and bid. Only winning bidders are required to provide their information."

"How about cameras?" Adele insisted.

He pointed at the ceiling. "Some on the floor, but not on the doors or facing the audience in the auction rooms. We find it spooks the guests."

"Seriously?" Adele said. She bit back any further comment. It almost felt like the small man was *trying* to make this impossible.

Now it made sense, though, why the killer had chosen Leon Antiques. He could have come, sat among the audience, completely anonymous. He would've been able to watch the other customers as the auctions were held.

Did he get off on it?

Was that part of the MO?

Paige was watching Adele now, turning her back to the auction-house manager as if she'd had quite enough from him.

For her part, Adele was struggling to think of their next move.

"Maybe we should get some rest," Paige was saying, frowning as she watched Adele, her eyes hooded, her expression indeterminable. "Come back to it tomorrow morning."

The manager nodded delightedly at this suggestion.

Adele, though, just stood there, frowning. Perhaps Paige was right. Perhaps some rest would clear her mind. They'd booked a couple of rooms just down the street.

But they were no closer to apprehending the culprit... And if the killer stuck to his pace, then another body would drop any time now. Another corpse on Adele's conscience.

She didn't want to face her conscience. Didn't want to face the silence of night, in a lonely room, with nothing but accusatory thoughts for companionship.

"Sure, sure," Adele said, nodding stiffly. "Some rest... Just, can I get what footage you do have from those cameras?" She pointed towards the surveillance equipment angled towards the items in the room.

"Then you'll leave?" he said.

"Yes. Then we'll leave."

"Done," he said, in an almost sing-song tone. "Just, be warned, most of the cameras are just for show. They aren't even on."

"Of course they aren't," Adele muttered beneath her breath.

***

Adele's hotel room had never felt so small... Where she sat on the edge of her bed, the darkness pressed in around her, and the sound of the dripping faucet from the bathroom sink echoed in the quiet space. *Drip. Drip.*

She scowled, her features illuminated by the blue glow of her raised phone as she cycled through the scant footage she'd been provided by the auction house owner.

Nothing. No one stood out. Most of the footage was too grainy to help, and most of the cameras had only been used as decoration.

Still, for the third time over the last three hours, she cycled back to the first video, squinting as she tried to make out the poorly pixelated forms moving through the auction house entrance. She thought she could just barely determine a bowtie on one of the figures—the manager no doubt.

"Come on...," she murmured, as if by speaking her frustrations aloud, she might coerce some cooperation from the technology.

But it was to no avail.

Night had claimed the horizon outside the hotel. The windows were shut, the door to her room bolted. It all felt so *small.* Claustrophobic, as if the night itself were pressing in around her, seeping into every crease and crevice of her t-shirt and slacks.

Another grainy image passed over her phone and she felt a flutter of sheer defeat. None of this footage would be of any use. No one's face was determinable. Most of the cameras—the working ones—had faced the merchandise, not the people.

Had the killer known this? Had he scoped the place out before?

They didn't even know who they were dealing with...

Her phone began to vibrate, and Adele yelped, dropping the device. It hit her knee, painfully, and flopped onto the bed between her legs. She scooted back, wincing and rubbing her knee before lifting the phone. The *drip, drip* from the bathroom sink was soon drowned by the ring of her device.

She stared at the name on the screen, feeling a slow prickle along her back.

For a moment, she considered letting it go to voicemail. But then she sighed, flopping back onto the pillows, her eyes closed in the dark. And she answered.

"Hey John," she said, trying to keep her tone bright and cheerful.

"Hang on, dear," a distant voice echoed on the phone. "Claudia—no—no, stop that!" Then she heard John belly laugh. There was the sound of splashing water and more laughter.

"Not soap!" a small, child's voice echoed. "No fair!"

John was still giggling like a schoolboy, though the sound was muffled over the device. "Keep it down—your mother said these dishes have to be as clean as she would make them. Come on—help me with the towel."

Adele stared at her phone, hesitant. "John?" she said.

But the only response was still muffled, distant. She heard another squeal of laughter and more splashing. John's booming voice, in mock anger, thundered, "You got it in my eye! Come here, you rascal!"

Another squeal of joy and the sound of thumping footsteps.

Adele tried a final time. "John?"

But clearly, he hadn't meant to call. She felt strange, sitting there in the dark, listening to a father play with his daughter. For a moment, she just wanted to keep listening. But then she sighed and shut the phone off.

It had been a long time since she'd ever felt *that* happy about anything. A pang of loneliness shot through her, and she pressed her head deeper into the embrace of the pillows.

She missed Robert... Missed her mother... Missed...

So much.

John was doing better now—better since the killer was dead. Since his daughter was still alive.

And while this seemed to bring Agent Renee joy, it only filled Adele with an even greater sense of guilt. The dripping sound from the bathroom continued to echo through the bedroom.

This case... this new killer... she'd hoped it might distract her from the plaguing thoughts... But now, again, she knew she was only in hiding. Slinking through the night, hoping Claudia didn't tell John what she'd seen. Hoping no one pried too close.

How much longer could she keep lying? She wasn't accustomed to lying—not professionally, and certainly not privately.

It ate at her insides.

But even more than that...

She'd allowed a man to die in front of her. She'd shot him, then watched him bleed and drown. She'd allowed him, in a way, to win. She'd given the one thing he hadn't been able to take by force. The part of herself that could only be surrendered willingly. And she'd done it.

To save Claudia. To save a life. He deserved it...

She wanted to believe this voice. Wanted to agree...

But things were never so easy. The Painter had spent his life playing games with others. And even in his death, he was still playing.

Eventually, she had to tell someone.

John? Perhaps this phone call was some sign. If anyone would understand, Renee would.

Adele closed her eyes, breathing slower now, trying to calm herself. The *drip, drip* from the bathroom only brought back thoughts of the swirling stream beneath the park bridge.

She twisted, turned, pulling a blanket over her heard to block out the noise.

Her own breath felt warm against her upper lip, her nose. Her back prickled with sweat beneath the blanket. The hotel they were staying at was far, far too quiet for Adele's taste.

She fidgeted again, shifting the other way.

In the dark, in the night, as sleep slowly came...

She pictured the scene beneath the bridge. The swirl of mist about them. The steady sound of churning water. The gurgle of the drowning killer.

Then, the body in the water went still. A hand flopped onto the shore. The face turned, twisting, staring up at her, sodden and damp...

A face she didn't recognize...

A face of some innocent...

Adele twisted again, growling as she hovered between sleep and rest. She was too hot... Too distracted.

Sleep would be elusive tonight.

Drip. Drip.

She snarled, throwing her blankets off, grabbing a pillow and stomping into the bathroom. She jammed the pillow beneath the faucet, catching the droplets now. As she returned in the dark, flopping back onto her bed, the sound finally faded.

Leaving Adele alone with her churning thoughts.

CHAPTER TWELVE

Night had come, but with it so had complications. He was no longer crying, but neither was he smiling. He scowled through the tinted window of his sedan, now parked further up the street, where he'd been forced to move to preserve his anonymity.

Ahead, under what should have been a dark, cloudy sky, lights were beaming. Headlights, windows, lights from the front door stretched across the long driveway and manicured lawn. Lights flashed from other cars as doors opened and closed and guests moved in and out.

The light bothered him almost as much as the people. He preferred coming out at dark, and now they were ruining this pitch-black tapestry. They were ruining his next visit.

He double-checked the doors were locked, his fingers scraping against the small plastic knob. He made sure the child lock was on, then slumped down in his seat, his back pressing into the firm cushion. He scowled through his windshield, watching as the guests entered the main house. Laughter flitted from the direction of the open door. Another sound of a slamming car trunk.

No doubt Mr. Schitt was showing off the new item he'd won at auction. "Schitt, Anders," the man murmured beneath his breath, trying the name on for size, reciting it in the same way he'd read it. He always had a knack for reading. There had been a time, not long ago, when he hadn't had any interaction *besides* his books. And even those had been dusty, old, falling apart and weather worn.

Now, slumped in his seat, he made sure his buckle was tightened, the seatbelt across his chest in a comforting way. Even though he was in park, the car unmoving, he felt a shiver of delight at the securing strap.

Schitt was showing off the old piano, no doubt. He'd paid a king's ransom for that hunk of wood and keys. The man in the car snorted, shaking his head in derision. The things people spent money on these days... pathetic.

And that was why he was here after all...

He twisted at the strap over his chest, flattening it. Then, he reached back, still slumped in his seat, groping around in the darkness behind him. It took a second, and he knocked aside some clutter of old fast-food wrappers and empty water bottles. Then, he found the hem of his thick, large blanket. The sort of blanket one might use as the backdrop for a stage.

He pulled it, grunting from exertion due to the sheer weight of the hefty thing. As he did, he continued staring out the window, watching, waiting.

Time would pass, night would fall. Eventually, even these partygoers would leave. Eventually, everyone would have to sleep. They always did.

Not so with him.

He hadn't slept in nearly two decades. Not since it had all started so many years ago.

Sleep was for the weak. Sleep was a distraction. Sleep, sometimes, held the fear at bay. It allowed you to swaddle your consciousness in neglect, and comfort. But without sleep... nightmares still came. Except in his mind, the nightmares were all too real.

Another flash of memories. Of being trapped in that horrible, horrible space. The stench of dust, the constant sneezing. The air was thick with mildew. He'd choked and vomited—how he'd been beaten for that mistake.

Years he'd spent tight, locked, trapped. He hadn't slept a wink.

And now, it was sometimes difficult to tell if he was simply wandering around life in a daze, or if he was well and truly asleep. Perhaps all of *this* was a dream.

He would help Schitt sleep, too. It was the least he could do to repay them for all those years.

He grunted and yanked the thick blanket a final time. The thing smelled familiar, also of dust and mildew and mothballs. An old blanket. The faint hint of BO and urine tinging it.

A comforting blanket. He pulled it over himself, still staring out the window, wrapping the blanket over his head, allowing it to drape down his form. He swaddled himself in the thick fabric until it wrapped around him, tightly. He pulled it fast, securing it *beneath* the belt buckle with more tugs and insistent grunts.

Then, like that, cocooned in his own blanket and seatbelt, his arms barely above to move, his legs secured as well from the thick fabric, he sat... and waited... and watched.

Lesser others might have panicked from the claustrophobic confines of the dark, small car, the seatbelt, the constricting blanket.

But to him?

This was home.

This was security.

Like a turtle's own shell—he could take it wherever he went.

And while he couldn't sleep, he could think... he could remember.

Violent, hateful memories flashed through his mind—two decades of movies to draw from. Twice as much life as most other humans in the same time frame. He'd never been given the anesthesia of slumber—he'd had to endure.

And so he sat there, not quite awake, not quite asleep, still living a two decade-old nightmare he'd never been allowed to wake from.

Now, he contented himself by simply dragging others into the horrors he saw.

Mr. Schitt would be next.

Eventually the guests would leave. Eventually, as always, he'd be the only one awake.

CHAPTER THIRTEEN

Adele wasn't sure she'd slept much the previous night. Her limbs felt heavy, her eyelids laden as she sat propped on her bed, staring towards the door to her hotel room. *Tap. Tap.*

The same sound that had woken her. At first, she'd thought the sink had started to overflow, but then she realized it was coming from the door. Another polite double tap, then a pause.

"H-hello?" Adele called, her voice hoarse from poor sleep. She blinked again, wincing against the faint strands of sunlight coming through the lowered blinds behind her.

"Adele?" Sophie Paige's voice came brusquely through the sealed door. "Are you ready?"

Adele groaned but muffled the sound as best she could. She wanted nothing more than to flop back on her pillows and allow her blankets to swallow her. She wanted to stare at the ceiling, at the immobile blades of the wooden fan. She wanted to drift away.

But sleep had other ideas.

So did Paige.

Perhaps the two of them were in cahoots.

Adele scowled at the thought. She pushed out of the bed, groggily, grabbed her suit jacket and pulled it on. She hurried into the bathroom, double-checking the sink hadn't overflowed, and, peering over a very damp pillow, she stared at herself in the mirror. Her dirty-blonde hair was disheveled, and it took some water and quick motions to smooth it as best she could.

She was nearly five foot nine, taller than most women, but now she felt hunched, her shoulders laden as if the weight of the world had finally found a preferred resting spot.

Once she'd brushed her teeth, mostly for the scent of mint, neglecting a proper cleaning of her molars, she hurried back into the bedroom, grabbed her phone from the nightstand and reached the front door in time for another insistent *Tap-tap.*

She flung open the door, her hair still somewhat out of place, one of her buttons done incorrectly on her suit, and her phone clutched in damp fingers.

Paige, on the other hand, looked like she'd just arrived from a business meeting. The older woman frowned, her lips pursed, her suit immaculate.

"Agent Sharp," she said briefly, peering past Adele into the bedroom.

"Paige."

"Ready?"

Adele blinked, trying to focus on the day. "I—yes... We're going to...," she trailed off, hoping Paige would fill in the blank, which she didn't. It was a difficult thing to *not do* something smugly, but Paige managed even this.

"Did you sleep?"

Adele shrugged. "Somewhat. Kind of."

"You look like death, dear."

"Thank you."

Paige sniffed. "Did you find anything on the camera footage?"

Adele paused, then shook her head. "No—no nothing. The footage was too grainy. Too many gaps."

"So we have nothing?"

Adele sighed, massaging the bridge of her nose. She wasn't sure she was ready for all of this. She glanced down at her phone, relieved to see the only text was from her father, making sure she was doing well.

"No other bodies in the night?" Adele said, feeling the faintest glimmer of hope.

Paige shook her head. "None we've been notified about yet."

"At least there's that."

"Sleep is important, you know, Adele."

Adele wrinkled her nose. "I know that. Just... was busy last night."

"With the footage?"

"Something like that," Adele said. The last person she wanted to get into her recurring sense of guilt and horror with was standing before her—five foot-two, with a face like a retired nun.

Paige didn't lean against the door frame, like John Renee might have. She wasn't nearly so physically confident or comfortable. Every time she took a step, or even a breath, it looked like it mildly irritated her. The only thing *more* irritating to Agent Paige was standing on the other side of the hotel room door.

"I imagine it's somewhat of a distraction," Paige said at last.

"Excuse me?"

"Killing the Spade killer. I read the report."

Instantly, Adele stiffened, an alarm going off in her mind. She shifted, nearly imperceptibly, into somewhat of a defensive stance, frowning towards the older woman in the doorway. “Oh?” she said as noncommittally as she could manage. Where was this coming from? This was the second time Agent Paige had started sniffing around.

“Yes,” Paige said, nodding. “You're being lauded as a hero back at the office. Quite impressive, Agent Sharp. To have survived what so many succumbed to.”

“Hmm,” Adele said. “Well, thank you, I guess? Look, I don't really want to talk about it.”

“I wouldn't either.”

“I was thinking about the case,” Adele said, intent to redirect this line of conversation. The less Agent Paige examined the shooting of the Painter, the better as far as Adele was concerned. If anyone might accuse her of a bad shooting, or failing to render aid, it would be this woman. Already, Adele felt enough guilt as it was. But not so much guilt that she wanted to spend the next twenty years behind bars for homicide.

“What about it?”

Adele winced. “Just... while they don't have registrations of all the guests who attended, they would have to take down information of all the auction *winners,* yes?”

Paige blinked. “I suppose so.”

“Well, we won't be able to find the suspect this way. But we might be able to find his next victim.”

“You're certain he'll kill again?”

“Aren't you?”

Paige blinked, hesitated, but then pressed her lips into a thin line. “And how do you suggest we use this information?”

“Well... we can cross-reference the winning bidders of *all* the items during both the auctions Mr. Foucault and Mr. Vosloo attended. They would have been winners of single items among many. Perhaps some of the other winners saw something. Or were targeted in some way. Hell, maybe the items themselves could have a connection.”

Paige shrugged. “Alright. I'll call the auction house for the information.” Adele began to step out of the room, but Paige held up a hand. The older woman snorted, waving back towards the bedroom. “Clean up, dear. You look like death.”

Adele blinked, but Paige grabbed the door handle and shut it in the younger woman's face, sealing her in darkness once again.

It wasn't until Adele heard the faint ringing sound of a phone connecting on the other side of the door that she frowned. Not just at Paige's feather-ruffling personality, but at her *words.*

You look like *death.*

Had she simply intended to be insulting? Or had she meant something more by the phrase?

Adele massaged the bridge of her nose, closing her sleep-deprived eyes a moment longer. She couldn't think like this, especially not while tired. She needed coffee—black. Two of them. Perhaps then she'd be able to face Paige.

Perhaps then she'd be of some use on this case. Foucault had called on her specifically. A sign of respect. But also, while it gave her the chance to curry favor, it also shone a bright spotlight right on her.

And the longer she stood in the limelight, the more likely spectators saw things she wanted hidden. Shadows and glimpses of skeletons in her closet best kept out of sight.

Paige's voice came muffled now from the other side of the door as she spoke on the phone. Adele turned, moving back to the bathroom to splash some water on her face.

Paige's inferences aside, Adele felt at least a little vindicated. Comparing the names of the auction winners was bound to yield *something.* Some lead.

One step at a time. That's how cases were solved. Just one step.

CHAPTER FOURTEEN

Adele sat in the car, in the back seat this time. She wasn't sure why, but somehow, it felt more comfortable to avoid sitting directly next to Agent Paige. At least this way, the older woman had to glance in the rearview mirror to see her.

They were sitting in the parking lot outside the hotel in their dark, rental hybrid SUV. Paige scanned her phone then her eyes bounced, reflecting in the mirror. "Anything?" she said.

Adele didn't reply at first. For the last hour now, they'd been combing the records provided by the auction house manager.

Names and addresses and item numbers for the winning bidders of unique antiques. "No overlap," Adele murmured. "Here's the closest, two men with the last name Bardem—but one lives in Spain, and the other Italy."

"Related?"

Adele shook her head. "Already checked. Nothing."

"So we don't have any connection between the two auction days?"

Adele sighed, her eyes still bleary. The large Styrofoam cup, exuding the bitter aroma of black, no sugar, sat in the lowered divider across the middle seat. The second cup-holder also had a coffee, this one already drained, and half crumpled.

Paige hadn't grabbed anything from the hotel lobby, as if intent on making a point.

For Adele, all she cared about now was their next step. The gentle nudge of caffeine cycling through her system prompted her to scan the excel sheet on her phone a second time. She was surprised at how many names there were. The small, auction house had sold nearly thirty items in just those two days.

A few of them priced in the tens of thousands. Some, though rare, even higher.

"I have a woman in Germany and another from Leon who share a birthday," Paige said, glancing in the mirror again.

"Either of them connected to our victims?"

"No."

"I checked the birth dates, too—no connection."

The air of frustration was now mounting in the car. Adele and Paige were frowning where they reclined in their seats, stationed in the dark parking lot outside the hotel.

Though her eyes stung from the screen, Adele refused to give up. Something would have to click. Something had to—

"Let's visit someone," Paige said suddenly.

Adele looked up. "Excuse me?"

"Someone on the list." She raised her phone, wagging it.

"Who?"

"I don't care. Anyone. Someone local. There's that woman from Leon. Let's see her."

"And how is that going to help?"

Paige turned in her seat, scowling. "Do you have a better idea?"

"No. I'm just trying to get a sense for the tactic here."

Paige turned back, huffing a breath as if the explanation were beneath her. But then, in a somewhat patronizing tone, she said, "They don't live far from here, so it won't cost us much time. Plus, as you mentioned, the cameras were grainy—poor footage. Perhaps, with the help of an eyewitness, we might be able to stir something up. You know these sorts—bidders at auctions. Nuance is important. Collectors of antique? They pay attention to detail. I think we should speak with someone who was actually there."

Adele stared at the back of Sophie's head, her own phone still half-raised. Her eyebrows inched up, somewhat impressed. It wasn't a bad plan. It wasn't great, but it felt more like making the best of what they had, squeezing water from a rock. Only a few droplets, yet still impressive given the tools available.

"Huh," Adele said.

"Huh," Sophie returned. "You're not the only one who can follow a hunch, Agent Sharp. Here, we can visit Ms. Charis Bigarny. She lives twenty minutes from the auction house. Are you buckled?"

Adele sighed, but leaned over, grabbing the buckle and listening to it whir as she clicked it in place. She settled back in her seat. Once Paige was sure her passenger was secured, only then did she put the car in gear and, far, far slower than John Renee ever would have, began to roll out of their parking spot and circle down the ramp towards the street.

***

Adele stared at the old, archaic house behind the large, silver gate. Given how much Ms. Bigarny had paid for a stuffed owl on an old coat rack, Adele wasn't surprised the woman came from wealth. But the estate itself looked almost like an old cathedral, with sandstone turrets and even—what looked like—a belfry.

But the silver gate, the rows of trimmed hedges and the giant marble fountain centering a roundabout made it clear this was a private residence.

Paige was rolling her window down as they pulled their vehicle towards the closed gate. Adele was struck at just how quietly they moved on the perfectly maintained blacktop—no stray stones, nor gravel. The smooth ride was interrupted only by a faint jolt as Paige put them in park and pressed the buzzer.

The woman frowned up at a camera situated above the buzzer, facing towards the front of the car.

Adele watched, waiting, occasionally glancing through the window towards the enormous cathedral-styled mansion beyond the pond. She wondered what sort of permits were required to construct something with honest-to-goodness, stained glass windows like Ms. Bigarny's home.

"Hello!" Paige said impatiently. She waved a hand towards the camera. "DGSI!" she insisted.

At this last part, the buzzer suddenly crackled. A voice emanated from a speaker above the camera. "DGSI, you say? Who is this?"

A male voice. A snobby, male voice in Adele's opinion, though perhaps that was simply her own biases coming through.

"Agent Sophie Paige with Agent Adele Sharp," the woman replied. She flashed her credentials, holding them up to the camera, then lowered them again.

"No, no!" the voice snapped. "Hold it higher—I can't see."

Paige scowled, but lifted her laminated ID again, holding it long enough for the camera to see. Then, she lowered it once more.

Again, Adele was struck by how differently this might have gone with John Renee in the driver's seat. Both Paige and Renee were impatient. But in Paige's case, while she was often frowning or grumpy, she still *acted* professionally. John, on the other hand, probably would have tried to batter through the gates with the hood of the car.

Different strokes for different folks, took on a whole new, cardiac event-inducing meaning where Agent Renee was concerned. Still, Adele missed her boyfriend. Things were far, far *chillier* in the back seat.

"We're here to speak with Ms. Bigarny," Agent Paige insisted.

Another crackle. Then the same voice. "Is the mistress in *danger*?"

"Nothing like that," Paige returned. "Open the gate please. We can speak in person."

"Do you have a warrant?" the voice replied.

Paige scowled. "Do we need one?"

Completely unphased, the voice said, "Yes. I recommend Judge Bigarny. I'm sure he'd love to let you intrude on his daughter's privacy."

Adele winced. Paige leaned back, rubbing a hand across her forehead. "Is she there?" Paige said. "This shouldn't take long."

Another pause, another crackle from the speaker, but this time with no response. The silver gate remained sealed. The flash of sunlight across the red, blue, yellow windows beyond seemed to taunt them now in vibrations of resplendent color.

Adele shifted a bit in the back seat, adjusting her seat belt—it was far too tight. But when she'd tried to remove it on the drive over, the overly-safety conscious Agent Paige had pulled to the side of the road until Adele had replaced it. Now, Adele was worried if she tried to remove it again, she'd get a tongue-lashing in front of a witness's home.

Paige waited an appropriate amount of time but then reached out for the buzzer again, before she managed to press it, though, a far different voice came over the intercom.

"Hello," the voice said, sounding somewhat sleepy.

"Ms. Bigarny?" Paige replied, staring at the intercom.

"This is Charis, yes. You are with the police, I'm told."

"Agent Paige. We would like to speak with you."

"Yes."

"...Inside, perhaps?"

"No, thank you, this is fine. How can I help you? I'm not in trouble, am I?" The voice tried to laugh airily, but there was an undercurrent to the words that made it sound desperate.

"No, Ms. Bigarny, nothing like that. We don't believe you're in any danger, either. We would like to speak with you about the Leon Antiques auction house."

Adele was staring through the windshield now, trying to spot any movement in the big house. She briefly thought she saw a flicker of shadow across one of the lower, stained-glass windows. But the motion might simply have been the movement of trees planted ten feet apart throughout the courtyard.

Adele wondered where Charis Bigarny had stowed the antique coat rack she'd won at the auction. In a place that large, there were many rooms to choose from. Rooms, by the sound of things, the two agents were never going to set eyes on.

“I'm not comfortable inviting strangers in my home, Ms. Paige,” replied the voice in that same airy, sleepy quality.

“Agent Paige,” Sophie stressed. “Alright, fine then. Would you be willing to come out here and meet us?”

A pause, then murmured voices. Finally, a long sigh. Adele watched from the back seat as a sliding terrace door opened, and a figure stepped out onto a patio, curlers in her hair, wearing a long, flowing silk sleeping gown. At this distance, the woman looked somewhat squat and shaped like a barrel. Still, she moved with grace and poise as she approached the rail of the terrace, leaning against it and overlooking her immaculate garden, waving one hand across the expanse between the house and the sealed gate.

“I can see you,” the woman murmured, her voice still echoing over the speaker. Adele peered through the windshield and spotted the way the Ms. Bigarny cupped something against the side of her face, like a phone receiver or some sort of walkie-talkie.

“We can see you,” Agent Paige said. “Would you mind coming to the gate?”

“No, thank you, agent. I don't have all day. What can I help you with?”

Paige shot a look into the mirror which Adele returned with a shrug. She'd never conducted an interrogation over an intercom before. Then again, at least the woman was willing to chat. With the filthy rich sorts. one could never really tell.

The woman was leaning against the marble terrace rail now, one of her hair curlers having fallen in front of her eyes. She was adjusting her bangs and waiting patiently.

Paige frowned and said, “I really must insist you—”

But Adele, knowing a losing battle, cut in, calling from the back seat, “We wanted to ask you about your visit to that auction house. If you remember anything of the day.”

The woman on the patio hesitated. Then said, “Who is this?”

“Agent Sharp—I'm in the car too.”

“Hello Mrs. Sharp. What are you asking about specifically?”

Paige was frowning again but at least held her tongue, allowing Adele to speak. “I want to reiterate, ma'am, you're not in any trouble. But we're wondering about other bidders on the day of your auction. This would've been... three days ago, yes?”

“Mhmm. I won this lovely little barnyard owl. I love owls, you know.”

“Right—well, do you happen to remember an old grandfather clock?

A really big thing. It was won by a middle-aged man."

"Umm, yes, I think so. It was a few slots before my purchase. Why do you ask?" The woman had finally adjusted her hair curler and was now standing straight for modesty's sake, as her nightgown was drooping a bit low.

Adele stared through the windshield, between the wide bars of the silver gate, down the long driveway between the hedges, her eyes fixated on the single figure outlined against a tall, stained-glass window. The oddness of the interview was only challenged by the line of questioning. "Just—honestly anything untoward? Perhaps other bidders," she said, suddenly struck by a thought, "people who bid on that same grandfather clock, but missed out."

"You want to know about the clock or my owl?"

"The clock, please."

"My owl was more expensive, you know," the woman said, sounding petulant all of a sudden. Another figure was standing just inside the sliding glass door, a silhouette, beckoning towards the woman. "Look, I'm afraid I have to go. If you want to speak with me, please make an—"

"One more, sorry—I'm sure the owl is lovely," Adele said quickly. "I like owls too."

"Oh, yes? What's your favorite type?"

"Tawny," Adele said, making a complete guess.

"Ah—well, I see. Yes, they can be quite—"

"Mhmm. But look, about the auction. You said the grandfather clock was a couple of slots before yours, yes? Well, I was wondering if you noticed anything about the customers who were bidding on that thing? Did anyone stand out at all to you?"

"I—I mean I can't say they did. Well..."

"Anyone suspicious? Anyone who looked out of place?"

"There was this very, very smelly woman. She took up a seat in front of me. I could see her neck sweat."

"Anyone else?"

Ms. Bigarny sighed, nodding towards the silhouette in her home as a gloved hand fluttered, gesturing for her to step back inside. She lowered the device from her face a bit, but then murmured, "Well—now that you mention it, I do recall one thing."

"Yes?" Adele perked.

Paige had gone still as well, her lips sealed, watching with raised eyebrows in the small, rearview mirror.

"This very rude man—he didn't care at all about the owl. Not that

I'm complaining, but I remember him saying it was ugly." She snorted, shaking her head and causing her curlers to swish. "No taste, mind you. He was quite ugly as well. But this man only seemed to want that stupid clock. That's all he talked about. Kind of like you."

"I see. And this man—how did he react when the clock was sold?"

"He lost out—didn't have enough money, I imagine. It often comes down to money." She snorted, shaking her head again and patting a hand against the marble rail. "Silly to show up at an auction while poor. Not that I mind poor people, of course. Some of my best friends are poor."

"Of course. And this man, once he lost the bid, did he say anything? Do anything?"

"Why yes, in fact, he did. He told the man who won the clock that he'd regret it. He was very, very angry at missing out for the second time that same week."

"Wait, hang on? He missed out another time?"

"I don't know the details, Mrs. Sharp. I just remember him screaming like a banshee, yelling and flailing. Quite unsightly. But he was upset about losing the clock. And also kept saying how the whole system was rigged against him. Just like Saturday's auction. That was what he kept saying. Just like Saturday. The whole thing is rigged... Of course, it isn't. He just was out of his depth. Anyway, Mrs. Paige—no, sorry, Sharp? Yes, Mrs. Sharp. I'm sorry but I must be going. Have a wonderful—"

"Hang on, just one more—"

"—day."

The intercom went silent. The woman on the patio turned, her silk robe fluttering behind her as she moved back into the house towards the beckoning silhouette. The screen door slid shut, and once again, Paige and Adele were left alone, facing the long driveway and the old mansion.

"Well then...," Adele began to say, but Paige was holding up a finger and, in her other hand, a phone.

Adele went silent, frowning and watching as Paige's phone vaguely rang in the background. A second later, a voice answered.

"You again?" the voice groaned, muffled over the speaker.

"Yes, me," Paige said firmly. "How come you didn't mention the disturbances this last week?"

"The—what?" Adele recognized the voice of Mr. Ettiene, the auction-house manager. "What disturbances?"

"We've just been speaking with a reliable witness."

"Who?"

"Confidential. But we've been speaking with them, and they give testimony that there was an outburst from one of your clients after the auction of the grandfather clock. How come you didn't mention this?"

"What? An outburst—no don't be silly. That sort of thing happens all the time, Agent Paige. All the time. Emotions run high at auctions. It's like a sport to these people. To *us.* A little bit of emotion is to be expected, smiled upon, in fact."

Paige frowned but pressed the issue. "According to our witness this went a bit beyond frayed tempers. The angry customer threatened the winning bidder that they'd regret it. Apparently, he suggested the auctions were rigged."

"Rigged? Now—now that's ridiculous! Who would—hang on, wait, do you mean Mr. Cabellut?"

"Who?"

"Just a local businessman. We've had him in before. He always sets his eyes on things a bit out of his price-range, if you catch my drift."

"I see—and why would he accuse you of rigging bids?"

A long sigh, and for a moment, Adele thought the manager might have hung up, but then the voice returned. "I think I know what he's referring to. He lost out on another bid on Saturday, a couple of days before the Monday auction."

"What bid?" Adele and Paige said simultaneously.

"I—well... damn. Now that you mention it, perhaps I should have recollected. Mr. Cabellut has been doing this for years now, though. He's like a grumpy uncle. Certainly harmless."

"What bid?" Paige insisted.

A long, whistling sigh. Then, "The wardrobe. The one Mr. Foucault won."

Paige perked up. Adele went stiff in her chair.

"You're telling me this Mr. Cabellut bid on the wardrobe, lost, then bid on the grandfather clock and also lost, then threatened our second victim?"

"It didn't even cross my mind. Mr. Cabellut has been coming regularly for years. He's complained in the past. It's just how he is. A little bit too much drink if you catch my drift."

This was the second time the manager had stated something blatantly while treating it as an inference. Subtlety clearly wasn't the fellow's strong suit. But neither was critical thinking if his testimony was to be believed.

"What is this Mr. Cabellut's first name?" Adele called.

"I—umm, I don't—wait yes... David, I think. Mhmm. David Cabellut. He sells furniture... A boutique store—not antiques mind you. Cheap furniture." The manager enunciated this last part clearly as if it were quite important.

"He sells *furniture*," Adele pressed. "And our two victims bid on items he lost. He threatened one of them. And then later, both victims were found shoved *into furniture.* Is that what you're saying?"

"I—well when you say it like that... But no, no—hang on... Victims? What do you mean shoved into—"

"Focus!" Paige snapped.

"Oh my... Oh dear... My... Mr. Cabellut is not a violent man. He's all bluster no bark. He isn't particularly successful in his business but likes to flaunt as if he is. He enjoys the attention."

"So he's vain. And by losing out on those items he bid on, his vanity was threatened. Is that fair?"

Another, even longer pause over the phone. Then a mumbled, "Perhaps it is best you ask him yourselves. His shop is in the city—simply called *Cabellut's Repeat Boutique.*"

Paige was already putting the car in gear. Adele was no longer listening to the faint chirps and protests over the phone. She frowned, scowling out the window and watching the stream of asphalt and tree lines as they hastened away from the old mansion.

A man who flaunted wealth he didn't really have, and who was prone to outbursts of anger, was exactly the sort of person who might finally *do* something about their sense of ego. Something like murder? Quite possibly.

There was often no telling what made someone snap.

Paige picked up the pace, still sticking to the speed limits, but clicking off her phone and tossing it on the side seat to grip the steering wheel and focus as she moved back through the city.

"GPS," she called over her shoulder.

But Adele had already typed the furniture store's name into her phone. Now, she had clicked the address and raised her device so Agent Paige could hear the directions.

CHAPTER FIFTEEN

The *Repeat Boutique* was located between Leon and Linxe. Only a half-hour drive from the antique store. As they approached the place, Adele was struck by just how similar it looked to *Leon Antiques.* The window displays had nearly identical lettering, advertising products within. The door even had a little brass bell that jangled when they entered the store.

Adele blinked for a second, staring at a nearly identical wooden greeting podium at the end of the room near a cash register.

The woman behind the register was even wearing a polka-dot bowtie like the manager at the auction house.

"Spooky," Adele muttered beneath her breath.

Paige didn't comment, perhaps didn't even notice the obvious similarities, and instead marched right up to the receptionist, leaning in and slapping a hand against the varnished counter. "Hello," Paige said towards the older woman sitting in the desk chair behind the counter.

The receptionist looked up, beaming—though there was something a bit too *toothy* about the smile. "Hello," the woman replied with a nod. "Welcome to—"

"Forget about that," Paige interjected. "We're here to speak with Mr. Cabellut."

The woman continued smiling, her hands resting out of sight behind the counter. Adele approached around the podium, slipping past an assortment of small tea tables with a big discount placard.

"Oh?" the woman asked. "And do you have an appointment?"

As seasoned as Paige was, she had already anticipated the riposte. Her laminated ID card was slapped on the counter before the sentence had completed. She tapped a perfectly manicured, unpainted nail against it.

The woman glanced down, her plucked eyebrows going low over long, paste-on lashes. Then, she looked slowly up, her gaze bouncing from the ID to the women. "I see," she said. "And is there a reason the DGSI wants to speak with Mr. Cabellut?"

"Yes," Paige said curtly. "Where is he?"

Her gaze flicked down a hallway, leading into the back of the store, but she just as quickly returned her attention to the agents. "I'm afraid," she said with a delicate cough, "Mr. Cabellut isn't in right now. He's out for lunch."

"At ten AM?" Adele countered.

"Sorry, did I say lunch? I meant a business meeting." The woman folded her hands primly besides a keyboard on the desk. "I can take a note, though—what is this all about?"

"Do you have a way of contacting him?" Paige asked insistently.

"Oh—I mean, certainly. But he doesn't like being interrupted in business meetings. Perhaps its best if you came back another—"

"Paige," Adele said curtly, frowning down the hall.

Someone was moving on the other side of a glass, office door. The shadow disappeared a second later, but it was the same door the receptionist had looked to moments before. Adele glanced at the woman's hands which were back in sight. She frowned, then started moving, around the counter space towards the long hall.

"Excuse me!" the woman called. "You can't go back there."

"Did you tip him off?" Adele snapped, looking over her shoulder.

"Sharp," Paige said.

"He's here!" Adele replied. "He's back here."

The receptionist was still squawking but Adele was no longer listening and instead picked up her pace, breaking into a jog as she hastened towards the office door at the end of the hall. The shadow was no longer moving inside, but it was nice to put her body through rapid motion again. Normally, she spent a couple of hours every morning going for jogs or doing some sort of cardio. In recent days, she simply hadn't found the motivation...

Normally, running or any sort of physical movement helped keep her mind off things. But things were different now. Perhaps they'd never be the same again.

Regardless, caffeine cycling through her system, feet picking up the pace, arms pumping, Adele felt at ease for a brief moment. Paige was calling after her, the receptionist was shouting. And then, just from within the office, Adele heard a faint, muffled oath.

"He's here!" Adele yelled. She reached the door, not bothering to knock, and flung it open. "DGSI!" she called. "Mr. Cabellut, you're—"

She froze. So did the man straddling the windowsill. His red tie had caught in the frame and he was hastily yanking at it. In one hand, he'd managed to grab a pair of scissors from the nearest desk and was busy cutting at the tie.

Now, though, scissors frozen, tie extended, the man trying to make his getaway just stared at her.

He had dark features, with oversized, bugging eyes. His hair was prickly and sheered closed. At first, it seemed like his barber had done a poor job, but on closer inspection, Adele assumed the man's head was oddly shaped, with strange divots or the faintest of bumps. Whatever the case, it gave him an odd, thuggish look.

The man cursed at last, cutting his tie, tossing the scissors to the floor and hefting himself out the window.

"Stop!" Adele yelled.

But he had clearly already determined his course of action. She heard more yelling from the direction of reception. Agent Paige was still calling after her.

"He's running!" she yelled down the hall. "The parking lot! Go! Go!"

She heard a shout then the sudden sound of rapid footsteps. For her part, Adele couldn't pause to determine what Paige had decided to do. Instead, she was now rushing to the open window as well. Beyond, as she hastily approached, she spotted Mr. Cabellut stumbling through a hedge lining his office building and tracking strands of dark mulch across the pavement as he shook his shoe, trying to dislodge some of the offending organic material.

"Stop!" she tried again.

But the furniture store owner was hastening towards a flaming red Maserati parked in a designated space beneath a metal sign. Behind her, Adele heard the jangle of the brass bell, suggesting Paige was hurrying around the building as well.

She hurled herself through the window, slipping over the sill and landing in the freshly mulched landscaping. Stumbling over strands of bark, and kicking through a prickly hedge, she raced up the sidewalk, cursing and breathing heavily. The caffeine circling her system was now joined by a jolt of adrenaline, propelling her rapidly forward.

"DGSI!" she tried again. "Mr. Cab—" But she cut herself off, preferring now to conserve her breath. The man had clicked the locks to his sports car and was hastily slipping into the front seat. She heard a squeak of fright from the man as he peered through his window and spotted another figure emerging around the side of the building. Agent Paige emerged, paused on the sidewalk, assessed the situation, then spun on her heel, racing back towards their parked SUV, keys jangling as she pulled them from her pocket.

Mr. Cabellut pulled his Maserati from his parking spot, tires squealing and lending rubber to the road. Adele rushed forward, stepping off the sidewalk onto the asphalt. She watched as, through the windshield, the business owner glanced in his rearview mirror, spotting Agent Paige enter the SUV. His already oversized eyes widened in panic, and instead of heading towards the road, he instead turned his wheel sharply, custom rims spinning, as he rushed towards the alley.

Directly in Adele's direction.

She paused, briefly, standing in the road. The headlights flashed; the horn blared as the sports car hastened towards her.

Agent Paige's SUV was now pulling from its spot, angry rear-view lights glaring. The Maserati put on a burst of speed, horn still screeching.

And Adele...

Stayed put.

She'd never played chicken with a speeding sports car before, but in that moment, feet set on the asphalt, she knew she wasn't going to move.

Her hand went to her holster, resting there, but she didn't draw her weapon—didn't even have time. She just glared, feet at shoulder width, standing directly in front of the fleeing Maserati, blocking its path.

She saw the whites of Mr. Cabellut's eyes widen in horror beyond the windshield. Watched the front bumper of the bright red vehicle rush towards her motionless form.

But she didn't blink—didn't flinch.

A small, much darker part of her subconscious whispered strange and sweet promises as the car approached. In some ways, this could solve her problems.

One way or another. She was so tired of worrying, of spinning her own wheels. Tired of constant motion without progress. Tired of fear.

She stared at the car, almost smiling now. At the very least, feeling completely at peace.

Then the sports car veered sharply. Through the cracked window she heard a shouted curse. Mr. Cabellut spun the wheel, avoiding her at the last moment and plowing with a sickening *crunch* into the side of his own office. The hood of the car crumpled, crushed like a tin can against the brickwork.

Adele stood there, breathing heavily, eyes wide as she stared at the steaming hood of the ruined sports car. From within the front seat, through the cracked window she heard low moaning and a series of faint curses... "Crazy... bitch..." the voice was saying.

For a moment, she stood rooted to the spot, her mind mid-capitulation, trying to keep up with her own sparking physiology. Sweat dampened her palms; her spine tingled. Agent Paige's SUV screeched to a halt behind the smashed sports car. The older woman leapt from the front seat, glaring at Adele.

"Are you crazy!" she yelled.

Adele blinked, glancing back towards the Maserati. "He seems to think so," she murmured.

Paige just growled, handcuffs emerging from her belt. Adele remained rooted, not quite sure she had the strength to take a step.

She'd been braced... preparing for... for what?

She wasn't sure she wanted to admit what she'd been thinking.

Wasn't sure she even remembered.

She watched, a spectator, adrenaline receding like the tide as Paige barked instructions, checked to make sure their suspect was still coherent, then pulled him from the front of his car, yanking his arms behind him.

"Stop whining," Paige snapped. "You aren't even scratched. Mr. Cabellut, you're under arrest."

Adele felt a flicker of gratitude at these words. Arrest. That was one of the ways the game of chicken could have ended.

The other way...

She shook her head, finally stepping from the asphalt, back onto the sidewalk, moving as if in a dream state towards Agent Paige.

At least they now had their suspect.

Mr. Cabellut had been seen bidding on the same items as the two victims. Had been heard threatening the second victim.

Adele's mind was slow at first, like a train suddenly switching tracks after a stop. But now, breathing steadily again, on the sidewalk once more, she passed a hand over her face, feeling the effect of the caffeine aid her mind. The suspect—he was their suspect. Yes...

Focus damn it, she thought to herself.

She watched as Paige pushed the furniture-store owner back towards the waiting SUV. "I'm driving," Paige snapped towards Adele. She muttered beneath her breath, "Insane... absolutely insane..."

Adele winced but instead of commenting, simply fell into step, slipping into the front seat and already rehearsing the interrogation in her mind.

CHAPTER SIXTEEN

Anders Schitt winced against the pounding headache. Groggily, feeling the soft bunny rabbit slippers beneath his feet, he padded to the kitchen sink, glass in hand. He allowed lukewarm water from the faucet to fill his glass, his head still aching. He took a long swallow, closing his eyes against another throb of pain.

The previous night's celebrations had come with a cost. Normally, Anders didn't think of himself as much of a drinker. But his friends always knew how to entice him. Moscato. Cheap, sweet wine, little more than grape juice with fizz. And now, a few hours after a bottle and a half, he was reaping the reward.

How embarrassing. A wine headache.

He glanced across the kitchen, his eyes moving over the island counter, towards the large couch in the high-ceilinged living room. One of his friends was still sleeping on the couch, having stayed the night before. But the slumbering man's face was buried beneath a duvet, and Anders couldn't make out his features. He couldn't even remember who he'd invited the previous night. He groaned again, massaging his temples, taking another long sip of water, and then grabbing a piece of bread from a pack next to the toaster. Jamming the bread into his mouth, he stumbled in his bunny rabbit slippers towards the front door.

The guest sleeping on the couch tossed, groaning, likely suffering a similar pounding head.

Anders stepped down the long hall, beneath an ornate chandelier over the doorway. Two marble pillars flanked the entrance on either side. A bit ostentatious, but he liked making an impression. He pushed through the door, stepping out in front of the house and wincing as he glanced towards the mailbox at the end of the driveway

His head still hurt. But he'd often been told the best way to get over a hangover was to get the blood flowing. Still, he had to grab the mail anyway, so he shut the door behind him and began to make his way blearily down the driveway towards the mailbox.

His home was situated on a double lot, and the stone façade was the envy of the neighborhood. Rightfully so as he'd paid an architect from Belarus for the designs. He reached the mailbox, grabbed a couple of bills, and the magazine for a charity he had once donated to, and hefted the items in one hand. He scowled at the magazine. It didn't sit well that generosity was repaid with constant nagging for more. He made a mental note to never donate to that particular charity again. Secretly, he suspected they shared contact information among charities whenever someone made a sizable contribution. Served him right for trying to do the right thing.

He grumbled, his head still pounding as he moved back down the driveway, bills and magazine clutched in one hand.

As he returned to the house, he paused, standing next to a lilac bush, and staring across the stonework of the large home. He smiled. One had to take moments of gratitude for the small things in life. And now, he was grateful for the design of the sculpted bricks, and the way in which the veneer curled around the trickier portions of his home. The sun, nearly reaching its peak in the sky, shone down on his home, illuminated the flowerbeds around him, and warmed his skin. He gave a satisfied little nod to himself, and then moved back up the driveway, one padding footstep at a time, the bunny rabbit slippers hopping along the tarmac.

He reached the door, and then paused, staring.

He frowned. He had closed the door, hadn't he?

He stared at the open doorway. The large double doors, normally so impressive, seemed a bit flimsy in the daylight. The right side was open a couple of inches.

He scratched the back of his head with the rolled-up magazine and glanced over his shoulder down the long driveway

He looked back at the door. He'd closed it. He was certain. He could remember the *click.*

Maybe that was just the alcohol, though. It had been so long, he wasn't sure what the side effects were.

Who was sleeping inside on the couch? He wished he'd got a better look at their face.

"Santi?" He called into the house. No answer. "Mateo?" He tried again.

Silence.

He scratched at his chin with his magazine and then sighed, pushing back into the house, muttering to himself about his failing memory. He was only middle-aged, barely a day on the other side of fifty.

His fiftieth birthday was why he'd held the party. Was why he'd purchased the Steinway piano. He paused in the hall, glancing towards the music room off to the right. He smiled through the glass doors at the amazing, sleek, hundred-and-fifty-year-old original. It had cost him more than the house. But all the guests had fawned over it. Of course, he could barely play, but he'd always wanted to take lessons. He already had his first one scheduled for next week.

He took another step into his home, double checking over his shoulder this time the door was shut.

And then the lights went out.

One moment, he'd been moving down the well illuminated hallway. The next, the chandelier above went dark. The lights in the kitchen, and the glow from the TV screen, as well as a couple of lights visible at the long end of the hall also turned off.

He frowned, hands bunched around the bills and magazine.

"Dammit," he muttered to himself. When was the last time they'd had an outage? He supposed his fiftieth year, turning over a new leaf, was being introduced with all manner of new experiences. Many of them, it would seem, quite unwelcome.

Muttering darkly to himself, he began to move down the hall. The breaker was in the basement.

He glanced towards the couch and watched the figure still slumbering, head in his hands.

As he moved in the dark hallway, past the glass doors of the music room, and his new Steinway, he felt the strangest of chills up his back. As if, somehow, he were being watched.

He wasn't sure why he did it, and the moment he did he felt quite foolish, but he paused and murmured into the dark, "Hello? Is anyone there?"

No response.

How stupid could he be? No one else was here. He lived alone. He'd never married. Didn't have any children, at least not that he knew of. And the only friend who'd stayed was still sleeping on the couch. He was just being paranoid. Was that another side effect of a wine hangover?

Suddenly, despite his own excoriating thoughts at his timidity, he balked at the thought of venturing into the basement, in the dark, without a light. Surely he kept a flashlight somewhere.

He still felt the strange prickle up his spine. Still felt as if he was being watched somehow. Maybe that was just his own self-awareness at how silly he must have looked. He gritted his teeth, looking past the coat rack towards the small shoe bench. No flashlight. An umbrella dangled from one of the hooks. He felt certain that was where he used to keep the light.

"Stop being silly," he muttered to himself, massaging his head against another throb. In a fit of frustration, he tossed the mail onto the bench, bunched his fists, and stalked towards the basement door. He wasn't going to let a little bit of darkness scare him.

He reached the door, gripped the handle. And paused.

It took him a second to realize what had made him hesitate...

Why was the brass handle warm?

He hadn't gone in the basement. None of the guests had. Metal should be cold, shouldn't it?

And yet this handle felt warm. Almost, oddly, damp. As if slicked with sweat.

He held it for a moment, the same prickle of horror rising up his spine. He stared at the sealed door, suddenly having second thoughts. Perhaps he should wake his friend from the couch. But if he did, he would never hear the end of it from his work buddies. Big bad Mr. Schitt, scared of the dark. He *wasn't* scared.

He set his teeth, and yet somehow, his fingers wouldn't move. He needed to turn on the lights, but he didn't want to go down there.

He stood in the hall, beneath the dark chandelier, motionless on the other side of the basement door. And then he heard a faint *creak*.

The sound was coming from the other side of the door.

Another *creak*. Like a footstep against wood.

He released the door handle. His eyes widened.

"Hello?" he whispered at the closed door, staring at the painted white wood.

Another *creak*, then silence. For the faintest moment, in the belly of his large home, there were no more sounds. Not even the sound of his own breathing, as he had gulped air, and now held it in a strange panic, waiting for the next sound.

Nothing.

His fingertips were trembling. His lips pressed together. Perhaps he should call an electrician. He nodded to himself faintly. Yes, that was best. An electrician. An electrician would solve the problem. It wasn't fear. It was just propriety. It wasn't like he knew anything about wiring.

He nodded to himself, grateful for the excuse to turn away from the door to his basement. The moment he did, the door swung open.

It slammed into his shoulder, sending him spinning with a painful cry. He tried to get a glimpse of the shadowy figure rushing from the top of the stairs, emerging from the black basement like a bat out of a cave.

A hand found his lips: a sweaty, warm hand. He tried to cry out, and then something buried into his chest.

A rapid jolt of pain. Another. Then a blossom of agony and warmth.

He stumbled back, gaping, not quite able to draw breath. Paralyzed with fear, his head still pounding from his hangover, he felt the shadowy figure grab him by the throat, throttling the air, and the scream from his windpipe. Then the same hand grabbed his collar and began to drag him.

A faint, murmuring, rasping voice above him whispered, "One eye, two eyes. Sightless. Good boys are allowed outside. Bad boys get locked away. You've been a very bad boy."

His chest was still pounding in agony. He could feel the warmth, wet, spreading down his ribs. His heart pounded, but weaker, faint. He couldn't scream, could barely move. Dark spots were dancing across his vision, as his consciousness threatened to flee.

He tried to cry out. Tried to speak. Suddenly, he couldn't even hear. He felt himself pulled through the glass doors of the music room.

The only sound he heard now was faint, rasping breathing, and then the banging of piano keys. Dear God—not the Steinway!

He had paid so much for that piano.

His thoughts weren't coherent. His heart fell still. And vision faded completely. The last thing he heard was the creak of the lid on the piano, then he felt strong hands tugging, lifting, pulling insistently, shoving him. His back against wood. An arm against taught strings. He tried to cry. But he was gone. Everything was gone. It was all over now.

"Get in there," the voice whispered in his ear. "You've been a bad boy. Get in there."

The darkness was complete. He couldn't see a thing. He couldn't feel. He couldn't hear. There was no *he* left to do any of it. Just a corpse.

CHAPTER SEVENTEEN

The precinct in Leon was one of the nicer ones Adele had ever been in. Even the interrogation room looked more like a waiting room for a job interview rather than a place to question suspects.

The table was wooden. The chairs were padded. The lights above were bright, but not oppressive. The walls had flowery paper, and the air itself held the faint fragrance of cinnamon. Adele couldn't quite place the origin of the scent.

But now, as Agent Paige settled in one of the padded chairs, Adele remained on her feet, arms crossed, leaning against the metal door and facing their suspect.

Mr. Cabellut was scowling at them. His oversized, bulging eyes gave him the look of some amphibian. His lumpy, shaved head didn't do him any favors either. He wore a suit, but it didn't quite fit his frame. His tie, which he had cut with scissors to dislodge it from the window, rested against his chest, only so far as the top of his chest. The rest of it was missing.

Agent Paige was still shooting Adele the occasional look of suspicion. Clearly, she hadn't liked the stunt outside the furniture store.

Adele herself was still processing the impromptu game of chicken. She wasn't normally in the habit of standing in front of oncoming traffic. It simply had felt like the right thing to do at the time. At least that was what she was telling herself. Another, smaller, darker part of her psyche kept whispering other things. Fouler things.

She didn't want to die. Did she? She had never felt that way before. Not really. But things were different now. It was almost as if her story had ended. The thing that had motivated her for nearly a decade had finally come to a close. She felt, and she hated to admit it, aimless. In a way, this all felt pointless. He was dead. She'd killed him. He'd *made* her do it. He'd won. But also, she was safe. Her mother's killer was in the ground. She should be happy about that. And yet she couldn't manage it. John and her father seemed to be doing quite well. But this only made her feel worse.

And now, after another long, hooded glance from Agent Paige, Adele wanted to leave the room, go find a bathroom stall, and hide. But this wasn't an option. The car hadn't hit her. She was still there. She still had to solve this case. The executive was counting on it. A lot was counting on it.

"You ran," Paige said, blunt and to the point.

The man with the severed tie just glared at them.

"You don't want to talk?" Paige said. "Fine. Let me. You were seen at two auctions, bidding for the same item as victims in our homicide cases."

The man blinked. He glanced at Adele, as if trying to determine if they were being serious. He looked back, cleared his throat, opened his mouth, but then paused, closing it again.

To Adele, he looked surprised. Not a good start. Then again, he clearly wasn't on the up and up. People could act. They thought they were better at it than they really were, but first impressions didn't mean anything. Not until they were confirmed by follow-up queries.

Paige knew her job. She continued. "You nearly hit a federal agent with your car."

"I didn't," he protested suddenly. "I didn't hit anyone." Despite his odd appearance, he had a rich, chocolaty voice. The sort of voice that belonged in advertisements, or narrating mystery novels. The voice did not fit the bug eyes and the lumpy head.

"So why did you run?" Paige tried again.

"I didn't. I was going out for lunch."

Page snorted. "Out the window?

"I didn't see you."

"So you're a murderer and a liar."

He shook his head violently. "I didn't murder anyone. You're mistaken."

Paige pressed her fingers together. "You bid for an antique wardrobe on Saturday. And then the grandfather clock on Monday. Remember them?"

The furniture store owner shrugged. His nose flared, and he let out a long breath. "That's it? I bid on a lot of items."

"And do you often threaten people who win the bid from you? You were heard telling one of our victims they would regret their purchase. That you would make them regret it."

He waved a hand, the handcuffs glinting beneath the soft light above as his other hand was forced to rise as well. "Nonsense," he said. "I say things. That's part of the fun. These are lively events."

"Where were you Sunday? Where were you on Tuesday?"

The man stared at her. "This week?"

"Yes. We've already checked your flight records."

"My what?"

"You've been to Switzerland."

"Hang on." The man was becoming more animated now. "Switzerland? That was like two years ago. What does that have to do with anything?"

Adele interjected now, if only to contribute something. "Belgium and Switzerland," she murmured. "That's where the victims were killed."

He shook his head adamantly, and his finger arose as well, wagging back and forth. "I was in Switzerland *two years ago*. I've never been to Belgium. Check my passport. It sounds like you already have."

"Planes aren't the only way to travel," Paige said, insistently. "Why did you threaten Mr. Vosloo?"

"Who?"

"The man who won the grandfather clock from you."

"Like I said, I was blowing off steam. I didn't know that was his name. I didn't care. I just wanted to win the clock. That's all. Things have been rough at the business for the last few years. Sue me. It's fun. Harmless."

"Not harmless," Paige retorted. "Two men dead."

He was getting agitated now, shaking his head so violently Adele thought he might twinge a muscle. "And I had nothing to do with it. Listen to me. Read my lips. I didn't kill anyone. I haven't left the country in years. Check my passport. Check with my receptionist. I was working all week and was saving up for another auction."

Adele had never heard of an addiction to auctioning before. Perhaps it was similar to a gambling dependence. The man seemed insistent when he spoke. Passionate. And more than a little angry. But anger could disguise other emotions. Passion could hide rage. Practiced killers were often psychopaths. They could lie through their teeth.

"Do you have proof that you didn't leave the country?" Paige insisted.

"Like I said, check with my receptionist. She can verify."

"You'll forgive me for saying, but she's not exactly a reliable witness. She warned you we were coming."

"Bah. Prove it."

Paige shot Adele a look. This time, mercifully, it wasn't one of suspicion. Rather, it seemed inquisitive. As if looking to see if the younger agent had any questions to add. For a moment, silence hung in the flower wall-papered interrogation room.

"Is there anyone else that can verify you were in the country this week?" Adele said.

The man's fingers were trembling now. His face had gone pale. He licked his lips nervously; with his big eyes and moving tongue, he looked more frog like than ever. At last, he gave a little rasping sigh, and then muttered, "My accountant."

Paige leaned in, putting a hand to her ear, "Come again? I can't hear you?"

"I said my accountant!"

Page wasn't ruffled by the tone. "Why would your accountant be able to vouch for you?"

"I was with him for like fourteen hours Sunday. We were going over some books."

Adele perked up. Something else had crept into his tone. Something besides outrage and anger. Was that shame? Guilt?

Adele pushed away from the door now, taking a couple of steps towards the table. "Why were you meeting with your accountant for that long?"

"Just routine. He can vouch. If he says I wasn't there, he's lying."

"Why would your accountant lie about you being in the country?"

"I don't know."

He was glancing off now, refusing to meet their gaze. Adele paused, and then her eyes narrowed. "Why did you run Mr. Cabellut?"

His head dipped, his chin pressing against his chest.

"If we speak to your accountant, what's he going to tell us?"

The man looked up suddenly, some of the anger returning. "Complete bullshit. Just like what you're bringing up. Absolute crap. I didn't steal anything. My numbers have all been accurate for years."

Paige and Adele shared a look.

"Are you saying your accountant found something untoward about your books?" Adele said. Even as she spoke it, she felt a jolt of frustration at just how predictable a man like this suspect was.

"No," he snapped. "You wanted someone who could vouch I was in the country; he can. Anything else he says is shit. All of it can be explained. I already have a lawyer going over it. You said you wanted to know where I was on Sunday. Well, I was speaking with him. And my lawyer. For hours. There is no way I could've left the country. You can ask them. Here, I can give you their numbers."

Paige was already pulling out a pad of paper and a pencil. But Adele said, "Is that why you ran? You thought we were there about embezzling?"

Now, he looked like he'd been slapped. "Embezzling?" He shook his head violently. "Prove it. Prove it. That's why you're here! I knew it. I didn't do anything. This is a fabrication. Bullshit lies—my accountant's been stealing. He did it. I'll prove it."

Adele weathered the storm of the outburst and waited for him to draw breath. Then, she said, "Your Maserati looked quite expensive. You've been visiting these auction houses and bidding on items; you don't seem like you're strapped for cash, Mr. Cabellut."

He jutted his chin out. "I'll spend my money where I want. I didn't do anything wrong."

Adele shook her head. "I was just observing."

She'd encountered men like this before. Men who used their money to make an impression. But that path only ever kept going. It never ended. More impression meant more money meant more people to please, meant an even greater impression, meant even more money, meant even more people waiting for one's downfall. The cycle continued and continued like a hamster wheel. There was only one solution Adele had ever seen. Her old mentor, Robert Henry had lived it nearly perfectly. He didn't allow the opinions of others to shape his spending habits. He refused to live to impress humans.

She felt a lump in her throat at the thought of her old mentor. She looked away.

Agent Paige was tapping the pencil against the paper. "Names and numbers," she said. "Your accountant and your lawyer. Until we get your story verified, you're staying here, so no funny business. The more accurate your information, the quicker we can resolve this."

Their suspect was grumbling now, but he didn't refuse. He extended his cuffed hands to accept the pencil.

This only confirmed what Adele was beginning to suspect. Perhaps they really did have the wrong guy. An embezzler with spending issues and a temper problem, no doubt. But he had veered away instead of plowing into her. If he was a killer, why hadn't he just slammed into her?

And in a way, while this information was important, it was also demoralizing. For one, Adele didn't want to think much at all about the incident with the car. But on the other hand, if Mr. Cabellut wasn't their suspect, then all they had left to go on was word-of-mouth. People who had seen others at an auction. But there was no way to narrow down the list. What were they missing? This was just another dead end. Mr. Cabellut was a criminal, but hardly a killer. The motive didn't fit either—with his money problems, targeting an accountant made more sense than other antique collectors. The latter would only draw more attention. But they had no other leads to go on, and no way to tell who was at the auction other than vague recollections interspersed occasionally among unreliable witnesses.

Even as these morbid thoughts cycled, a phone began to ring.

Cabellut was busy writing on the pad of paper. Agent Paige reached into her pocket, removing her phone. At the same time, Adele's own phone began to ring as well. She stared at Paige, allowing the older woman to answer hers first.

Paige frowned, listening for a moment. Her lips pressed tightly together. Her mouth became much smaller. She waited, paused, said, "All right. Understood."

Then she looked up. Adele's phone was no longer ringing. Mr. Cabellut was still scribbling dutifully on his pad of paper, as if it were some sort of lifeline. Adele just watched her partner. "Bad news?" she said, feeling a cold and absolute certainty she knew what the call had been about.

Paige's next words proved the premonition. "Another body was found. Outside Madrid. The victim was stabbed in the heart twice then stuffed into a grand piano."

Adele wasn't shocked. Wasn't stunned. It all felt so inevitable.

They had failed. And so, another body had fallen. Another human lost.

She sighed, and nodded, turning and moving towards the door. She had been in Spain recently, and she wasn't particularly eager to return, especially not under such circumstances

A third body, two more stab wounds, and another disposal in an antique. What was the killer playing at? What was his endgame?

CHAPTER EIGHTEEN

The plane ride to Madrid had passed mostly in fitful slumber for Adele, and now, the heated glass of their rental from the airport warmed her cheek as she leaned against the window, watching the flash and blur of color in the countryside outside Madrid.

Agent Paige was driving again, content—as ever—to take the wheel. Some people just liked taking the lead. Adele and Paige hadn't spoken to each other for the duration of their journey to the third crime scene. Occasionally, Adele caught Sophie watching her out of the corner of her eye, as if worried Adele might do something rash. For her part, Adele didn't return the glance, keeping her expression impassive, her posture as docile as she could manage. She wasn't sure what the older woman thought of her, but the less Paige was allowed to pry into Adele's life, the better.

Now, as they pulled to a halt outside a large, stone house, Adele was grateful to be free from the confines of the sedan. Her door sprang open first, and she whipped her seatbelt off in the same motion as she exited the car. A long driveway led from a mailbox through two flowerbeds towards the brickwork facade. Police officers were stretching caution tape across the door, replacing a couple of sawhorses that had already been set up. Other officers moved around the side of the large house, searching the garden. Through the open doors, Adele spotted more figures moving in the hallway.

She didn't wait for Paige to join her, preferring to set out first, brushing past someone wearing the lab coat of a forensic unit, and stepping over one of the wooden sawhorses.

One of the Spanish officers frowned in her direction, reaching out a hand as if to stop her, but Adele ignored the interference, her movements confident, her expression impassive. She stepped under the caution tape and entered the house. The officer shot her a look, but then was distracted by one of the forensics agents in the yard and turned away.

A voice said something in Spanish from a room off Adele's right-hand side. When she just looked over, frowning in confusion, the man in question switched to English. "Can I help you?" he said.

She turned and found herself facing an older man with white hair, and a thin, curling mustache. He watched her quizzically. "I don't know you," he said. "Are you the Interpol agent?"

Adele nodded. "Yes. Is the victim in there?" She said this part more as a formality than anything.

She could see the body.

Not only that, but she could also see the trail of blood leading down the hall, over a thick carpet, along tiled ground, splashed on the upright piano, and then pooling beneath the piano in a thick puddle.

"Mr. Schitt," said the white-haired Spanish policeman. "A good citizen. I was told this might be a serial case."

Adele glanced past the officer towards where two men in lab coats and gloves and protective gear were starting to move the body

“Wait!" she called.

The forensic team looked over. The Spanish cop gave a brief nod and stepped aside, gesturing for Adele to sidle past him. "Careful where you step," he warned.

She glanced over her shoulder to see Paige moving slowly up the garden path, frowning into the flowerbeds. The older woman was always more meticulous, preferring to pay closer attention to details. Adele, on the other hand, like to get straight to the point. And so she did, stepping over the trail of blood, sidling past the frame of the glass door, and entering the room with the large piano.

The victim's arm was bent at an odd angle beneath the lid.

Adele stepped between the two forensic techs, and frowned at the body

Her stomach twisted. No matter how often she came across corpses, it was always unnerving.

Feeling foolish, she almost wished, now, staring down at the corpse, that she would feel a pang of regret or sorrow. A reminder that she was human. Her stomach twisted at the blood, at the odd, grotesque way in which the man had been stowed in his own piano but that was it. Not sorrow. Not regret. She shivered at the thought, wondering just how calcified she had become.

"See anything?" the Spanish officer asked from the door.

Adele didn't look back but kept her eyes on the body in the piano.

She frowned, looking at the way the man's sweater was pulled past his wrists. He wore suit pants, which didn't quite match the sweater, but the slacks were wrinkled, as if they had been slept in

She glanced under the piano at the pool of blood. "When did he die?" she said quietly.

In a far heavier accent, one of the Spaniard lab techs muttered, "Not sure, in the morning most likely—we're placing the time of death within four hours maybe six."

Adele nodded briefly. “Cause of death?”

The man just pointed. They had been busy trying to lift the body, and in doing so, they had raised the man's chest where it pressed against the strings inside the piano.

Adele stared at the two angry reds blotches against the man's sweater over the heart.

"He let out fast," the heavily accented man said. "At least there is that mercy but judging by the blood, he was still alive when dragged."

Adele sighed, nodding vaguely. She glanced back towards the cop with the white hair. "Do we know anything about the victim? You said his name was Mr. Schitt?"

The officer gave a faint nod. He looked somber, but in control of himself. "Yes. He had a break-in a few years ago, and I took the call. Friendly man. He lived on his own. He just turned fifty according to the one of the witnesses we found on the premises."

"Hang on, we have a witness?"

"He was unconscious when we arrived. Drunk—no blood on his hands, no recollection of anything. He didn't see or hear the killer. Also, when we arrived the lights were off.”

Adele bit her lip. "The breaker?"

The officer nodded once. “I'm afraid so. Was that what happened at the other crime scenes?"

"Our killer seems to like the dark. This witness, can I speak to him?"

"We're already interrogating him. We had his blood alcohol checked. He's been drunk for nearly six hours. To stab the heart so meticulously would've required a clear head."

One of the Spanish lab guys crossed himself, muttering beneath his breath.

Adele sighed, nodding. "Can I at least get a report of that interview?"

"It might take some time. We're speaking with him as we can, but we're mostly waiting for him to sober up. We'll give you what information we're able."

Adele nodded in gratitude, turning away from the piano now, grateful to look in any direction except the body

She had consciously avoided looking the man in the face. She didn't really want to know what he looked like. The preliminary report had already filled her in on most of these details. Fifty years old, lived alone, wealthy and again, he'd been pushed inside an antique.

She pointed at the piano "Know anything about this?

"You mean what it is? Or where it's made?"

"Do you know when he got it?"

The Spanish officer hesitated. "Is that relevant?"

"It might be. I'm not sure. Anything?"

He shook his head. "I'm afraid not. I can start looking into it. We're still sorting through some of the items in the house. Our victim here threw a party last night by the looks of things. We're having to clean through more than the usual amount of discardable materials."

"Found it," a voice called from the hall.

Adele looked over and watched as Paige stood by a wooden bench under a coat rack. She had knocked a magazine off a pile of mail. And now, she was holding up a single envelope. "It's a bill," she said.

Adele's heart skipped a beat. "From where?"

Agent Paige kept her distance from the trail of blood, preferring to stand near the bench and the coat rack. "Not Leon Antiques," she said. "It's a local store in Madrid, by the address. It's called Casa de Subastas."

Adele glanced to the Spanish officer, but there was no recognition in his eyes. "When is the bill from?"

The Spanish officer, in answer, reached out, and tore the top of the envelope.

"There. What are you looking for?" he said, handing the letter to Adele. She unfolded it, stepping daintily over the trail of blood back towards the door. She frowned, and said, "I didn't know a piano could cost that much. He bought it a couple of days ago."

"You think it's connected with our other purchases?" said Paige.

Adele considered this angle. She couldn't think of a reason to refuse. It seemed like the next best bet. She ignored the curious glance of the Spaniard. "It's in Madrid. Not far. Maybe our best bet is to see if there's a link between the places."

Paige just grunted.

The killer was striking at a rapid pace. Adele wondered what the executive would think of another body dropped by the man who had killed his cousin. In all of it, Adele felt distracted. But also, she was finding, more than anything, she wanted to solve the case.

It wouldn't make it better, but it might help her guilty conscience ease a bit. She had always prided herself on saving lives by putting bad people behind bars. But now, it felt even more personal than that. As if who she was hung in the balance. The executive had asked her specifically, but now, more than that, Adele wanted to prove to herself that she had the motivation, even with her mother's killer dead, to still do a good job.

"All right," she said, reaching a conclusion. "We can visit the auction house. Maybe they'll have a connection. I'm driving" she said, adding this last part with a forceful nod. She stepped over the trail of blood, moving past the Spanish officer. She marched back towards the car outside the old home.

CHAPTER NINETEEN

Agent Paige wasn't accustomed to sitting in the passenger seat. And yet she could tell Adele was tense. The younger woman had been acting oddly ever since the incident outside the furniture store. She had put herself in front of the car on purpose. Paige had seen it with her own eyes.

She had always known Adele was reckless as they had worked cases before. While Paige like to follow the rules, to stay by the book, Adele often seemed to find her own interpretation for long-held agency protocol.

But Agent Paige could sense something out of the ordinary was off with the younger women. They had never seen eye to eye, but this was different; she shot a look towards the driver side, where Adele was following the final directions of the GPS to pull them into the multistory parking lot outside the auction house in Madrid.

The antique store was at the top of an industrial building. Adele pulled into the parking lot, circling the ramps, taking them higher; she refused to look at Sophie. This had never been the case before.

Adele had always been defiant, rebellious, confrontational sometimes. But now she was avoiding it entirely. As if, somehow, she were ashamed. Ashamed of what, though? Paige frowned in thought.

Adele pulled into a parking spot, coming to a quick, jolting halt.

Paige got out of the car, following Adele towards the sliding glass entrance at the top of the old industrial building. On the side of the glass doors, she spotted golden lettering, marking the various offices that occupied the space.

Adele took the lead, entering through the glass doors and emerging on the top floor of the industrial complex that housed Casa de Subastas.

Adele didn't push through the door, however, but instead glanced at the brown and gold placard next to the door, designating the other office spaces with numbers. Agent Paige frowned as Adele passed the auction house, and started moving down the hall, towards the back of the industrial building.

Adele took a left turn, heading towards another door, set in the furthest wall, and now Agent Paige realized what she was up to.

A door centered the wall, marked by a sign that read *shipping*.

Adele and Agent Paige pushed through the dusty and unobtrusive entrance, like the back door at a grocery store.

Now, as they entered the shipping area of the auction house, a faint scent of dust lingered on the air. Agent Paige caught a sneeze, holding a hand to her face. All around them, there were boxes. A few figures were moving through shelf spaces, one of them holding a red label maker, another a clipboard, marking down entries as they followed from box to box.

Another figure, taller, with a severe face like a librarian, was shaking her head, a brown bun swishing back and forth. "No," the woman was saying in accented English. She was blonde, with pale features, suggesting perhaps a northern European descent. The employees she spoke to looked local with swarthy features and dark hair. "These were supposed to go out last week. Look at the date. If you can't read your own handwriting, you're better off printing the address.

Paige came to a halt by a large floor-to-ceiling silver rack. “Hello,” Paige said in English, clearing her throat.

"Excuse me," the tall woman said suddenly glancing towards them. "This area is off limits to customers. Please head to the main entrance."

Paige noted two security guards standing near another door. Both of them wore gray uniforms, with lapel mics and firearms in holsters at their hips. She remembered just how expensive some of the antiques were. She glanced back and noticed two security cameras above the door behind them. She also noticed another security guard was sitting behind a cubicle adjacent to the door but had fallen asleep, evident by the way his head was bowed over a newspaper and a cup of coffee on the desk in front of him.

"Interpol correspondent," Adele said, raising her identification.

The woman with the clipboard frowned, surveying the two unwanted guests. Her gaze slipped past them towards the security guard reclining in his chair behind the desk, and her brow dipped.

“You shouldn't be back here,” the woman said a bit more forcefully.

Paige, though, returned the clipboard-wielding woman's scowl with equal gusto. She stepped past Adele, affixing her best 'angry-mother' glare and snapped, “We're here on a murder investigation; unless you would like us to shut this place down, you'll answer a few questions.”

The woman stiffened, her fingers tensing against her clipboard. The other employees at her side shot each other uncertain glances. The security guards all watched but remained by their posts.

“We need to know about a piano you sold a couple of days ago,” Paige pressed on. She raised her phone, turning it and showing an image she'd captured of the Steinway. The body wasn't visible from the angle she'd chosen.

The tall, blonde woman shook her head. “What about it?”

“So you remember it?”

The woman nodded once. “Every item we sell comes through here. That one was an absolute hell to package and ship. Had a 24-hour rush delivery. What's this about murder?”

Paige lowered her phone and crossed her arms. “We need to know who else bid on this piano.”

“The winner? We have that information, but—”

“Not the winner. Who else bid on it. Other customers in the auction.”

Now, though, the lady shook her head severely. “We don't have that information. We host public auctions. What was your name again?”

“Agent Paige. This is Agent Sharp. By public auctions, you mean...”

“No registration required. What's this about?”

Adele cut in, though, glancing at the two other employees. “Did either of you see anything strange in the last couple of days? Anyone that stood out—any altercations?”

Paige could tell they were grasping at straws now, taking a shotgun approach and hoping to peg something. But both employees shook their heads. The one with the label-maker gestured back in the direction of the doorway that led into the main auction house. “We don't work up front,” he said in hard-to-discern English. “But nothing we heard.” He shrugged.

The other employee nodded in affirmation, preparing to keep his lips sealed.

Paige and Adele shared a look, both of them displaying sour expressions. Another public auction—another lack of registration. The killer could have been anyone present.

“Do you have cameras?” Adele said suddenly.

The woman in charge scowled now. “Do you have a warrant?”

“We can get one.”

“Do that, then. I must request you leave.” She gestured with long fingers back out the door they'd come through.

Adele glanced towards the phone in Paige's hand, then back up suddenly. “One last question.”

“Please, you really have to go. We're busy.”

“Just one question: is anyone missing today? Did someone call in sick? Or call in vacation days? Someone who was here the day before..."

"I don't know. Now really, you should go—"

But Adele was no longer paying attention, her gaze shooting towards the two security guards at the back of the room. Paige also followed the younger woman's attention. She had seen it too. The guards, at Adele's question, had leaned in, murmuring to each other. Now, they were both shifting uncomfortably under the scrutinizing attention of the others in the shipping warehouse.

Paige frowned, pointing towards one of the guards. "You know someone missing?" This guard just held up his hands, shaking his head. The other, though, coughed delicately. He shot an uncomfortable look towards the tall woman with the clipboard as if seeking some sort of permission. Paige didn't give her the chance to interrupt, though, and said, more insistently. "Who?" she demanded. "Is someone on sick leave? I saw you react—what about?"

Again, the guard look uncomfortable, but Paige began striding towards him, closing the gap. The woman in charge protested, but Paige ignored this. She pointed at the guard. "We're investigating three murders," she said. "I don't want it to be four. What do you know?"

Now, the guard let out a long sigh, hitching his belt and shifting in a way that caused his shoulder mic to sway. Slowly, with painstakingly pronounced words, his heavy accent communicated disjointed speech. "Say missing? Hmm? Sick? No—but Gutierrez." He winced, shrugged, and rattled something off in Spanish, looking to his partner for help. But the other guard just shook his head more adamantly.

" Gutierrez?" Paige asked firmly. "He took a sick day?"

But the man shook his head adamantly.

"What do you mean, then?"

The man tried miming now, an up and down hammering motion. Paige just wrinkled her nose, but Adele called out. "The auctioneer?"

Now, the guard nodded quickly, pointing towards Agent Sharp.

"What about the auctioneer?" Paige said. "He's not here today?"

Now, the tall woman finally interrupted. "It's nothing like what you're imagining, agent. Thank you, Mr. Ortiz," she said quickly, scowling towards the guard. "That's quite enough."

"I'll say when it's enough," Paige retorted.

"You don't have a warrant. Which means I'm in my rights to make you leave."

Paige snorted. "You are somewhat insistent about that, aren't you? Not hiding anything, surely?" She shook her head. "You're not going to make me do anything. What isn't unusual? Who is Mr. Gutierrez?"

She faced across the dusty, warehouse floor, glaring down an alley of stacked boxes and old, packaged items in Styrofoam.

The woman sighed wearily, but then said. "It's nothing unusual. Mr. Gutierrez sometimes runs auctions for the company. He isn't here today, *but*," she added emphatically, "that's just because he only comes when necessary. We don't hold auctions every day. Tonight we are, but tomorrow we're not. Mr. Gutierrez has been a long-time, loyal freelancer. He travels to hold auctions and comes from a reputable firm."

"Travels?" Adele said, perking up. "And he was the auctioneer who presided over the piano?"

"Yes. He does most of our work. We're a smaller company. Now, really, we have to get back to work. Please..."

Adele shook her head. "I don't mean to take up more time. I'll let you go, just last thing: he travels to other auction houses, that's what you're saying?"

"And convention centers, and farm appliance auctions. Wherever he's needed."

Adele gave Paige a sharp look. She said, "And do you know if he's ever worked at *Leon Antiques* in France?"

"Possibly. You'd have to contact them directly. Now, I must insist. *Leave.* We're horribly behind schedule as it is."

Adele held up her hands, nodding in gratitude and turning on her heel to return back to the main floor. Agent Paige moved slower, but also left, frowning towards the tall woman as she did. She didn't like being told what to do. Especially by someone acting as a roadblock on an investigation.

As they exited the room, filing past the sleeping security guard whose eyelids fluttered now, Agent Paige fished her phone from her pocket again, already cycling through the stored numbers. The doors shut behind them, and a sudden burst of tongue-lashing echoed through the glass in Spanish.

Adele glanced towards the doors, winced sympathetically and returned her attention to the phone in Paige's hand.

"Are you—"

"Yes," Paige said. Pressing the number and waiting for it to connect.

"Will you—"

"Of course."

"What if—"

Paige held up a finger, shushing the younger woman while pressing the phone to her ear. She waited for a shaky voice to answer on the other line. The response started with a long, heavyhearted sigh. "You again?" the voice said.

"Mr. Ettiene?" Paige replied brusquely. "I have a couple of questions for you."

"I'm busy," the manager of Leon Antiques groaned. "Can you bother someone else?"

"Mr. Ettiene this is a federal investigation. If you'd like we can bring you in personally for questioning. Would that suit your needs better?"

Another long sigh and more muttering. Then, "What do you want?"

"Thank you, Mr. Ettiene. It's quite simple, really. We want to know if you hire itinerant auctioneers, freelancers to work at your house."

"I—sometimes... It isn't cost-effective to keep one on full-time. We only hold auctions two to three times a week."

Agent Paige's eyes narrowed. She could feel Adele watching her closely where they stood in the hall outside the closed warehouse doors at the top of the industrial complex. "Do you know a Mr. Gutierrez? An auctioneer?"

"Paulo Gutierrez? Yes—why?"

Paige nodded once and she heard Adele intake air sharply. "He worked for you as an auctioneer?"

"Occasionally. What's this about? What did he do?"

"Nothing we know of yet—just checking our bases. When was the last time he worked for you?"

A pause, a swallowing sound, then, "I hope it's clear I don't know the man very well. He *barely* works for us. Only now and then. If he's got himself mixed up in anything—Just so you know, the items we purchase are all verified by—"

"You're not implicated in anything, Mr. Ettiene," she said her temper staring to rise. Her five-year-old was better at answering direct questions than the auction house manager. "When did he last work with you?"

"Sometime last week," the man squeaked. "But look, look, no—I'm checking now. He wasn't presiding over either the wardrobe or the grandfather clock! Those two items you flagged? He didn't touch them. Wasn't on his floor." The tone suggested he'd only left off the part where he declared *Ha! So there!*

"Alright, so he wasn't presiding over *those* auctions. But as an auctioneer would he have had access to winning bidders and addresses?"

"I—well—I suppose so..."

"I see."

Adele was tugging at Sophie's arm, but the older woman scowled, yanking her sleeve away and taking a couple of steps down the long, echoing hall.

"Ask him if he knows where the auctioneer is going next," Adele whispered.

Paige held up a finger. "I was going to," she snapped.

"What?" Mr. Ettiene squeaked.

"Not you. Listen, do you happen to know where Mr. Gutierrez is going to work next?"

"I... I mean I don't *know*, but if he sticks to the schedule his agency provided then I have an idea."

Paige tensed, and Adele seemed to sense the woman's excitement. Adele leaned in, eyes wide, watching.

"And on that schedule...," Paige said, trailing off. "Mind filling me in here, Mr. Ettiene."

"I... Do you—"

"If you say *anything* about a warrant, I'm going to scream, sir."

He swallowed.

"Look at it this way," Paige said, simmering. "If you give me an address, I'll be someone else's headache. You won't have to see me again."

He sighed. But then she heard what sounded like a drawer being opened, then the ruffle of papers. Finally, a smack of lips as if the man was preparing to read lines in a play. He cleared his throat and said, "This is the list his agency gave me—I don't know how up-to-date it is. I don't know if he'll actually be there. You can't hold me—"

"We won't. Where's he supposed to be next?"

"Presiding over another auction. In Spain, in fact. Northern Spain. Looks like he should be at a farm auction in Santander at five o'clock. So a few hours from now. Is that all?"

Paige was busy texting the address to herself to store in her phone. Speaking louder, so the speaker would pick her up, she said, "Thank you, Mr. Ettiene, you've been a great help." Then she hung up.

Paige finished copying the name of the new location, then looked at Adele. "Got all that?"

"Every word."

"Then let's go. This time *I'm* driving."

Adele didn't protest, but instead was pulling her own phone out. "I'm going to call the locals to see if they can put someone on Mr. Gutierrez. I'm tired of jumping around the country."

“Don't spook him. Tell them just to keep an eye, to keep him in place.”

Adele flashed a thumbs up, picking up the pace and moving down the hall with her phone now pressed to her ear.

CHAPTER TWENTY

The drive north passed far too slowly, and Adele was once again wishing for Agent Renee at her side. Paige seemed to follow every speed limit, every traffic light, every turn signal to the point they almost overshot their window of time as they pulled into the parking lot outside the large warehouse.

Around them, farmland stretched as far as the eye could see just shy of the Santander coast. Farming implements, tools, tractors, combines and the like were organized in front of the large barn-shaped warehouse. Other, smaller devices were set on long tables being passed over by auction-goers perusing the wares. About fifty people moved through the items, examining machinery, testing tire-pressure, or conversing with the auction representatives for further information.

A small, wooden stage was set up just inside the barn, and folding chairs had been placed facing the stage.

Adele felt her pulse skip as she glanced towards the clock on the dashboard. Nearly fifteen minutes late. The auction should have already started by now... So where were—

And then Adele spotted it. Beyond the empty seating, and the empty podium, was a much smaller gathering of people in the back of the warehouse, near a large whiteboard with numbers written on it. People were raising brochures or occasionally nodding as a man in neat suit with choir-boy hair was rattling off bidder numbers and prices.

"There!" Adele said sharply, pointing.

Agent Paige angled the car, slowing down to make sure she parked between the lines next to an old, rusted truck. Adele could feel her frustration mounting. Beyond the warehouse, near the main road, she spotted the police cruiser that had been parked, waiting.

So far, the locals had kept their distance per instructions.

But now, Adele could feel her heart hammering. The small group inside the warehouse were beginning to disperse. A private auction before the main event? Something else entirely?

She couldn't be sure. She didn't wait for the car to come to a full halt before shoving open the door and pushing out onto the asphalt. She broke into a jog, rushing towards the open doors, passing tractors and old farming implements. She avoided an usher who came to great her, brochure extended, and instead stepped through the warehouse doors.

The small gathering by the whiteboard had completely dispersed now, save the man with the suit and choir-boy hair and another, older fellow who was shaking his hand. The two beamed at each other, flashing white teeth and crescent smiles.

It looked as if the older man might have won a bid. The auctioneer in question, with the neat hair and suit, matched records of Paulo Gutierrez—he looked nearly identical to his very photogenic driver's license picture.

Now, though, as he shook the old man's hand, Adele felt a spark of concern. Was he marking the winning bidder as his next victim?

"Hey!" Adele called, racing around the empty folding chairs and wooden stage. "Gutierrez!" she yelled. "Yes, you!"

The man looked up in surprise, his eyebrows meeting his perfect fringe. His eyes went suddenly round, and he frowned in Adele's direction. She met the expression, raising her ID and beginning to call out again. "DGS—"

Before she could finish, the man turned sharply away from her, pretending he hadn't seen her. Then, he began marching through the small gathering of people near the whiteboard, stepping hurriedly in the opposite direction of Adele. He wasn't quite running, but he was power-walking.

"Stop!" she called.

But this only prompted him to pick up his pace.

"Why do they always run," she muttered to herself, breaking into a jog and calling, louder, "DGSI! Stop! Mr. Gutierrez, stop where you are!"

But now, half-jogging, half power-walking, apologizing profusely as he bumped into a couple of elderly auction-goers, he reached out, steadying an old lady, gripping her shawl-laden arm, but then using the same motion to propel himself around her, back towards a rear-facing exit in the far corner of the large space.

"Mr. Gutierrez!" Adele barked. She glanced back but had lost sight of Agent Paige. The local police were still on the main road, watching the entrances but holding fast.

Now, it was up to her to intervene before he made good his getaway. She sidled past the same elderly couple who seemed quite perplexed by all the yelling and the motion. A few other auction-goers were looking in Adele's direction, frowning.

The auctioneer though, realizing now that he hadn't shaken her, broke into a sudden sprint, head down, arms pumping. He raced towards the rear exit. This time, he bowled into a young man carrying a briefcase, sending the fellow tumbling with a shout.

"Stop!" No use. Adele broke into a sprint as well, keeping her weapon holstered in these crowded quarters, but fixing her eyes on the man's fleeing form.

He shoved through a gaggle of customers, sending two women screaming in alarm. He bolted towards the back door, his neat hair still—somehow—keeping its shape. Such was the wonder of modern hair spray.

Adele's own hair whipped about her as, breathing heavily, she hurtled a fallen auction-goer, racing towards the back exit. Twenty paces away. Ten.

He reached it first, shoving through.

A fire-alarm started blaring, red lights flashing above the door.

Five feet.

She reached it now, too.

Mr. Gutierrez was in an all-out sprint. He yelled over his shoulder, incoherently, hastening out onto the tarmac behind the main building. A new row of older, rusted looking farm appliances was gathered in an overgrown portion of the auction-space.

The auctioneer rushed between two green-red tractors, huffing as he did, his tie flapping over his shoulder.

Adele spotted a blur of motion around the other side of the tractor. A flash of dark hair ,tinged silver ,and a neat suit.

Agent Paige. She'd come around the back of the building.

Now, the two of them converged, both racing forward. Paige circled the first tractor and Adele came between the two, preventing a retreat.

Mr. Gutierrez shot a look back, eyes wide, sweat slicking his face. He looked panicked. His shoulder ricocheted off a large wheel-well and he spun but didn't fall, cursing as he did. At the same moment, Adele lunged in, trying to snag his arm. But he ripped free, spinning around the front of the rusted tractor.

Then, Agent Paige emerged with a shout. "Sto—"

But her words were cut short as the larger man slammed straight into her, his shoulder catching her solar plexus. She grunted in pain, the air whooshing from her lungs as she was sent tumbling. But to her credit, in the same motion, she managed to grab the man's tie, yanking *hard.*

Paige hit the ground with another grunt, but the auctioneer went stumbling over her. She flung a leg out, still gasping in pain but catching his feet and tangling them.

The man tried to steady himself, stumbling a step, another, reaching out to try to steady himself against the large tractor cabin.

He managed to stay on his feet.

For another couple of seconds.

But then, Adele, who vaulted over the groaning Agent Paige, slammed shoulder first into Mr. Gutierrez, giving him similar treatment to what he'd provided her partner.

He didn't even have time to gather enough breath to grunt—rather, she slammed into him, pain arching up her shoulder, and the two of them hit the ground in a tangle of limbs.

Dirt scraped beneath her, grass stains on her suit sleeve, but she managed to wrangle the kicking auctioneer, holding him down and twisting him on his back. He'd had the energy for the sprint, but not the ensuing tussle.

He was now heaving and gasping like some wounded creature, huffing like a bellows. Agent Paige was still groaning but, in flashes of motion as Adele rapidly tried to subdue their suspect, out of the corner of her eye, she spotted the older woman push up in the mud between the tractors. Then, testing her ribs, she pulled her handcuffs from her pocket and extended them.

"Sharp," she wheezed. "Sharp!"

"Got it," Adele returned, snatching the cuffs and holding Mr. Gutierrez beneath one knee while breathing heavily above him. "Stop it!" she snapped. "Stop struggling."

Finally, as Paige, wincing, joined Adele, the man beneath the two agents went still, moaning into the ground and still gasping heavily.

Together, the two women cuffed him in place, pulling his hands behind his back and refusing to let loose until he stopped resisting.

CHAPTER TWENTY ONE

Adele tried not to glance towards Agent Paige as they sat in the back room of the barn-shaped auction house, but it was difficult to ignore the faint wheezing puffs of air the older woman released every couple of seconds. Now and then, though she pretended it didn't bother her, Adele spotted the way Paige massaged her ribs, wincing and glaring at their cuffed suspect.

They had decided not to immediately return to the precinct. The room had been cleared, and beyond them, they could hear the auction in full swing. One of the owners of the farm implements had stepped up now that their auctioneer was in cuffs.

The two policemen who'd been keeping an eye on the road were now stationed outside the door. Adele glimpsed their shadows under the gap beneath the wooden frame. Occasionally, she heard a faint murmur or a response, in Spanish, over a radio as they informed their precinct what had happened.

Agent Paige had been the one to insist they interview first before returning to the station. The auctioneer seemed sufficiently discombobulated and was glancing around frantically in the small, back-office room, not glaring at either woman but looking as perplexed as he could manage as if he didn't know why in the world they'd cuffed him.

The act might have been convincing if he hadn't fled federal officers. What was he up to? What did he have to gain by playing games?

Adele took a moment, gathering herself, listening to another painful gasp from Agent Paige before shooting the man a long look.

"Mr. Gutierrez," she said firmly, "I take it you know why we're here?"

He blinked, hesitant. His choir-boy hair was still immaculate, almost a miracle in and of itself. He gave a faint shrug then a long sigh.

"Is that a no?"

"Because of the murders?" he said slowly in perfect English.

She blinked. "I—yes... So you admit it?"

He shook his head adamantly. "Admit? No—I just know about the murders. It's been all the talk on the auction circuit. Why else would you be here?"

Now, his eyes narrowed and he watched her closely without blinking. *This* question seemed more important to him than the initial one. Why else would they be there, indeed? A strange query.

Adele wasn't sure what to make of it, realizing it wasn't rhetorical. Instead, she stayed on task. "We realize you were present for the auctions of all three murder victims. How do you explain that?"

He didn't seem surprised by this line of questioning. He had bright, intelligent eyes and though he was a bit out of shape, he carried himself like someone who processed their emotions quite quickly. Now, he just watched her, speculative. "I don't believe I have to explain anything. That's your job, yes?"

"So you're not denying it."

"I don't know exactly. I run a lot of auctions. But if you say so, it must be. What other reason would you tackle me, otherwise?"

Again, it was stated like a rhetorical question but again Adele felt as if some authentic curiosity lurked beneath the surface. He was fishing for something. Just as much as she was, he was looking for information. But what?

He wasn't denying it. Didn't even seem to really care about the murders—why did that make sense? Unless, of course, he really was the killer. Perhaps he thought he could get away with it if it made it to court. Maybe he was looking for what evidence they had in order to construct his own story.

Still, things would go far more smoothly for a prosecutor if they had a signed confession.

She said, "Did you kill Mr. Vosloo, Mr. Foucault, and Mr. Schitt?"

He blinked, hesitated then said, "I—no, of course not."

"So you *do* deny it?"

"I deny I killed anyone. I don't deny I was likely in proximity to them. Do you see how those claims are different, agent?"

She frowned. "Which brings me back to my initial question. How do you account for it?"

"Coincidence," he said simply. "In what way was I supposedly connected to them?"

"You were at Leon Antiques on Saturday and Monday. You were then at Casa de Subastas where Mr. Schitt purchased a piano."

"I remember a piano. But I've been to Leon many times. It's part of my job."

"It also happens to be the preferred haunt of a serial killer."

Again, he didn't look at all surprised by this. Was it because news had made the rounds, or because he'd already known all about it?

"Come now," he said at last, shaking his head, "What is this really about?"

She blinked. "Excuse me?"

"We both know I'm not actually a murder suspect. What are you fishing for?"

"I... Hang on...," she trailed off, studying him. He looked entirely sincere. She bit her lip slowly, trying to make sense of this. "Sir... You are a suspect. Just so we're clear. You were in contact with all three victims; you were present during the auctions. You would have had access to their names and addresses."

"Yes, yes," he said, sounding amused. "All quite rehearsed. I know. Who are you really with? Commerce? The agency? I've seen your tricks before, lady."

Now, Adele leaned back, truly flummoxed. He didn't seem at all concerned with the accusation. In fact, he looked almost coy, playful as if participating in some big joke.

Paige, who had gathered her breath, but was still massaging her ribs, sat straight-backed as if so much as a twitch might bring pain. She glared at the man who'd slammed into her. "I've never heard of an accused murderer being so amused. I'll make sure the judge hears of it."

He looked at her now, rolling his eyes emphatically. "You're really committing to the bit then, are you?" he insisted.

"What bit?" Adele said. "You're a suspect in a triple homicide. I wouldn't be so dismissive if I were you."

The man paused, a faint smirk twisting the corner of his lips. He glanced back and forth between them, partly anxious but also partly smug. Neither of the agents blinked, both returning his glance with the severest of expressions.

He hesitated a second, his smile fading, but then widening again, then fading. He seemed at a conflict, his mind traversing two paths at once. He hesitated, his smile dimming a moment. Then he met Adele's gaze, looking her in the eyes. She didn't look away, didn't blink, her brow somewhat furrowed, quizzical. But her disapproval still radiated from her glance.

He went still now. His smile faded completely. His brow darkened somewhat, and his eyebrows dipped.

"I...," he hesitated. "You're not... Hang on—you're actually law enforcement? Wait—wait... What branch?"

"DGSI," Adele returned. "French federals. We're working with Interpol and have jurisdiction on international cases."

"International..." Suddenly, the blood seemed to drain from his face as he reached a conclusion all at once. His eyes bugged and he practically wilted in his chair across the table, his shoulders slumping. Adele noted the shadows of the police officers beneath the door shift. And now, Mr. Gutierrez glanced towards the door and back to her, horror widening his gaze. "You're serious...," he said. And this time it wasn't a question. "You really think... You think I *killed* someone? Holy shit. No! What? No-no! You've got it all wrong."

Adele wasn't quite sure what role she was meant to play in this strange monologue. The man had gone through a series of heightened emotion all in a short space of time. Clearly, he thought something else was going on here. Or, perhaps, he was a very good actor, trying to use confusion as a weapon.

"How about we start from the beginning," Adele said. "Why did you run?"

He just gaped at her. "I didn't kill anyone! You've got to be kidding—who said I did? I didn't—I knew about the murders. Everyone did."

"Yes. Murders of three victims that you were connected to during your auctioneering circuit."

"But that's just a gimmick. An excuse for you to come and look into—"

"If you say embezzling," Paige growled, "I'm going to lose my temper. Of course we're looking into you for the murders. You travel for your job. You're connected to all three of our victims."

"So you keep saying, but I didn't even know them. I barely would've recognized them. I helped at auctions, but I do hundreds of them per year!"

"What did you think we wanted from you?" Adele said still somewhat confused by the man's originally lackadaisical manner.

"The shills," he said suddenly as if reaching a conclusion. "I didn't murder anything. I've never so much as harmed a fly. I *like* flies. I used to befriend them as a kid. I like living things. Like keeping them living. Holy shit. I didn't kill anyone! You're insane!"

Adele folded her hands, still confused and now more than a little irritated. In part, on behalf of Agent Paige who was still massaging her ribs. "Innocent people don't run. You were confident we were here about the murders. What am I missing?"

"I was confident you were using the murders as an *excuse,*" he declared, his forehead now prickling with sweat. "An excuse to investigate me!"

"An excuse? Mr. Gutierrez, you're going to want to start making sense. I'm getting a headache."

"Agent Sharp, I'm telling the truth. Look, I didn't even consider. Didn't think... The idea of me being a killer is so laughable I just assumed you were...," he shook his head. "It didn't make sense. When I heard about the murders, I knew it was going to give the agency a chance to look a bit closer at some of my," he coughed delicately, "business practices. They've been—you've been... *They've been* looking for an excuse for years. I knew with the murders it was only a matter of time..."

"A matter of time to use the murders as an excuse to investigate you? Over what?"

"My... some of... nothing serious mind... I know it's not necessarily appropriate but... Look, just so we're clear, I didn't have anything to do with murders."

"What did you think we were investigating?" Adele pressed, frowning deeply.

He squeaked, glancing towards the door, then back at the agents. He let out a sound like a leaking rubber ball, then winced and stared at the ceiling, his head tilted. "It's nothing...," he murmured.

"By your own admission, you were at the auctions where the victims were targeted," Adele pressed. "You're going to want to provide an alibi. Why did you run, Mr. Gutierrez?"

"Because!" he bellowed in frustration, his tone suddenly increasing in volume like a dam finally collapsing under mounting pressure. "It's just an old auctioneer's trick. Everyone does it! Everyone—I can give names. Happy to give names. Let's cut a deal."

Adele just waited, massaging the bridge of her nose. She was tired of asking for clarification. The look of disgruntlement on her face seemed to prompt the auctioneer to pause, gathering himself with a few huffing breaths. Then he said, "Look... They're not exactly shills. They're just interested parties. Not actors—mostly friends. People I bring in to help stir up the auction-goers. Just for a little bit of competition. It's all part of the fun."

"Hang on," said Paige scowling. "What are you talking about? What shills?"

"No—just... Look, that's what I was accused of. But I like to think of it more as a marketing tactic, see?" He flashed a weak grin, his weak chin trembling.

"And how does this tactic work, exactly?" Adele said.

"I... It's all perfectly legal. Well, mostly. Well, it should be. It's hard to keep track with all the countries I work in. But—remember, I had nothing to do with the murders... And... yes, alright, an explanation." He swallowed, his Adam's apple bobbing. "It just...," he murmured something so quietly, both Adele and Paige had to lean in.

"What was that?" Paige demanded.

He sighed, then tried again, "It helps drive up the prices. The actors... I mean *friends* I bring with me. It just helps. It helps me get more jobs, too. Clients pay attention to that sort of thing."

Adele was completely out of her depth, frowning in confusion and glancing from Paige to the auctioneer and back. But Agent Paige's lip had twisted in scorn now and she was glaring at the auctioneer with hooded eyes.

"I see," Paige said. "That's why you tackled me? Because you've been planting shills at the auctions?"

Adele glanced over. "I'm not sure I understand," she murmured.

Paige just gave a weary shake of her head. She pointed an accusing finger at Mr. Gutierrez. "It's against the rules, of course. Which is why he ran. Essentially, our friendly auction-man here has been hiring people to bid on items and drive up the prices. It makes a higher commission if the item sells for more, doesn't it? You're leaving that part out, aren't you?"

He winced but shrugged, glancing off to the door again and looking as if he wanted to make another break for it. And he might have if not for the officers still waiting in the hall.

Adele finally leaned back in her chair, listening as the old wooden thing creaked beneath her. "Oh," she said simply.

Now it was beginning to make sense. Mr. Gutierrez had run because he'd thought they were investigating his illicit tactics. Which was why he'd been so cheeky at the start of the interrogation. He had thought they were part of the financial investigation bureau, pretending to be concerned over the murders in order to peg him on a lesser crime.

This provided multiple issues.

For one, if he was *that* confident that they weren't here about the murders... Then it suggested perhaps he *wasn't* involved. He'd seemed so certain at the start he'd had them figured out, like a child watching a bad magician's trick. Now, though, he looked downright stunned.

Adele folded her hands, looking at the auctioneer. "Fraud is still a crime," she said firmly. "But just because you're guilty of it doesn't clear you on the murder charges. You need to provide an exact and detailed account for your whereabouts. Specifically, Sunday night of last week, Tuesday evening. And last night. Can you do that?"

He stared at Adele for a moment, his jaw unhinged, his eyes still wide as if in shock. But then he swallowed, his features turning red. "I was in Leon on Sunday and Tuesday. You yourself said you knew I'd worked at Leon Antiques."

"Can you prove it," Adele replied.

"Prove... but you just said—"

"Can you prove you were there all three days? Without leaving?"

"Why would I leave... You just said—"

"Our first victim was in Belgium," Adele countered, seeing no reason in that moment to withhold the truth. He was already on the ropes. Perhaps by offering him an outlet, he'd make a mistake. "Our second was in Switzerland. Our third was here, in Spain."

Now his mouth formed a circle, and he began to shake his head. "Not possible!" he declared. "I worked at Leon Antiques on Saturday, then had another auction on Sunday, working for the park district. I couldn't have been in another *country.* You didn't mention anything about skipping countries! Impossible!"

Adele bit her lip but folded her hands now. She glanced to Agent Paige for a moment, considering her words. Then, feeling her heart pound, she leaned in, whispering, "The agency itinerary," she said, her voice barely a whisper. "Do you have it?"

Paige raised an eyebrow but then began to reach for her phone. Adele straightened again, watching Mr. Gutierrez. "And how about Monday through Tuesday?" she said.

"Leon again," he replied reflexively, and then I took a plane here. I needed to be in town for the first auction at Casa."

"You took a plane directly after the second auction?" If this was true, he wouldn't have had time to fly over to Switzerland first.

"Yes. And that *I* can prove. It's only my phone. Which she stole from me!" he added, his tone somewhat petulant as he jutted his chin in Agent Paige's direction.

Paige, meanwhile, had pulled out her own phone, pointing towards a screenshot of a print-out from Mr. Ettiene. On the paper, it showed the list of Mr. Gutierrez's recent stops. Paige was now tapping a finger against a line between two lines that both read *Leon Antiques.* In between was the phrase: *park district.*

Adele looked away now feeling the wind slowly leave her sails. She made a hesitant sigh. "I see," she murmured. "I'm going to need access to your phone sir, to confirm this flight of yours."

"Happily," he retorted. "Just as soon as I get my lawyer. I've given what I can, but you're insane if you think I killed anyone. No—no more.

Lawyer. Now."

Adele shared a look with Paige who was frowning. "We can confirm if you were on a flight on Monday another way," Paige cautioned. "If you're lying—"

"I'm not!" he said belligerently, his eyes narrowed, his chin tilted.

Adele and Agent Paige both seemed to reach the same conclusion simultaneously, rising slowly from their seats. Paige called to the door, "We're done!"

The shadows shifted under the frame and the Spanish officers pushed the door open and entered the room.

The officers waited, hesitantly, watching Adele then Paige.

At last, Paige gave a disgusted snort and pointed towards the man. "All yours," she said. "Book him on fraud. We can give a full report by this evening. Take him away."

The officers nodded, beginning to move over. But one of them paused and, though he didn't speak English, he surreptitiously held up two fingers and quirked an eyebrow.

"Don't book him on the second charge," Adele said, interpreting the gesture. The officer hesitated but she gave a brief nod, and with it felt her own heart sink.

Mr. Gutierrez was muttering on about his lawyer, but now that he'd been booked, some of his original fire had returned and he was scowling from one woman to the other.

Paige stalked over to Adele, joining her by the door and frowning. "I'm checking with the airports," she said quietly. "If he was on a plane Monday, we'll know it."

"If he was," Adele replied beneath her breath, "Then he's not our guy."

CHAPTER TWENTY TWO

Adele was sitting on a tractor's wheel behind the auction house, staring across the farmland in Santander when the news came. Paige marched over from the back office, frowning as she drew near, her phone clutched in one hand. As she approached, Adele's heart plummeted.

"No good?" Adele asked.

"None," Paige returned. "He had a plane ticket on his phone, and the airline confirms he was present. He couldn't have been in Switzerland at the time."

Adele let loose a lung puff of air. "So he's not our guy," she murmured.

Agent Paige stood straight-backed for a moment, massaging her ribs, but then, with a sigh, she let out a long breath and slowly lowered onto the toppled tractor wheel next to Adele, staring out across the landscape. Vast swathes of flat land were illuminated by the fading sunlight above. Rows of trees and dirt roads cut the land into sections.

Adele admired the compartmentalization. Each place for its proper use. No crossover...

She wished her own mind could be nearly so regimented.

The two women sat with a gap between them, yet still facing the same direction. This felt appropriate somehow. Adele shifted uncomfortably, frowning as she did.

Another dead end.

They were once again back at square one. Twice now, their suspects had provided solid alibis. Her phone was now on vibrate, and part of her wanted to shut the damn thing off. She wasn't sure she could face a call from Foucault yet. Not now.

Agent Paige released another painted sigh, and Adele glanced over.

"Are you okay?" she asked.

Paige straightened again, throwing her shoulders back. "I'm alright," she said curtly.

"Mhmm... he hit you good."

"I've had worse."

"Did he say anything else? Anything we might use?"

Paige just shook her head.

Adele twisted at her sleeve, wishing she'd brought a change for her jacket now that the thing was wrinkled, and stained with mud and grass along the sleeve.

"Hear from Foucault yet?" she asked nervously.

"He's keeping low," Paige replied. "Doesn't want to talk about it until we have good news. I've been respecting those wishes."

Adele winced, nodding. Framed like this it only meant one thing. They *didn't* have good news. But even as she considered this, a jolt of curiosity redirected her attention.

"What's the deal with you and Foucault anyway?" she said with a frown. She'd never so bluntly asked the question before. The executive and the senior agents had been friends for more than a decade. Not just friendly, but seemingly close. Rumors had circulated the office about the nature of the relationship. Some had suggested an illicit affair, others whispered that the two were somehow related, but they hid it to avoid accusations of nepotism.

Foucault had been the one to get the Paiges out of a tight spot ten years ago when evidence had gone missing. Adele had played a part in all of it as well. Somewhat regrettably as it had turned out.

Paige gave Adele a look, and normally it was a cold enough glance to prompt Adele to retract the question or change the subject. But she was just too tried to care about the older woman's disdain. So she said nothing, remaining quiet and allowing the silence to fill the space between them.

"What about us?" she said.

"You seem close," Adele replied.

Paige scowled. "What are you accusing me of?"

"Nothing. Absolutely nothing. I was just making conversation."

"Is it... you're not jealous are you?"

Adele's eyebrows shot up. "Wha—no."

"Because I've seen the way you've looked at him. You're not his type. Too young."

Adele tried not to choke on her next breath, hastily shaking her head. "That's not it at all," she stammered. "I wasn't saying... I didn't think. Dear Lord, no. Not Foucault. I'm not jealous."

Paige shook her head, her hair swishing. "It's alright. I don't intend to reveal your secret."

"There's nothing to reveal! I don't like him."

It took Adele a second longer but then she realized Agent Paige's expression was a bit *too* fixed, her eyes unblinking but twinkling with mirth.

"You're... you're joking," Adele said, stunned. She hadn't known Paige had the capacity for humor. "Aren't you?"

Paige snorted, shaking her head. "I know about you and Renee. Yes, I'm teasing. Foucault is a family friend. We've known each other since we were children. Is that sufficient?"

"So you're not—I mean to say—"

"The same answer as yours to the same question. We're just friends. I did a favor for him once."

"What favor?"

Paige turned now, shifting on the old, toppled tractor tire, her brow low. "I'll tell you," Paige said quietly, "in return for an answer of yours."

Now, Adele felt blindsided. Something about the severe way in which she was being watched made prickles creep up her spine. "Answer about what?"

For a moment, everything seemed to go still. Adele held her breath, her heart feeling as if it went suddenly silent. Paige considered this a moment, masterfully moving from the interrogated to the interrogator with seamless precision.

Then, she said, clearly enunciating each word, "What happened in that park?"

The words hung between them. The fields beyond beneath the sun seemed somewhat dimmer now. Adele swallowed, trying her best not to let the gesture seem nervous. At first, she didn't speak at all. This more than any topic was one she didn't wish to broach with Agent Paige. On the other hand, if she said nothing it would only exacerbate any suspicions. Not that Paige had reason to be suspicious, did she?

Choosing her words as carefully as she could manage, Adele said, "What do you mean?"

"I think you know what I mean."

"I very much don't."

"I'll tell you about the favor I've done for Foucault, and in exchange you tell me about shooting the Spade killer. You've been acting strangely, Agent Sharp. Ever since."

"I don't think I have."

"You have." Paige left no room for disagreement. She shook her head severely, looking every bit like a woman of the cloth.

Adele just shrugged, keeping her lips sealed while her mind raced. She wasn't sure what else she could add that would make a difference for Agent Paige. So she kept silent.

Paige, though, pounced on the opportunity. "I wasn't forthright."

"Oh?"

"I have heard from Foucault. Briefly. Last night. He wanted to know how you were doing. Was frustrated the case was taking so long."

"Did you tell him—"

"That you're not yourself? Yes."

"No," Adele protested, surging to her feet now, and turning to face the seated older woman. "Did you tell him it was difficult? That we were following a lead?"

"I told him the truth. What I felt was the truth, at least. And the executive agrees."

Adele wasn't sure she wanted to know at all what this meant. But her curiosity tempted this next question. "Agrees about what?"

Paige shrugged, but then winced and remained sitting straight on the old, toppled tire, somehow—with posture alone—making it seem a throne. "You returned too quickly to the field. You're not mentally present. You're lagging, Agent Sharp. Foucault agrees. He's considering replacements."

Adele's mouth hung open and she didn't know what to say. If anything, this felt like a slap to the cheek. "I... I don't...," she stammered.

"It's not that we haven't solved it—we haven't had enough time for that. But it's how you've been acting. It's why Foucault assigned you a lead on this one. It might hurt to hear. But it's true, and you know it. If you'd like to stay on the case, I need to provide the executive with a valid reason for your lethargy up to this point."

"Nothing happened in the garden!" Adele retorted. "I already gave my report. Foucault read it. He cleared me."

"Yes. Which is why you were assigned. But we both know this isn't your best, Agent Sharp. You're good at your job, whatever else you may be. But recently...," Paige waved a hand towards the barn-shaped auction house. "Proof is in the pudding?"

"What about you!" Adele retorted. "You're on this case the same as me."

"I received my tongue-lashing as well," Paige said crisply. "Foucault didn't hold back on account of our friendship. He loved his cousin. Trust me, I want to solve this too. But I'm trying to decide if you're a liability or not, Agent Sharp. Well?"

Adele felt her hand bunching at her side, not that she knew what to do with it. The ground was soft, scattered with dust and straw beneath her feet. Part of her wanted to fix her glare on Paige a final time then turn and stalk away. But another part of her knew this wasn't the sort of thing someone could just run from.

"What do you want from me?" Adele murmured, feeling a cold, tightening sensation in her chest.

The same cold she'd felt the previous week. The same sort of misty chill lingering on the nighttime air back in that park.

Vaguely, if she strained, she even heard Claudia's trembling voice calling for help. She heard the gurgling and bubble of the stream and the Painter lying face down in it. She heard the swish of water, the splash of desperation and then...

Cold indifference.

The way she'd watched. She'd known he was going to die. He was helpless, defenseless. She'd shot him after all... His legs wouldn't move. He wasn't strong enough to push out of the creek.

But she'd just stared, willing him to die. Wanting him to die.

It hadn't been a matter of neglect, nor shock. She'd known what she was doing.

More accurately, she'd known what she wasn't doing.

Perhaps Agent Paige was right. Perhaps Foucault's reservations were deserved. Maybe she truly *didn't* know what she was doing. Maybe part of her had died back there as well. She didn't want to face the truth... but was it the truth?

"Nothing happened," Adele said coolly.

"What do you mean *nothing*? You killed him, didn't you?"

"I shot him twice to save Claudia," Adele said robotically, dissociating from the whir of emotions, "then he drowned."

"That's the part you glossed over in the report, wasn't it? You said he was shot, then while you were rushing to help Claudia, he drowned...," Paige had gone cold all of a sudden, her tone more analytical than anything.

Adele felt the faintest of shivers up her spine at the sheer analytical nature of the older woman's attention. It was as if Paige had slipped into a new gear, starting slowly to put on the pressure but now increasing as she sensed her destination nearing.

But what destination? What did Sophie Paige want from Adele? To get even? To throw her in prison? She was fishing, surely, she didn't know anything. She was going off a gut instinct.

"Killing a man has an effect," Adele said simply. "Especially the man who murdered my mother. I'm fine, but it will also take some time for me to get out of my head." Adele allowed some of her emotion to creep through now, an intentional feint. Her voice cracked and she swallowed a lump in her throat. "I'm trying my best," she said hoarsely.

"And I can focus..."

Can you? The small voice in her mind whispered. *Can you really focus?*

Part of her had been taken in that park... At least, so her subconscious believed. But Adele didn't think it was so simple. She refused to simply fall prey to the Spade killer and his designs. She wasn't his pawn. She wasn't like him. Not unless she allowed herself to think so.

She hated the way her thoughts went back and forth. Wished she had someone to talk to. But John was so happy, her father the same. She didn't want to rob them of it. Would they ever see her the same way if she told them?

Her mother was gone. And Robert Henry had died.

Been killed... by the same man she'd buried.

"You're not yourself, Agent Sharp," Paige said crisply, standing up now as well and dusting off the seat of her pants. "It would be best for everyone if you would admit it."

Adele wet her chapped lips, eyes narrowed as she faced the older woman. "What do you think I should admit?"

Paige studied Adele a moment longer, tilting her head and then nodding once as if reaching a conclusion. "Remorse," she said simply. "I can't quite understand why. But you're remorseful, regretful."

"I killed a man."

"To save the life of a little girl. The man who killed your mother, your mentor, your ex... So why do you regret it so much, Adele? That's what I can't seem to quite understand."

Adele just met the scrutinizing stare. She wasn't sure she knew what to say.

Wasn't sure, either, that she even knew the answer to such a simple question. *Why* was she remorseful? Because she'd killed him? Or because he'd won a final time?

"Do you wish you'd killed him sooner, is that it?" Paige murmured frowning.

"Perhaps," Adele returned. "Maybe you're just digging too deep. Maybe this is just difficult."

"I admit that it is. But how can you focus?"

"I've always been able to focus," Adele retorted. Not so much because she believed this posture, but because she was sick of being questioned. Especially by Agent Paige. The older woman had always been jealous of Adele. That was it, wasn't it? It had to be the reason she was this way. It explained everything...

Does it really?

She ignored the calmer, more rational part of her brain. "Jealousy..." she muttered beneath her breath.

Paige went rigid, scowling. "What was that?" she asked, placing a hand to her ear in a mock pose.

"You heard...," but before the scornful words could fall from Adele's lips, she went suddenly still, staring at Agent Paige. "I... Jealousy," she murmured, her gaze no longer focused, staring off into the distance now. "It's...s" She placed a hand against the back of her head, the sleeve with the mud and grass stains even more wrinkled now. But a thought had suddenly struck her.

A thought from somewhere completely separate. A thought that had nothing to do with Agent Paige...

But everything to do with jealousy...

"What is it?" Paige said, her tone also switching now as she realized the change in the younger woman's posture. "What's the matter?"

"It's...," Adele trailed off, swallowing. "They all are so... vain. Aren't they? Not the wealthy—people spend money if they have it, I get it. I'm not blaming them... But look at Mr. Gutierrez. The way he dresses, the way he looks... What he'll do to get ahead. All for money."

"What's your point, Adele. Don't switch the subject. I need an answer—"

"This is your answer, Paige," Adele retorted, nodding firmly. "The auctioneers, the managers... their neat hair, their stupid bowties. Even the furniture store owner—his dumb Maserati he couldn't possibly afford."

"What are you saying? You think one of them did it?"

"No," Adele said. "Not at all... I'm saying an atmosphere like that creates two things. Two things for certain."

Jealousy...

"What?"

"Covetousness," Adele said simply. "Jealousy. Envy. That's for one."

"Are you quite alright? Adele, look, I don't mean to be harsh but—"

"Then don't be. You're not listening. All the auctions were open to the public, yes? This is the reason there was no registration. But if the auctions were open to the public, what if there was someone there just to watch... Or to lose? Someone who would be around this wealth, this posturing, this vanity and be left out?"

"Adele, you're not making sense."

“Perhaps not... But there's just something about these suspects, Paige. Surely you see it?”

“I don't. And I'm starting to think Foucault is right. Maybe you should head back to France.”

“Fine. I'll do that, but only *after* we ask them all one question.”

“All who?”

“The auction house manager, the auctioneer, even the furniture store owner.”

“And what are we going to ask them?”

“About the nobodies,” Adele said simply, with a smile. *Like my mother,* she thought to herself. Elise Romei had been a nobody. Nobody had come to her rescue. Nobody had cared enough to try and solve her case. The nobodies fell through the cracks on the fringes of society.

They were also, among the vain, among the wealthy, among the posturing, very, very easy to spot.

The exact sort of people that an auctioneer or a manager or a blustering store owner might notice.

The sort of person who *never* won a bid because they never could afford to.

“They wouldn't have to register if they never won,” Adele murmured. “Would they?”

“Adele, seriously, what are you talking about?”

“They'd be perfectly anonymous... Perfectly in the dark.”

“Adele...”

She nodded her head once and spun on her heel, marching back in the direction of the barn-shaped auction house. “I have an idea,” she called over her shoulder. “Get Mr. Ettiene on the line.”

CHAPTER TWENTY THREE

Adele decided Mr. Gutierrez's hair wasn't so neat now, where he sat shoved in the back of the police cruiser in the parking lot. The tractors were still lining the front of the barn, but the occasional auction-goer kept glancing curiously towards the parked police car and the two officers standing by the hood, speaking to the agents.

"Just a few minutes," one officer was saying.

Adele was already nodding, waving away the protest and leaning to peer into the backseat, staring through the open door at the auctioneer. His cheeks were somewhat puffy now beneath his eyes, and he looked equal parts unsettled and furious.

"What?" he snapped. Now that he'd been placed in the back of a police car, some of his original decorum and caution had faded.

"Mr. Gutierrez, I have a question for you."

"No questions until I speak with my lawyer," he retorted.

"Adele," Agent Paige suddenly called. "This is silly, Adele."

Adele just glanced back at the other agent, gesturing with her hand for her to draw nearer. "Is he on the line?" she asked.

Paige sighed but then nodded, marching forward with her cellphone in one hand, extended forward. A face was on the screen, staring out quizzically. Even as Paige approached, Adele could hear the exasperated sigh over the speakers from the man on the video call. He wore a different bowtie today, but judging by the backdrop of glass counters and golden watches, he was once again in his auction house, eager to be free of the meddling of federal agents.

A weak, warbling voice echoed from Paige's speaker. "You said this would only take a minute!" The voice was complaining. "I don't have all day...," beneath his breath, the auction house manager muttered, "you also said you'd stop pestering me."

"I'm sorry, Mr. Ettiene," Adele said quickly, glancing from the phone to Mr. Gutierrez. "It shouldn't take long. You two know each other, yes?"

Paige didn't quite roll her eyes, but it was a near thing. She angled the phone down so Ettiene could get a good look of the auctioneer in the back of the police car.

"Oh my," Mr. Ettiene said, holding a small hand dramatically to his lips. "My dear Paulo, whatever have they done to you?"

"It's nothing, nothing," Gutierrez said quickly. "Everything is fine, truly. Just a little misunderstanding."

Ettiene nodded in conciliation, but then in a stage whisper addressed Adele. "He didn't kill them, did he? I should've known..."

"What does that mean?" Gutierrez demanded.

Ettiene pretended like he hadn't heard.

Adele, though, wasn't concerned with the exchange. Rather, she cleared her throat and said, "Look, I need both of you to listen closely and tell me... Think back to this last week, at the auction houses. The one in Leon and in Spain."

"I wasn't in Spain!" Ettiene piped up.

"I know, I know. Just focus on the location you were at."

Paige was still not quite rolling her eyes, but now her foot was tapping rapidly in clear frustration.

Adele ignored it. This wasn't as much of a long shot, though, as Paige seemed to think. There was more than one type of evidence. Physical evidence could help in a court of law, could narrow down a list of suspects. Material evidence was valuable. But on the other hand, there was *human* evidence. Humans were far more predictable than they liked to think. Paige had proven this, hadn't she? Simply following her instincts where Adele was concerned to question about the park.

Adele didn't think the auction scene was any different. High school, middle school, lunchrooms all over the world spoke of a pecking order. Spoke of gaggles of gossipers murmuring behind others' backs...

The sorts of people who enjoyed gelling their hair, wearing polka dot ties while bidding on extraordinarily expensive items were also the sorts that *noticed* details.

The sort of details Adele was interested in.

"Who was the fish out of water," she said simply as both men listened, one from the back seat of a police cruiser, and the other over the cell phone's spotty connection.

They both stared at her blankly. Ettiene a bit more so due to pixelation.

"Who," Adele said, now that she'd set up her terms, "at the auction was never going to win an item. Who was the unwanted guest? Who didn't belong?"

Gutierrez just cocked an eyebrow. Mr. Ettiene cleared his throat and declared, "I'm afraid I don't know what you mean. We value *all* our guests equally."

Adele shook her head. "Cut the shit. That suit is tailor-made, yes? You would know if someone ordered off Amazon. Or if they wore hand-me-down shoes, yes?"

"What are you implying?" the face on the video screen demanded.

"I want you to think back to your auctions. Think back and tell me, *who* didn't belong? You first Mr. Ettiene." Adele's eyes narrowed but she held up a finger. "They would have been sitting in the back row or leaning against the wall. They would have bid on items they couldn't possibly have afforded. It might have irritated you or annoyed you. They would have been sitting alone. Definitely male. Something about them would have seemed off—the sort of person you wouldn't want to introduce in polite company."

Ettiene and Gutierrez were both staring at her now, strangely silent.

"Well?" Adele demanded. "Someone is coming to mind—it's only been a few days. Who? Who are you two thinking of?"

Adele could feel Paige staring still, but she didn't care. Not all evidence was material. People were predictable. People with a memory for the 'losers' in life were doubly so.

Ettiene spoke first. "I don't know what you're implying. But here at Leon Antiques..."

"He would've bid until the end," Adele said just as quickly, cutting him off. "The man I'm speaking of would've wanted the items but would've lost in the end. An underbidder, but he would've lasted. Ignore the room of a hundred. Ignore the fifty. Then ten. Focus on the last few. Picture the paddles going up... Someone in the last few—someone who didn't belong at that auction. Someone neither of you would want to associate with outside of business. Who was it? You must know."

Ettiene had gone silent now, biting his lip. He looked far less certain, but again, he said, "At Leon Antiques we *do not discriminate* against—"

"The man in that stupid, frayed sweater," Gutierrez interrupted.

Ettiene went quiet, scowling. Adele noted this. A scowl. Not surprise, but a scowl.

"What sweater?" she pressed eagerly.

"Just a weirdo in the back of the room," Gutierrez snorted. "He was wearing an ugly wool sweater with a hole in one sleeve. Showed up to a couple of auctions. Everyone noticed him. Don't pretend you didn't Ettiene."

Mr. Ettiene sighed but then shrugged. "It was a very ugly sweater, yes."

Adele felt her stomach twist, her eyes widening. "So you did notice someone?"

Both men paused but then shrugged, nodding.

"He had poor taste," Ettiene said.

"Was ugly," Gutierrez added.

"And poor," both men said at the same time.

Gutierrez added with a note of scorn, "A loser—a perpetual loser. I noticed because he kept bidding on items that I knew he couldn't afford. I was going to have him escorted out, but thankfully he bowed out of each auction *before* he won. He never could've afforded anything. Not even a decent sweater."

Adele felt a flicker of excitement at the exchange. Not because she was particularly impressed by either man's interpretation of another person, but because she'd been *right.* In front of Agent Paige, no less.

"Last question," she said, her breath coming slowly. "What, exactly, did this man look like?"

CHAPTER TWENTY FOUR

Adele sat in the passenger seat of their rented car, listening as Agent Paige played the voice memo again, for the third time, over the Bluetooth speakers. The two of them were alone once more.

The voice memo, from Mr. Gutierrez, crackled over the car's speakers. "He was short..."

"No—average height!" Ettiene's far fainter voice called over the recording.

"Fine... Short to average. Brown hair."

"Yes, yes, a muddy brown."

"He had glasses."

The recording went silent, then Adele's own voice crackled out. "Anything else?"

Agent Paige clicked the recording off, glancing across the divide between the two car seats. "Well?" the older woman said. "Average height, brown hair, glasses... Not exactly a photographic description."

Adele was leaning forward in the passenger seat, one arm resting against the open window, occasionally glancing in the rearview mirror. They were parked up the road now, having left the auction house behind them. Evening was quickly approaching, and with it, a heightened sense of urgency. The killer was still out there, still on the move.

But her hunch had paid off...

Or, at least, had yielded bait.

"The sweater," she added quietly.

"Right," Paige said. "I forgot. A ratty sweater. We might as well put out an APB."

Adele knew the other agent was being sarcastic, but she didn't have the energy to respond. Most of her attention was fixated on the problem at hand.

Both Ettiene and Gutierrez had remembered this out-of-place auction-goer. Not just in Leon, but also in Madrid. It couldn't be a coincidence... could it?

She supposed some people like to auction-hop, simply for the enjoyment of the event, sort of like fans following their favorite sports teams around the region.

But when connected to a murder investigation...

"The best way to find him," Adele said carefully, "is going to be at another auction."

"And where do you suggest we find one of those?"

"It might be worth checking one of the auction houses we know he's already visited," Adele said, turning to watch her partner. "Leon Antiques is done for the week."

"So?"

"So...," Adele said softly, "Casa de Subastas has another auction tonight."

Paige frowned, staring at the dashboard between them, her hands on the steering wheel of the motionless vehicle. At last, she let out a long sigh, only wincing towards the end and rubbing at her ribs. "You want to drive back to Madrid? To go to this auction?"

Adele bobbed her head. "That's exactly what I want. Yes."

"And what if this mystery loser of yours isn't there?"

Adele shrugged. "Do you have any better ideas?" Inwardly, though, she was confident he *would* be there. He had to be. This killer had already taken three lives. He wasn't done. Not yet. There was no evidence he was slowing down. It was either up to Adele and Paige to catch up, or more people would die.

Paige closed her eyes for a moment as if trying to compose herself. Her fingers tapped against the steering wheel, and she shifted her shoulders, settling against the cushioned backrest. Then, she muttered darkly beneath her breath and put the car in gear, slowly pulling out of their parking spot at the side of the road, kicking up dust as they turned back onto a meandering, countryside road.

The two women dwindled off into silence, the gulf between them far wider than simply the armrest. This time, Adele's arm pressed against the cushioned divider.

Not that she cared.

Agent Paige had been prying, Foucault was once again questioning her—she needed to solve this case. Not just for her career, nor just for her freedom, but as an act of redemption. She'd watched as a life was snuffed in front of her in that park, and now she couldn't sit idly by as others were taken by this auction-house killer.

"Faster," Adele said through gritted teeth. "Faster!"

To her surprise, against all expectation, Agent Paige actually increased the speed. Only going a few over the posted limit on the empty road... but at least this was progress.

They hastened through the countryside, across farmland, racing back towards Madrid and towards the second auction house.

CHAPTER TWENTY FIVE

They arrived at the industrial building auction house as night fell across the city. Adele and Agent Paige exited the third-floor parking lot, hastening through the sliding glass doors that lead to the auction floor.

This time, they didn't head to the back towards shipping, but stepped through the front entrance, emerging in a long, entry room that reminded Adele of a fancy restaurant she'd once visited with John in Venice.

Tiled floors beneath faux candlelight was lined by coat racks and laminated pictures of various items that would be up for auction over the course of the night. Two young women, both impossibly attractive, were standing at the back of the hall, near a beaded curtain, holding stacks of pamphlets.

One of the women smiled and said something in Spanish.

Adele winced, catching her breath from the brisk walk through the parking lot and shook her head apologetically. "French? English?"

The second young woman smiled genially and said, "Yes, English, of course. Are you two here for the auction?"

Paige remained a step back and didn't say anything, preferring to allow Adele center floor. Adele said, "Yes, please. Has it started?"

The woman bobbed her head, her silky, smooth, dark hair swishing. She glanced back towards a digital clock over the beaded doorway. "Yes, but you still have time for the last three bids."

"Great, great," Adele said quickly. The most expensive items would often be saved for last to keep as many interested parties in a room at the same time. "What might those be? The final items?"

The woman continued to smile congenially as she glanced down at one of the stacks of pamphlets. She flipped it open, the glossy cover flashing, and then she cleared her throat and recited, "A sixteenth century marble bust. A photo album of Robert Fulton, the inventor. And a large, handcrafted Ottoman carpet. More details are included within." She handed the brochure to Adele who accepted it gratefully.

Of the three items, the final one stood out most. If someone was going to hide a body, it could easily be stowed in a large carpet. "How much time do we have?" Adele pressed.

The woman glanced at the clock and said, "Two minutes, and then the final items will be queued."

Adele nodded gratefully, slipping between the two women, through the beaded curtain, which rattled around her, and into the main auction floor.

Nearly a hundred persons had gathered for the auction. Two security guards were positioned inconspicuously in far corners of the room, flanking the elevated wooden stage upon which an auctioneer was rattling off something in Spanish, pointing to members in the audience as he did.

Another gorgeous woman was standing by a display podium which carried a large, HD photograph printed on metal of the item in question. She kept her hands extended as if displaying it. Bidders continued to raise brochures or paddles as the auctioneer motored through his words, nodding and pointing and keeping the energy high.

Adele beckoned for Paige to join her in the back of the room, near some coat racks draped in garments. As they drew nearer, moving quietly, Adele was already glancing rapidly through the crowd.

The Spanish auctioneer suddenly exclaimed something and beamed, pointing towards an older woman wearing a big, blue hat. The woman standing by the metal print-out of the marble bust smiled towards the woman but then moved hastily off stage.

A second figure appeared, this time a young man, wearing a black suit. He was carrying a new metal photograph—this one of the old photo album.

The new display picture was placed on the easel in front of the sold bust and the auctioneer paused long enough to gather his breath. The young man cleared his throat and began projecting his voice, speaking in a rehearsed fashion and pointing to various parts of the photograph. Once he'd finished, he smiled and nodded back to the auctioneer.

The gathered crowd, all seated in wooden chairs, waited on the edge, and then the auctioneer began to speak again, waving his hands and pointing.

Adele's Spanish was regrettably poor. It was all quite strange to witness an auction in another language without the benefit of translation. She found she could trace intention, emotion, regret, frustration simply by watching body postures, or expressions or the speed at which paddles were raised.

She stood with her back to a large, fur coat, scanning the audience.

Paige suddenly nudged Adele from the side, surreptitiously nodding towards a man sitting only a few seats in front of them. A hunched fellow with dark hair, scowling at the ground.

Adele began to move, cautiously, circling to get a better look. She faked a sneeze. A couple of auction-goers frowned, glancing back at her. The auctioneer even looked over, but she gave a quick shake of her head. The man on stage scowled but continued seamlessly.

At the same time, the dark-haired, hunched fellow shot a look back, frowning.

No glasses.

Adele forced a smile and a nod and continued strolling as if she'd been intending to all along. She turned, once attention lifted from her once again, and rejoined Agent Paige by the coats.

"No glasses," Adele murmured beneath her breath. "No sweater."

"Glasses and sweater," Paige snorted. "How ridiculous."

Adele couldn't help but agree. People rarely went around wearing the exact same sweater, and glasses could be replaced with contacts. The character sketch was iffy... at best. But it was also the only lead they had. Another bellow from the auctioneer. A new figure, the same attractive young woman from before, returned, carrying a third metal print. This time of an antique carpet with resplendent, colorful thread patterns.

She placed this final metal photo of the item on the easel and took a moment to announce the thing. This time, a couple of patrons were getting to their feet, shaking their heads and heading to fetch their coats from the racks. Others just watched with excitement, hands tensed on brochures or paddles, waiting for this final leg of the event to commence.

Adele could feel a faint switch in the atmosphere, and her eyes narrowed as she quickly studied the figures scattered throughout the room. Some of the bidders sat straight, eyes on the auctioneer. No one, who was currently bidding, took to their feet. Adele wasn't accustomed to auction etiquette, but she supposed blocking the view of anyone would've been greatly frowned on.

This suited her just fine, as *her* view of the participants was only aided by the seated patrons.

She scanned the rows as the auctioneer rattled on, motor-mouthing through his spiel. Paddles rose, fell, paused, then rose again. A couple of disgusted clients dropped their paddles, shaking their heads and pushing angrily from their seats to march out of the room.

Eventually, the auction came down to five people. Adele's eyes bounced around the room, trying to spot them hidden in the rows of spectators.

Paige was similarly posed, her attention fixated on the faintest of motions in the tall-ceilinged room.

Then, Adele spotted another one of the figures drop her paddle in disgust, leaning in to speak to an older gentleman who nodded his head in commiseration.

Only four left.

Two were seated up front, both moving with casual gestures, occasionally nodding, and occasionally pausing long enough to consider their next moves. These two seemed well versed in auction tactics and remained poised. Another figure, an excited younger woman with a flat face and a big smile kept eagerly waving her paddle, often times back-to-back, outbidding herself. An older woman at her side kept trying to pull her arm down, cautioning her, but the excitement of the moment was getting to this patron.

The final remaining bidder was sitting in the second to last row, his brochure raised, his head tilted as if to get a better view of the metal print-out of the item. Adele frowned at this man as the auction continued. His hand was shaking where he gripped the paddle, and she visibly saw him swallow as the bidding continued.

The woman with the flat face glanced back towards this man, raising her paddle high towards the lights. The man muttered darkly beneath his breath, glaring back and pausing long enough so it seemed as if he might have dropped out. But then, with a grunt as if from physical pain, he raised his paddle again as well.

The bidding continued. The two professionals up front kept leaving it until the last moment. The eager young woman continued to jump the gun.

But Adele's attention was fixated on the man in the second to last row. His face was obscured from her angle, and so now, surreptitiously, she began to shift around the seats, gesturing at Paige and nodding towards the fellow.

The two of them moved around the back of the seated patrons, away from the coat racks and jackets.

The bidding continued, the auctioneer's voice raising in volume as if to signify some sort of crescendo.

The man in the back raised his panel a final time, nodding in certainty. One of the professionals at the front shook his head, bowing out. The eager, flat-faced woman hesitated, glanced towards the back of the room, frowned as if gauging something.

Adele hastened towards the man in the second to last row. He had dark hair. He seemed of average stature. And he was wearing a sweater...

She picked up her pace, moving around the chairs. Ten feet... five...

She just needed a look at his face.

She dipped down the aisle next to him, glancing surreptitiously off to the side. The man let out a long gust of air, glaring towards the woman who'd outbid him and then gave a petulant shake of his head.

Adele kept moving past, not wanting to draw attention just yet.

The fellow in question was stowing his paddle behind the seat in front of him, a look of disgust on his face as the item he bid on was eventually claimed by the young woman.

The man wore glasses. And there was a small tear in the sleeve of his sweater.

Adele stared at the fellow, her eyes wide.

He finally noticed her attention and looked up, scowling. "What?" he demanded in French, suggesting he wasn't local to Madrid. "Get out of my way!" he snapped.

Adele considered her options briefly. On one hand, the man matched the description and the activities of the fellow Gutierrez and Ettiene had noticed at their auctions. But on the other, he hadn't done anything illegal. Bidding on an Ottoman carpet that was large enough to stuff a body in wasn't a crime.

Adele glanced towards Paige, whose hand was at her hip, near her cuffs. The angry auction-goer was still scowling at her, waiting for a response.

What was the right call?

She hesitated, then simply dipped her head. "Apologies," she said in English, purposefully avoiding French. "The battle was well fought," she said, nodding towards the stage.

The man grumbled, looking away from her. As he did, though, Adele noted the way his lips just as easily curved from a frown into a thin line. An expression of supreme indifference, or caution even.

She frowned but began retreating back in Paige's direction.

"What was that?" Paige murmured beneath her breath.

"We don't have him on anything," Adele replied in the back of the room, her eyes fixed on the back of the angry man's head. "Wait. Watch. We need to follow him. Call in some locals to protect the winner of the carpet. She might be in danger."

Paige sighed but nodded, fishing for her phone.

Adele, for her part, leaned back against the wall, crossing her arms and glaring directly at the suspect, refusing to look in any direction. He matched the description, even, of all things, down to the tattered sweater. He'd been bidding on a final item and then lost out. It had to be him. Vanity was offensive. But envy just as much so.

Both could motivate someone to kill.

For now, though, Adele just waited, watched. What would his next move be? Would he try to get the address for the winner of the bid?

That's when she'd swoop in. Who would he speak to, though? The young woman herself? The auctioneer?

Time would tell.

Adele remained against the back wall, the dry paint cold against her body. She waited and she watched, unwilling to let the man out of her line of sight for even a second.

Patrons were beginning to rise, to move. Some stopped to congratulate each other or to admire, in the brochures, the items their friends or competitors had won. Others marched off, scowling, sulking, hastening away from the auction floor.

Still others remained seated, deflated or, in some cases, just watching as if enjoying the spectacle. The auctioneer on the stage was issuing some final instructions. The young man and woman who'd displayed the metal prints of the items were gathering the easel and the pictures, collecting them, then moving back off the stage, through a side door behind the elevated area.

Through it all, the man with the glasses just sat still, watching, waiting. The woman who'd won the carpet was at the front of the stage now, trying to catch the attention of the auctioneer.

That's when the suspect moved.

Adele froze, staring as he pushed from his seat and then began stalking between the chairs, moving towards the front of the stage.

Paige nudged Adele and together, the two women, as surreptitiously as possible, fell into step as well, moving after their dark-haired suspect, but not drawing any attention for the moment.

Adele slipped between a couple of auction-goers, nodding politely at an older man. Through it all, she kept her eyes on the man who was now approaching the eager young woman who'd won the carpet.

CHAPTER TWENTY SIX

Adele kept her eyes on the man as he approached the front of the stage. He paused for a moment, bending over as if to tie his shoe. She went still as well. The gathering of auction-goers continued to disperse, leaving only a few in the front of the room. The auctioneer had plastered a ten-watt smile to his lips as he addressed the woman who'd won the final item, nodding a couple of times and then gesturing towards the back of the stage in response to some question Adele hadn't heard.

Their suspect maintained his stooped posture, his fingers circling the laces of his old, worn sneakers. The hole in his sweater was visible from Adele's angle where he stooped. She frowned at his bent form.

Then, he got to his feet and stepped towards the auctioneer.

The young woman was moving around the stage now, towards the back door. The man in question didn't follow.

Adele stared, surprised, frowning. Paige was at her side and murmured, "He's not pursuing her."

Adele just quieted her partner with a shush and a nod. The two of them inclined towards each other, in line with the front row of seats, both pretending as if they were in conversation while watching the auctioneer speak with their dark-haired suspect.

The man adjusted his glasses, looking up at the stage and muttering something.

Instead of looking irritated or impatient, the auctioneer looked nervous. His eyes darted around the room, he swallowed and then he bent down, extending a hand as if in greeting towards the suspect.

Adele stiffened, unmoving.

The two men gripped hands now, one standing on the stage, the other below it, shoulders hunched. They exchanged brief words and then let go of their handshake. As they did, Adele spotted an edge of paper pass from one palm to the next.

"He slipped him something," Adele muttered beneath her breath.

"An address?" Paige returned.

But Adele was now moving again, hand going to her holster. Now the time for action had come. What had the auctioneer slipped the suspect? Information on the winning bidder? Was he in on it?

“Interpol!” Adele barked, lifting her credentials and leaving her hand on her holster. “Don't move!”

Both men turned to her, startled, eyes wide. The auctioneer went as pale as a sheet, coughed a couple of times and tried to hurry back across the stage, but Paige took the steps and caught his arm, blocking his progress. He met her gaze and then wilted, leaning against his wooden podium and nearly tumbling as if the strength had simply fled his body.

The suspect in the glasses was frowning at Adele, shaking his head, his hand turned conspicuously against his leg as he tried to reach into his pocket.

Adele reached out, snatched his wrist. “What's that?” she demanded in French.

The man swallowed, glancing back up to the stage, then back at Adele. His eyes blinked owlishly behind his round glasses. For a moment, he tensed, and Adele felt certain he might make a break for it.

But then, he just loosed a weary little sigh, followed by, “*Merde,*” and he released his grip on the paper in his hand.

Adele snatched the item and took a step back to maintain distance. The security officers on either side of the stage had noticed the commotion and were making their way over.

But Adele now stared at the rolled paper... Not a notepad. Not an address.

Money. Euro bills. Hundreds, folded in on each other. She stared at the stack of bills, then looked towards Agent Paige, frowning.

“What is this?” Adele demanded, shaking the money up at the auctioneer.

“I—money?” he said with a shrug. “I don't know.”

“Don't give me that,” Adele retorted. “You gave this to him. Why?”

The auctioneer looked miserable and was occasionally shooting angry looks towards the man in Adele's clutches. At the same time, the suspect was protesting his innocence in French. “That's mine,” he said. “You have no right!”

“What is it, Adele?” Paige called from the stage, glaring down. The two security officers were now standing back, waiting to see if their help was needed. Paige held up a hand to keep them at bay.

“Money,” Adele replied, frowning. “Five hundred euros.” She turned back towards the suspect in the sweater, “Why is he paying you five hundred euros?”

The man's lips were sealed now. He took a hesitant, shaking step back as if preparing to run again. “Don't do it,” Adele warned. She wasn't in the mood for another foot chase.

The two security guards, both thickset men with shaved heads, moved in, growling. And the suspect with the dark hair went still, giving a deflated sigh, and then shaking his head.

"I don't know," he said simply. "It's mine. It's all fine. It's mine."

"Why did he pay you?" Adele repeated, more firmly. "Hmm? *Why*?"

The man just glared at her, refusing to reply.

She scowled, shooting a look back towards the auctioneer. But his lips were sealed also. Adele gave a grunt of disgust, then reached into her belt, pulling the cuffs from their sheath. "Fine, you don't want to tell me here? Let's see if you'll prefer the station."

***

The police in Madrid had insisted on babysitting the interrogation. Adele could feel the eyes of the two officers assigned to their borrowed interrogation room at the police precinct. The two cops were standing by the glass window, behind Adele and Agent Paige. The Spanish police had also insisted on keeping the two suspects together until their lawyers arrived.

It was somewhat unusual now, as Adele settled at the metal table across from the thick, steel door, next to Agent Paige, that she faced *two* suspects in the chairs across from her. And two police officers watching her every move.

Adele glanced towards the two driver's license photos set on the table in front of her, frowning. She looked from one picture to the other, and finally looked up to meet the gaze of the auctioneer. The Spaniard had a thin mustache and ugly features, though his skin had a youthful quality despite his apparent years.

"Mr. Peres," she said, looking the man dead in the eye. "Why are we here?"

The auctioneer shifted uncomfortably, glancing towards the other man at his side. This second fellow, still wearing his glasses and ratty sweater, was Mr. Morales. He wore the more petulant expression between the two of them and slumped in his chair like a child being disciplined in detention after school.

"The money," Agent Paige demanded. "Why were you being paid, Mr. Morales?"

"I wasn't," he retorted.

"Do better than that," Paige said. It wasn't a request. "We saw you.

We caught you red-handed. How come you were being paid, hmm?"

The two men both shifted nervously, and this time Adele stepped in. "We're looking into three murders," she said with a significant tilt of her eyebrows. "Are you sure you want to keep lying to us? So far we're only looking at *a single* suspect. We never considered it might be two of you. But I'm happy to reassess if—"

"Murder?" Morales said, eyes bugged. "No, no, no... No one said anything about murder."

Peres, not to be outdone by his partner in crime, just gaped, his eyes like marbles. His mouth opened, then closed, but he couldn't seem to find the words for his shock.

"Yes," Adele replied, unperturbed, her fingers tapping against the driver's license pictures in front of her. "Murder. Exactly. Five hundred euros is a cheap price. But... I've heard of less."

Mr. Morales looked like he was going to be sick. Peres was still pale. Both men shared a nervous look. But Paige rapped her knuckles against the metal table. "Look at us, not each other," she demanded.

They did, both fidgeting now in their chairs. The two Spanish officers by the mirror remained silent, watchful, no doubt recording every gesture and word to report back to their higher-ups. Adele reserved judgment. On one hand, she could see the opportunity presented by two culprits. But on the other, did these two really have the constitution for murder? She frowned, studying them closely.

"I didn't sign up for this," Mr. Morales muttered, his face pale. He shook his head, tugging at the hem of his sweater. "Didn't sign up for *any* of this..." He looked adamantly away from the auctioneer now, his attention fixated on the two detectives. "I didn't know about... about...," he looked ready to be sick. "Murders," he whispered the word, leaning forward now. "I just was hired to bid on the items. That's it. I help create a... what was it you said, *atmosphere?*" Now he shot an accusing look at Peres.

The auctioneer scowled back, his mustache bristling. "I don't know what you're talking about."

"Ha! Bullshit. Don't try that. I've got the emails, *guy.* Yeah," Morales said, doubling down now and nodding at both agents. "This goof here hired me to bid up the more expensive items. That's why he paid me, for a job well done. Nothing to do with *murders.*"

Adele felt her heart sink as she studied the man. He seemed far too sincere for her liking. She bit her lip. "You were seen," she said. "At another auction house in Leon."

"Yes—Leon Antiques. He works there as well," the man said,

nodding towards Peres. "I follow around. It's easy money. He pays for the hotels too."

"Shut up," Peres snapped. "It's not true," he added towards the agents.

But Paige and Adele were both ignoring him now, staring at Morales. "He pays you to bid on items?"

"Yes! Of course! It helps his commission. What was it, Peres? Three percent now? Hmm?"

"I said shut up!" he auctioneer tried to shove the other fellow with his shoulder, his cuffed hands jerking with the motion. The Spanish officers barked sharply, stepping forward. Adele held up a hand.

"So you're saying you both can account for each other? You travel together?"

Now, the men seemed to realize they were cornered. The two of them paused, breathing heavily, shooting shift-eyed looks of irritation from one to the other. But then one at a time, they both nodded once. Peres interjected, "We didn't kill anyone. I don't know what he means about bidding. I sometimes pay him because he helps me with my bags when we travel."

"Oh shut up," Morales took his turn to snap. "They saw us! Saw us! Are you an idiot?"

"When's my lawyer getting here?"

Adele, though had heard enough. She pushed to her feet, glaring between the two men. "Hotels and dates," she said. "Any information you can provide. I don't give a shit about your fraud. That's up to these guys." She jerked a thumb towards the cops in the room. "I need receipts as well. Proof of payment."

Adele was shaking her head, but Paige moved far more slowly, rising and glancing between the two men. "I don't believe you," she said at last.

They both went still, watching her.

She shook her head. "It's too convenient. Too... rehearsed," she snapped.

Morales and Peres just watched her, both swallowing nervously.

"Paige..." Adele began.

But the older agent just scowled. "No, Sharp—they could be lying. Keep them here. Under our jurisdiction, waiting. We can keep them for twenty-four hours."

"While we look into it?"

Paige nodded. "Exactly. Perhaps our killer travels from country to country because there are *two* of them, no?" She raised her brow significantly, her arms folded and sleeves wrinkled.

Both men began to protest, but Paige slammed a hand against the table again. “Quiet,” she snapped. “You might have my partner here convinced, but you're going to have to do a *lot* better to convince me. I want movements, tickets, hotel stays, receipts for the last seven days. If I catch even a whiff of dishonesty, I'll lock you both away for as long as I can. Understand?”

Morales had sunk into his chair again, and Peres was wincing at the harsh tone, shifting uncomfortably under the scrutiny.

Adele sighed, glancing from her partner to the two suspects. She didn't buy it. Paige's suspicions were understandable but misplaced. If either of them was behind the murders they would have been much more covert about it. They’d exchanged money for everyone to see—additionally, they didn’t put up much of a resistance when the women had announced they were with Interpol. And as to her earlier thought… no. No she d’dn't believe either of these wilting daisies had the stomach for murder.

Which left one conclusion.

Adele had simply missed it.

’he'd pegged the wrong man. ’he'd thought her instincts had been right. It almost seemed miraculous that her line of questioning had led her to Mr. Morales only to be foiled in the end. The manager and their previous suspect had noticed someone in the audience... Someone who d’dn't belong. But it had just been a shill. The same sort that the last auctioneer had told them about.

Not a killer, just a conman.

Adele could feel her nerves twisting.

Her instincts had... had...

Failed.

She'd been wrong. Brutally wrong. Had that happened before?

Certainly. She'd been wrong before, but not when so certain... Something was different now. Something had changed.

Ever since that encounter in the park. Those two gunshots. The gurgle of the stream. Then silence.

She was losing her edge.

Adele passed a hand through her hair, listening to the sound of Paige questioning the men again. But the words didn't compute. It was as if the sounds were coming from deep down an echoing well. She let out a long huff of frustration, hand pressed against the back of her head.

The echoing sound only propelled her, tottering towards the door. She needed a breath of fresh air. Needed to think.

Maybe Foucault was right...

Maybe she couldn't handle this case. She'd bitten off more than she could chew.

Now... if another person was killed... it would be on her conscience. She gritted her teeth, ignoring the pointed stare of her partner as she muttered something about *coffee* and pushed roughly through the thick steel door, stumbling out into the corridor.

Eyes aching, head pounding, she rushed down the hall, towards the front of the precinct. Her hand moved towards her pocket, searching for her phone.

If someone had to tell Foucault about the failure, it had to be her.

After the call, she wouldn't be at all surprised if he took her off the case.

It wasn't like she could blame him. She'd just been so damn wrong.

CHAPTER TWENTY SEVEN

He sat halfway inside his car, one leg out, foot on the pavement, the other still nestled comfortably back in his tinted sedan. Sweat poured down his forehead, and he was breathing heavily now. Rapid, heavy breaths. In, out. In, out.

As the door to his vehicle opened, the tinted glass giving way to streams of sunlight, his heart hammered rapidly. He didn't like the outdoors... didn't like the light.

He blinked, raising a hand to block the glow. He shouldered the door open and carefully exited his vehicle, beginning to hyperventilate.

One eye. Two eyes. Blindness came quick. He closed one eye. Then the other. As he did, he pictured the way he stabbed them. One. Two. Eyes to the soul—eyes to the heart. He allowed things to see.

He shook his head faintly, blinking aside the final rays of sun. Even this, as evening approached, offended his senses.

He inhaled the cooling air, standing outside his car. He didn't close the door. He never liked to. Leaving the car door open gave him a path back, an escape route.

So he left it, the small little light in the ceiling glowing through the open door. The car wasn't nice enough for anyone to want to steal it. Once, someone had stolen his blanket, but now he stowed it beneath the back seat, out of sight.

Like this, leaving his car door open behind him, he took a hesitant step forward, then another. He looked up under the evening sky, his eyes uncertainly searching the figures moving along the sidewalk towards the main, circular building. This auction would be taking place in a museum. The curators were selling off some of their rejected stock—items brought world round from paleontologists and archaeologists. The sorts of items with better versions already in the museum.

It was rare for the museum to hold an auction of its excess pieces from history. And an excited air lingered over the wealthy guests moving down the pathway, beneath rows of neatly clipped trees. Music was coming from the open doors of the circular building. He forced a smile to his lips, walking slowly forward, matching pace with the attendees ahead of him.

One step. Two steps.

He blinked as he approached, his mind in its usual haze—a life without sleep played a number on the brain. As he drew nearer, he noted pictures in the concave windows, displaying the items that would be for sale. Some old pottery, mostly cracked, some pieces of archaic tools, and there... An item caught his attention. A large amphora. Far larger than most he'd seen. Large enough to hide a body? Large enough to fit into?

He felt a flicker of excitement as he stared at the old, dusty wine jar pictured in the window. But then his eyes moved on... not the amphora... No—no *this*. This was why he'd come.

He paused on the path, staring at the next item. It looked spectacular even just in a two-dimensional glossy photo. This was what mattered. As his eyes settled on the antique, he just as quickly forgot the amphora.

But he remembered *other* things... Things that had long since drifted to the silty floor of his memory. He lowered his head, still trying to smile as he strolled along the sidewalk, following the lead of the other guests moving from the parking lot, and doing his best to blend in.

He wouldn't be bidding on any of the items. They were far outside of his budget.

But he wasn't here for the items anyway... No. He was here for what happened *after*. He would watch them, watch the auction and then make his decision.

***

Adele sat alone in the car outside the police precinct in Madrid. Her phone rested on her lap. She hadn't used it yet. Couldn't bring herself to call Foucault. Agent Paige was still interviewing their two suspects. The Spaniards were busy investigating the two men's backgrounds, double-checking anything that might tie them to the murders.

Everyone seemed so determined to make it fit. Two killers, working together. They'd rehearsed their defense, their excuse. Admitting to under-bidding was just a way to deflect their actual crimes...

At least, so was the going theory in the precinct.

Which was why Paige still sat in that interrogation room, and Adele now found herself in her car in the parking lot with her laptop on her knees.

She'd made the mistake—she knew it. It had been her fault. Adele's instincts had led them astray, had snared the wrong criminal. But now, she refused to sit by and do nothing about it. Already, another corpse was on her over-encumbered conscience. She didn't need more guilt. Didn't need more blame to heap on her shoulders.

She scowled at the thought, considering her options...

Her fingers hovered over the laptop keyboard. Her back arched where she slumped in the passenger seat, having lowered the glove-compartment lid to serve as a bit of a desk where the laptop jutted past her knees. The warmth of the machine was becoming uncomfortable against her skin, and so she shifted, lowering the window a bit, and allowing the breeze to come through. The evening sky over Spain was clear, allowing a glimpse of the moon as well as the fading sun, as the two celestial bodies bid farewell to one another.

Despite everyone's belief that the under-bidder and the auctioneer were in cahoots (on Adele's say-so, no less) she was now more determined than ever to keep digging. It was all wrong. It simply didn't fit. Both the men in the interrogation room had been stunned. She'd found money exchange between them, not an address, not information.

Paige thought it was all a ruse.

But Adele's doubts were now eating at her.

She exhaled shakily, staring at the empty search bar on the computer. Her fingers rested lightly on the keyboard but didn't move just yet.

"The winners...," she said quietly. "Winners...," she murmured out loud as if trying the word on for size.

Perhaps that was the mistake. Winners and losers. She'd asked the vain to locate the least of these. She'd asked men who cared more about appearance than people to point out the hurting and the underwhelming.

But what if this wasn't about winners and losers?

What if that was the assumption she'd made mistakenly?

What if this wasn't about people at all?

As she thought it, she pressed her head against the cushioned headrest, and scowled at the ceiling, again trying the thought on for size.

She had to consider every angle. Not just the ones that first made sense. All three of the victims had been stowed in the items they'd won. A grandfather clock, a wardrobe, a piano... But Adele had sat through the Subastas auction... she'd seen the items. Most of them were small. A marble bust? A photo album?

One couldn't hide a body in these... So perhaps the people weren't the point at all...

She waited, allowing the consideration to linger. She tucked her tongue inside her cheek, shifting the laptop where it had grown too hot against her legs.

The point was the items.

Items big enough to hide a body...

And so she searched just that.

Auction items big enough to hide a body...

The moment she hit enter, she felt silly. The search engine displayed items of bodies, old marble busts, auctions with online retailers for sex dolls... This last search wasn't surprising given most of the traffic online.

She bit her lip, feeling silly but trying again. *Large auction items... Big items at auctions... Shipping for large auction items... Body-sized auction items...*

Suddenly, at this last search, she frowned... The top of the search engine offered a correction:, *Did you mean body in auction item?*

Her mouth turned down on either side in a sort of facial shrug. "Why not," she muttered. "Sure."

She clicked the blue link.

Instantly, she was taken to a page of an old article. The heading said the article was from nearly two decades ago. The title, though, in German, read *Body found dead in old auction item...*

Adele stared, feeling a cold shiver competing with the warmth on her legs from the machine. She scanned through the article, reading in German, piecing together the old journalistic style.

"Holy shit...," she muttered.

Nearly two decades, there'd been another murder much like the ones they were dealing with now. A man had been found dead in his own auction house. Stuffed inside an antique chest. The murder had gone unsolved, considered a theft gone wrong.

She read the last line of the article again, frowning.

The man was survived by his son. A boy who'd only been a young teenager at the time.

How old would that make the son now, she wondered. Thirties? About her age, in fact.

She stared at the computer screen, licking her lower lip against a patch of dry skin. She glanced at the name of the auction house owner, then towards the large box in the center of the text where a picture might have gone. The picture, online, had long since been deleted. Perhaps with the increased protection of child identities over the web.

But the caption remained.

It read, *"Anslo Burke 42 pictured left, Leif Burke 13 pictured right."*

Leif Burke. The auction house had been in Hamburg.

Adele quickly switched tabs on her computer, feeling the prickle along her back from earlier now return. She exhaled faintly, logging into the Interpol database, checking her phone, then using the sign in code for two-factor authentication. Once she'd entered, she quickly moved to the main database and entered the name. *Leif Burke.*

A few names popped up. None of them from Hamburg. None of them the right age.

She frowned... Leif Burke, the sole survivor from his family, didn't have an arrest record. Didn't have much of a record at all.

She switched to another database—this one coordinating with various DMVs in EU countries. She typed the name again. *Leif Burke.*

Hit enter.

A pause, longer this time from a less streamlined engine. And then suddenly, a list of names appeared. She scrolled down rapidly, scanning the birthdates. She narrowed the results by age, keeping it to men in their thirties.

Two results.

One from the Netherlands...

The other from Hamburg, Germany.

She felt a flicker of excitement and clicked the name, staring as a driver's license and a photo appeared. She scanned a few quick lines of text. The man still drove the same car he'd purchased nearly twenty years ago. Now that was commitment... or perhaps poverty.

Then again, it looked like little Leif had inherited the auction house from his father, and sold it. His bank accounts were hidden but color-coded green. Healthy. This was a man with means.

The sort of means to travel? The sort of means to bid on auction items? Perhaps not. But at least enough to take flights or trains from Switzerland to Belgium to Leon to Madrid... to Hamburg.

She looked up his address and only then, as she began to raise her phone, did she pause long enough to study the face of the fellow in question.

A strange thing it hadn't leapt out at first.

But he was a very ordinary-looking man. Rings around his eyes, bald, with a complexion like powdered pastry.

He didn't look particularly healthy at all.

"Alright then," Adele murmured to herself. "Let's see if you're home."

She frowned into those dark-ringed eyes, staring at Leif Burke. It was just a hunch... just another one. She'd already made a mistake.

But what were the odds of a case like this from twenty years ago? A case where the boy's father had been killed and shoved into an antique. A case where the boy had survived and inherited the auction house?

Was this some sort of revenge fantasy being played out? Had there been abuse?

Or was she just missing it again completely...

Adele lowered her phone suddenly, feeling a jolt of anxiety in her stomach. She reached up on instinct as if to slam her laptop lid shut, feeling a flare of guilt.

For a moment, she just sat like that, one hand on the top of the laptop, the other gripping her phone, caught in this sort of limbo... She couldn't trust her instincts. If she was really honest, the article had just been a lucky find. She was pulling at straws.

Then again... it wasn't like she had any *other* leads. Paige seemed convinced that she'd be able to crack the shill and the auctioneer. But Adele's doubts were at critical mass now.

No... No she couldn't give into the fear. What would her father think? What would John think? The thought of Renee brought back other emotions... feelings that she so often had to repress on the job. She hated to admit it, but part of her felt jealous at what John was sharing with his daughter. Was she going to lose him, too?

She frowned, pulling out her phone, staring at the screen. She pulled up Renee's number, fingers hovering. What would she say? What *could* she?

She wet her lips. For a moment, a small cowardly part of her wanted to hide the phone. But no—no Renee meant too much. If there was one person in the world who wouldn't judge her for what she'd done to the Painter, it was Renee.

She texted a simple message. *I miss you.*

Then she sent it.

But even this didn't assuage her thoughts about Renee or her father.

She was finding now, horribly, that even their opinion didn't matter as much. At least, not so much that it didn't matter, but that it *couldn't.* Not while she hid from them. Not while she *lied* to them about what had happened in that park.

Her stomach twisted again with even greater jolt of guilt.

She wanted to close the laptop, wanted to forget all about it. Perhaps Paige was right. Perhaps Adele was being silly.

But this felt personal now. Personal in a way she hated to admit.

She growled, audibly, her lips buzzing with the sound, and she tilted the laptop screen back again, almost angrily, and glared towards the license. She circled down to the address again, then lifted her phone, dialing quickly, feeling another jolt of nerves—not unlike stage-fright—in her gut.

If she got this wrong also... she wasn't sure she could do this again. If she failed again...

No... Think positive! Stop it! Think positive, she thought as loudly as she could to herself.

"Agent Marshall, hello? Who is this?" a voice crackled suddenly from the other line.

Adele wet her lips nervously, summoning her resolve. She still had time to hang up. Still had time to follow someone else's lead, to trust another's instincts.

But the moment she did that was the moment she'd decided to retire.

And for the moment, that wasn't an option. Three bodies dead. Maybe four, if this case from Germany was connected.

That was how investigations worked, wasn't it? Finding patterns? The time between the patterns mattered, but not substantially. The same MO—a middle-aged man killed and stuffed into a piece of furniture.

It wasn't a coincidence. It had to be connected. And if not, she at least had to scratch the itch of curiosity.

So, Adele summoned her nerve and, in a shaking voice said, "Agent Marshall, hello, this is Agent Adele Sharp, remember me?"

Another, longer pause.

Adele sighed inaudibly.

"I... Agent..."

"Adele Sharp," she tried again.

"I'm afraid I don't...," the woman on the other line trailed off.

"John Renee's partner," Adele said with a note of resignation.

"Oh!" the voice declared, excited all of a sudden. "How is John?"

Adele bit her lip against a jolt of frustration. She'd faced the same song and dance with the younger BKA agent in the past. Agent Marshall had made no qualms about hitting on Renee before. It seemed now was no exception.

"I'm sorry, Marshall," Adele said, scowling in the dark but keeping her tone as pleasant as possible. "But I need a favor. In Hamburg."

"Oh... Is John with you?"

"No—no he's not."

"Oh." She sounded disappointed.

Before the woman could hang up, Adele quickly said, "I just need you to send locals to check an address. Can you do that for me? Please?"

A longer, wearier sigh. The excitement had faded from the tone. Agent Marshall said, “I suppose... Can it wait—I was about to leave the office.”

“No—this is urgent. Life or death.”

“Isn't it always. Alright, alright. Who is this concerning?”

“It's the home of a man named Leif Burke. I just need to make sure he's home.”

“Shouldn't be a problem, I suppose. Send me the address.”

CHAPTER TWENTY EIGHT

Adele was stretching her legs now, circling the sedan in the precinct's parking lot. Her phone was glued to her face, her fingers pressed against the now warm metal as she rounded the bumper of the vehicle for what felt like the hundredth time.

"Come on... Come on...," she muttered beneath her breath. A lot was riding on this call. Not just her sense of self-esteem, which was more fragile than ever. But also, the lives of other potential victims. The killer stalked his victims then killed them over the course of forty-eight hours. In the case of Mr. Vosloo, less.

They didn't have time.

She circled the car again, the phone still against her cheek. Movement caught her attention from the sliding doors outside the precinct. She frowned, watching as a woman with silver hair and a tall man moved down the steps. It took Adele a second as she peered towards the figures. But the woman was shorter and rounder than Agent Paige. The man didn't look in her direction and the two figures moved off towards an idling cruiser.

The doors to the precinct sealed shut, and once again—as the police car rolled away—Adele was left on her own. She let out a faint sigh, returning her attention to a more proximate field of vision. Another rotation around her vehicle, her knee brushing against the rear bumper, did little to assuage her nerves.

Briefly, she'd considered boarding a plane herself and heading to Hamburg, but if the man really *was* the killer, then that meant Mr. Burke was traveling through Europe. He wouldn't be home.

If he was... she was wrong. Or he'd stopped killing.

She shook her head, muttering, "Fat chance..."

No. The killer would continue—all signs pointed to escalation. If Mr. Burke was home, he wasn't the killer and Adele was wrong again. She heard the screen door open behind her again and began to turn, wincing and half expecting Paige's disapproving glare. If Sophie was right, then it would solve her problems. If those two men inside were co-killers, then she hadn't been wrong in the first place... maybe that was the angle to approach—

Her phone rang. She turned, not quite facing the sliding doors. She heard the sound of footsteps on marble stairs behind her. But her focus had zeroed in again. She pressed a hand against the cold metal of the car in front of her, eyes wide.

"Yes?" she answered.

"Agent Sharp?" came a poorly connected line. Adele moved a bit to the right, hoping the motion might improve the connection.

"Agent Marshall?"

"Yes, can you hear me?"

"Yes, yes—what's the news?"

"None. He's not home."

Adele felt a prickle along her arms. She gripped her phone so tightly her fingers began to shake. "You're sure?"

"Locals said his mail is stacked up. He hasn't been home in days. No lights on. No car in the driveway. Mr. Burke isn't home," Marshall said. "Now—is that all? I'm heading home for the evening."

Adele sighed a long breath, making a whistling sound as she did. "Yes, yes," she added quickly, "Thank you, Agent Marshall."

"You're welcome," the woman on the other line said stiffly. Then, with a bit more energy, she said, "Tell John I said hi!"

Adele grumbled something noncommittal, bid her farewell and hung up. But her irritation at the fawning over her boyfriend was short lived.

Leif Burke wasn't home.

Piled mail suggested he hadn't been home in days...

Which meant the theory was still alive. The man was out there, somewhere. And while in part this gave Adele a thrill of vindication, or at least something close to it, it also came with a horrible realization.

If Mr. Burke really was involved, then he was out there stalking his next victim. Then again, there was no way of knowing he wasn't just on vacation somewhere, or perhaps visiting a friend. His absence from his home didn't mean he was a killer; it simply prevented him from being ruled out.

Adele still had to find the man.

She lowered her phone finally, her skin prickled with warmth and sweat from where she'd held the device. She blinked in the cool air, listening to the sound of footsteps behind her beginning to recede once more as a figure moved to the other side of the parking lot. She faced away from the precinct, frowning towards the street beyond.

They would have to put out an APB. If Mr. Burke really was the killer, then he'd been in Spain recently. Which meant if he was moving by car or train, he couldn't have gotten *too* far. Especially not after a kill.

Two-hundred-mile radius? Three hundred?

But an APB across countries wouldn't serve her purpose without a way to narrow it. Besides, if he was already at his latest hunting grounds, then checking roadways and trains manually wouldn't help. They didn't have time to try and check manifests for boats or trains... Planes, perhaps—that would be quickest. But if he'd been hopping from Switzerland to Belgium to France to Spain... Chances were he wasn't *only* flying.

The best way to catch the man would be to find his hunting grounds.

If, indeed, her hunch was right.

The man's father had been killed twenty years ago, the same way as the current victims. The father matched the MO—the disposal means as well. Mr. Burke hadn't been home in a while.

It fit.

No stone could be left unturned. Wasn't that what Robert Henry so often had told her?

Adele tapped her fingers against her leg for a second, scowling... And then she grabbed the door handle to the car, flung it open and slipped into the vehicle, pulling her laptop from where she'd left it on the dashboard, tilting the lid and settling in to begin typing once more.

She opened the same Interpol hub, pausing long enough to consider her options.

Then, she switched tabs, moving back to the search engine again. What she needed wasn't a criminal record or a driver's license photo. What she needed was another auction.

That was where they'd caught their last two suspects. That was where all of this took place. At auctions. It was getting late in Europe. Already passing through evening. How many auctions could still be open?

Perhaps too many in a three-hundred-mile radius.

She typed in “Auctions near me” in the search bar then moved over to the map feature, drawing the radius around an approximate location, using the last crime scene as the focal point.

Auctions held at night were fewer than those in the day. Secondly, Adele realized, the auction would have to be public. She added the keyword, “Public auctions near me.”

The last two auction houses had been open to non-registered guests. Anyone was allowed in. The killer wouldn't have to bid that way. If this was about the items, rather than the people, then Adele had to think differently.

Perhaps it was a combination of *both* the items *and* the people.

She stared at the red marks on the map matching her search within the radius but frowned hesitantly. Another criteria came to mind.

The final lot had to be a big-ticket antique large enough to hold a body.

As silly as it sounded, this would match the other cases. Including the one from twenty years ago.

The engine didn't have a search function for this, so Adele began combing through the results manually, her eyes bleary, her fingers moving as quickly as she could manage. Her head was beginning to throb from a caffeine and stress headache now ganging up on her subconscious.

The killer, whoever it was, had been on the move over the duration of his spree, preferring not to stay in any single country for too long.

As Adele scanned through the lists, she checked red boxes off the map feature, graying them out. One at a time, she searched through the results.

The narrowed parameters focused things.

Night-time auctions, within a three-hundred-mile radius, open to the public...

With a final item big enough to hide a body.

Adele growled in frustration, graying out red bubbles on the map for auctions of buttons, another auction for medieval knives. She completely ignored results for online auctions, which seemed far more popular than she'd first considered.

Finally, she found an auction for wooden carvings... Some of them were large, but not hollow. No way to hide a body. So she grayed this one out as well.

Her eyes ached, she sat in the dark confines of her vehicle, feeling the cold fingers of elapsing time pressing against her spine, sending tingles shooting down her back.

The longer she took, the more dangerous it was for potential victims.

Three results remained. She wet her lips. One of them was nearby, in Spain. She clicked the link but then cursed, checking the time. The auction was closing in three minutes, an hour and a half away. If the killer had chosen this one, they were too late anyway—along with the APB, they'd simply have to send police to investigate the auction-goers and protect the winners. Simple enough.

But the auction in Spain didn't fit the pattern anyway. The killer moved from country to country, didn't he?

Adele frowned, graying out this final option but making a mental note to send police units to check the site.

Only two options left.

One in Germany, the other in France.

No one had died in France yet. But Germany?

Burke was from Hamburg... The auction in question was taking place twenty miles from that very city...

Adele stared, eyes widening. It was taking place in a new museum. She scrolled to the page of the museum, checking the ABOUT section.

It had been constructed in the last fifteen years. An auction of excess items as a fundraising venture for a new wing.

"Holy shit," Adele said.

Still, she glanced at the second option in France, frowning. A Victorian-era ottoman was being sold as the final item. She glanced back to the German museum's website.

An ornate, hand-carved antique chest was up for the final bid. A chest...

Hadn't Mr. Burke been founded dead inside a chest?

She nodded to herself, slamming her laptop and slipping out of the car. She didn't even remember to shut the door in her excitement as she raced towards the precinct, hastening up the steps in search of Agent Paige.

The Spaniards would have to send cops to check out the local location. Paige could call Foucault to protect the French spot.

But as for Adele...

"Paige!" Adele yelled, calling down the corridor and ignoring the irate glance from the desk Sergeant. She hastened towards the interrogation room, rapping her knuckles against the metal door. "Paige!" she called.

A voice sighed from within. Muffled words said, "I'll be right back. Hold that thought..."

Then, Adele heard the sound of steady footsteps. The door began to open, and Agent Paige's face appeared in the gap, scowling. "I was getting somewhere," she hissed. "What is it?"

"Important. Come," Adele said quickly.

Paige just shook her head. "*This* is important," she jerked her head back over her shoulder. Adele glimpsed Mr. Peres sitting alone now behind the table. His would-be partner-in-crime had been moved to the adjacent interrogation room, it seemed, judging by the cop standing twelve paces away in front of a second door.

Another man, an older gentleman with a briefcase was standing next to Mr. Peres, whispering something in his ear.

“The lawyer?” Adele asked.

Paige scowled. “They share the same lawyer. Suspicious, isn't it? I'm telling you, Adele—I've almost got them.”

But Adele shook her head hurriedly, trying to tug at the older woman's arm to pull her into the hall. Paige yanked her hand back, glaring. “What?” she insisted.

“We need to go. Now.”

“Why?”

“Come and I'll tell you.”

Paige hesitated, dabbing a tongue against her lips. She huffed a sigh and glanced over her shoulder. Peres's lawyer shot her a dirty look. Paige looked back. “Can you make it quick?”

“I can explain it quick. But you need to come with me.”

“Come where?”

Adele winced apologetically, stepping back to allow Paige space as she reluctantly joined the younger agent in the hall. “Umm... well, Hamburg, actually.”

Paige just stared. “You're joking. Germany?”

“We really can't wait. You need to call Foucault to send a car to an auction house in Paris. We need to speak to the captain to deal with another in Barcelona...”

“Hang on, hang on—what are you talking about?”

Adele glanced at her watch, feeling a mounting frustration, wondering how to best summarize in a convincing fashion. The auction at the Hamburg museum would last another few hours, following a wine and dine dinner for the fundraiser.

They still had time.

But barely.

“Do you trust me?” Adele said.

“I don't believe so.”

Adele huffed. “Look, I think I know where the killer is.”

“Yes. Two of them. Here,” Paige insisted.

“No—no I don't think so. I think we have the wrong men. I think the real killer is someone named Leif Burke.”

“Who—what?”

“I know, I know... Can I at least show you an article? His father was killed the same way as our victims twenty years ago.”

“An article—Adele, start making sense. And stop trying to tug my sleeve!”

“Sorry, just, this is important. We need to hurry. The auction is still underway. We still have time.”

Paige bit a lip, glancing longingly over her shoulder towards the doors behind her.

"They're not going anywhere," Adele said quickly. "What could a few hours hurt? It might help them stew. Get them talking."

She could tell Paige was breaking. To the woman's credit, despite their differences, she wasn't as stubborn as Adele had often thought.

"Look, read this article. Tell me it's not suspicious. And get this, Mr. Burke hasn't been home in a while. I had the Germans check. His mail is piled up. No car. No lights on. He's not home."

"That could mean anything..."

"Read this!" Adele said, shoving her phone in front of her partner's face. She'd pulled up the same page with the murder report from nearly two decades ago.

Paige scowled, turning, and at last muttered, "Fine... Fine—no, give it here. You breathe too loudly."

She snatched the phone and began to read.

Adele replied with urgency. "No time! Read it in the car." She tugged at the older woman, guiding Agent Paige hurriedly after her.

CHAPTER TWENTY NINE

Adele could feel the doubt radiating from Agent Paige as the private plane Foucault had booked circled the landing strip. For her part, Adele was tapped into the live feed from the museum's auction on her phone, watching the video of the items go one at a time.

She scowled as the German auctioneer pointed with a pen towards members of the audience. "Five-thousand five hundred," he said in German, quite a bit more reserved than the other auctioneers she'd encountered up to this point. The pale-haired lady nodded once and pointed her pen to a new person. "Six thousand."

The item, in this case, had been brought onto the stage in a glass display case by two museum employees. Small fragments of pieces of ceramic of some old vase were scattered on a silk cushion, occasionally displaying a design or a swirl of paint.

"Seven thousand," the auctioneer continued in muted tones, pointing towards another figure. Adele sat glued to her phone, her eyes occasionally darting up to the small, blinking red dot above the video, making sure it was still live.

"Well?" Paige said testily, arms folded. "Anything yet?"

"No, no," Adele countered. "The dinner only just finished. Still early in the auction."

"How many items left?"

"Umm... Twenty-three by the looks of it."

Paige gave a harrumph and turned to peer out the window at the airfield in Germany. The pilot had been granted special permission to land out of schedule, and Paige was clearly somewhat flustered from her conversation with Foucault where he'd expressed his displeasure at the country-hopping.

Adele hadn't been brave enough to speak with her boss, but she'd heard his shout over Paige's speaker where he'd bellowed, "Just bring me the bastard's head, and do it by tonight, damn it! Stop wasting time."

Paige had weathered the storm well enough, but now she seemed to be having second thoughts about joining Adele in this excursion. She would also occasionally check her phone, mostly to keep track of any texts from the Spaniards regarding their suspects back in Madrid.

But the closer they got to their new target the more certain Adele became. “He's here,” Adele was saying, staring at the audience. “I know he is. At least... he has to be.” The video feed was only from the one angle, displaying the backs of the heads of the auction-goers who raised brochures or paddles or tipped fingers towards the reserved auctioneer.

“Damn it,” Adele said suddenly.

“What?” Paige demanded.

“It sold... They're going too fast.” Adele worried her lip and looked out the window again as the plane spun around and around and then finally broke into a descent.

Adele lowered her phone, her stomach twisting, feeling Paige's frustration radiating. At least the older agent had agreed to come. That meant something didn't it?

She'd read the same article. Had seen the same information. Adele wasn't crazy, was she?

There was something to this all. She felt certain.

***

The taxi from the private airport only had to make a quick, fifteen-minute trip to take them through Hamburg, to the new museum, but even so, Adele's nerves were firing like gunshots. No sooner had the cream-colored German cab pulled to a halt outside the round building, then Adele's feet hit the pavement and she broke into a rapid walk up the sidewalk, beneath overhanging trees towards the structure of glass and cement.

Paige came behind her, moving double-time to keep up with the taller woman.

Adele stepped through two, sleek, sliding doors that almost seemed to *curve* into the walls along with the curvature of the structure. She entered a large hall, with a couple of display cases settled tastefully near an information and greeting booth.

Two employees were standing behind the booth, watching the new arrivals curiously.

A young man, wearing a white uniform and an equally resplendent smile nodded to each of them. “*Guten abend,*” he said with a smile.

Adele bobbed her head in greeting. “Where's the auction?” she replied in German.

The man's smile became somewhat fixed, and he glanced towards the older man at his side. He hesitated, then returned his attention to

Adele. “It has already started, I'm afraid. Doors closed at 7:30.”

Adele waited a moment before reaching for her ID, preferring to gather information up front. “I thought it was open to the public.”

“Y-yes... On an invitation basis by members of the museum,” he said with a faint swallow and nod. “The dinner is over—which was three-hundred euros per plate, I might add.” He winced apologetically, glancing at Adele's wrinkled suit. She still had the grass stain on her sleeve.

“I see,” she sighed. “Alright, well, does this help?” She flashed her identification.

The man suddenly went still. He licked his lips nervously. “I—perhaps I should go fetch the director.”

“No, that's alright. The auction is this way?” Adele said, pointing down the only hall. “Hmm? Great, thank you. Don't notify anyone. Just stay put.”

Then, with that, and Paige in tow, Adele picked up the pace, moving down the hall in the direction of a faint voice.

Two double doors and an abandoned security checkpoint later, Adele and Agent Paige emerged in a large room with dinner seating. Rectangular tables laden with dishes had seating on only one side. The rows of dinner tables had been arranged to face the stage.

The older woman who Adele had seen on the video feed was still calling out numbers and pointing to various members of the audience, one at a time.

A few of the seated guests looked over at the new arrivals, flashing them disapproving frowns.

Adele ignored this, moving quietly, but glancing one way then the other. She lifted her phone, frowning towards the driver's license photo of Leif Burke.

“See him?” Agent Paige murmured as she also moved between the dinner tables at Adele's side.

A couple of auction-goers protested the blocked view, hurling an expletive after Paige which, thankfully, the older woman didn't understand.

“Bald, thirties, average-height,” Adele murmured beneath her breath. “Keep an eye for loners. Someone sitting on their own.”

Paige nodded to show she'd heard, and the two of them continued moving through the dinner tables, trying to remain as inconspicuous as possible while being the only two women in motion in the entire auditorium.

Still, most of the patrons were riveted by the auctioneer and only a few spared more than a passing glance at the DGSI operatives.

Adele scanned the participants, but none stood out in particular. She frowned, still glancing around, moving between the tables. But there were simply too many of them—too many auction-goers. A few hundred at least.

As she moved from one table to the next, another item was sold from the stage. She felt a jolt of frustration and glanced at Paige.

The older woman arched an eyebrow, watching expectantly. "Identifications?" Paige asked, quietly enough that the sound from the auctioneer nearly disguised the words.

Adele's fingers tapped against her upper thigh, and she fidgeted while considering this, but at last, she said, "No—too many. We can't ID them all."

She felt another flash of urgency. The killer was here... she knew it. Her gaze swept the seating, but no matter where she looked, Mr. Burke wasn't anywhere to be seen. Her eyes lingered on a blonde, bearded man sitting with a young family. But the eyes didn't match.

What if Mr. Burke hadn't come? What if he'd changed his appearance?

Adele felt a flicker of horror at this. "Shit," she said softly.

"What is it?"

But Adele was moving again, slicing between the rows of tables and now making a beeline towards the stage. She couldn't be wrong—not again. She'd come too far. The killer *had* to be here. The museum was in Germany! But what... what if he'd gone to the other auction? What if she'd missed it entirely?

Only one way to be certain.

She'd spent so much time over the last week hiding from what she'd done. She was tired of hiding. Tired of caring one rip what anyone thought. Besides... it wasn't often an investigator was given a captive audience.

And so Adele slipped past the final row of tables and auctioneers, avoiding treading on the hem of a woman's long, flowing black gown. She then moved to the stage, took the steps, and faced the auctioneer.

As she did it, Adele felt a jolt of nerves. She'd always hated stages.

The woman behind the podium glanced over at her, then did a double-take, her eyes suddenly widening as if she couldn't quite believe what she was seeing. She caught herself mid-sentence, declaring, "Increments of five-hundred only ple—excuse me? Ma'am, you're not allowed to be up here."

Adele could feel hundreds of eyes now fixed on where she stood on the stage. Could see the way the auctioneer just gaped at her, eyes wide.

A couple of security guards were beginning to move forward from the shadowed portions of the back of the room. Some of the dinner guests were murmuring in disapproval, but many watched curiously, impassively—how very German of them, she thought.

Adele cleared her throat, stepped towards the auctioneer, pulling her ID out and flashing it. "Interpol," she said stiffly. "I need this."

The woman looked like she'd been slapped. "I'm—this—highly—"

Adele nodded apologetically but extended a hand, placing it on the microphone. She didn't quite snatch it away but did wait expectantly for the older woman to take a step back.

Now, the voices around the room were rising. Someone was protesting, "Get down from there!"

The auctioneer looked towards one of the front tables, where a bunch of very important people in evening garments were sitting and staring in stunned silence.

"Don't blame her," Adele addressed the important-looking people at this nearest table. "I'm with Interpol." She cleared her throat, then, into the microphone, feeling quite isolated all of a sudden, she called out, "Please, everyone remain seated."

Adele blinked under the bright lights, wincing at the sea of faces gaping towards her. Agent Paige was standing near the front of the stage, frowning up at Adele, her arms crossed.

Adele inhaled shakily, swallowed then called out, "We'll return you to your evening event as soon as possible. But right now, we're looking for a man. He's involved in a serial murder case."

A low hiss of whispers spread rapidly.

"His name is Leif Burke," Adele called, her throat feeling very dry now, her legs somewhat unsteady on the stage. "Is a Leif Burke out there? Anyone?"

Only silence met her declaration. She'd hoped it might prompt him to up and run. That would've made her job much easier. But no one moved. Eyes stared up at her.

But Adele's gaze darted about like a hawk's, searching the members of the audience, looking for any sign of a reaction at the name.

But besides the frowns, and even a couple of shooing motions for her to leave, no one moved. No one got up and fled. Mostly, she was met with irritation and confusion.

"Excuse me," the auctioneer at Adele's side said, tugging at her sleeve. "But I'm looking on the guest registry, and no one by that name is here." The older woman had a phone in her hand and was scrolling through a list, shaking her head. Despite the odd interaction, Adele had to credit the auctioneer—she'd quickly regained her composure.

"You're sure?" Adele said, looking over. "Can you check again?"

"It's alphabetical, agent," the auctioneer murmured, tilting her face so she didn't speak directly into the microphone in Adele's hand. "There is no Burke. There is no Leif."

Adele pressed her lips tightly together. He must have been using a fake name. But even now, as she scanned the auction-goers, there was no sign of the man. For one, most of those in attendance were her father's age or older. Mr. Burke was still in his thirties.

For another, no one was sitting alone. All the tables were nearly packed, save one with only three guests, but all of these were women.

Adele's gaze swept the crowd, and only now, standing in front of a room full of people, did she start feeling her stomach twist, nerves beginning to rise.

"Shit," she said again, making sure to speak away from the microphone.

"You said murder?" the auctioneer whispered into Adele's ear, still tugging her sleeve.

"Yes, yes," Adele replied, still searching the audience... But nothing. No one. He wasn't here... She was nearly certain of it. He wasn't here.

He'd gone to the other auction. She'd missed it. Again. He wasn't here.

But it was as she considered this, feeling a sudden bout of stomach-twisting, knee-buckling stage-fright, her brow now slick, that Adele turned away from the podium, releasing the microphone and raising an apologetic hand.

At the same time, she glanced at the items up for auction, behind the glass display cases on the stage. Once an item sold, an employee appeared, placing a number on the item and wheeling the glass case towards the back of the stage. But they remained there until the end of the auction...

At least... All of them *should* have been there, judging by what Adele had seen on her video feed.

However, there was one display case, larger than the rest, that was empty.

"What's that?" Adele said suddenly, pointing. Now, her attention had refocused and she ignored the murmuring and dark comments from the crowd at her back.

"What is what?" the auctioneer asked primly.

"That case, the big one..." Adele scanned the items. "Where's the antique chest?"

"Pardon?"

"The antique *chest.* I saw it advertised online. You have a photo of it in the windows of the museum. Where is it?"

"Ah—I see. The chest was already sold at the start of the evening."

Adele felt her heart beat. "Excuse me?"

"Yes. A very generous donor offered an extraordinary sum at the start of the evening. Mr. Strobel, the proprietor, agreed to the terms."

Adele had now rounded on the silver-haired woman. "The chest is gone?"

"Sold. It should be in transit, now, in fact. Our event started nearly three hours ago. The purchaser came with his own assistant to move the item."

Adele's mind was reeling. She wasn't sure what normal auction etiquette was, but for a fundraiser, if the fee was high enough, perhaps it made sense that an item might be sold up front. But before the auction even started?

Would the killer have noticed as well? What if the killer wasn't here... because the chest wasn't here.

"A private buyer before the auction purchased the chest—you're sure?"

"Y-yes... I was there to witness the sale. It was only a few hours ago, agent..."

"Sharp. Agent Sharp. Look, I need to know the name and address of the purchaser. You at least have that information, don't you?"

"I—on payment yes. But in fact, he doesn't live far from here. He didn't want to wait for shipping, so he brought it home himself. I don't believe it would be appropriate... Look, I'm sorry, people are getting upset. Mr. Strobel is waving at me." The auctioneer forced a smile and waved back towards a man who was gesturing angrily at the podium. "This can wait, yes?"

But Adele caught the woman's arm, her back still to the crowd, her expression severe. "This is a murder case. Three of them. About to be four unless you give me the name of the purchaser."

"I don't think he'd appreciate—"

"Lady, his life is in danger! He'd appreciate the help. Trust me."

The auctioneer swallowed.

"If you don't, the body count will be four, and I'll have you to blame. Understand?"

She glanced past Adele towards her boss, who was likely still gesturing. The sounds of the disgruntled guests were now echoing through the room. Adele's back prickled from the unwanted scrutiny, but she remained fixated on the woman.

Finally, the auctioneer sighed, lifting her phone again and shaking her head. “Fine,” she said. “One moment. It's on another list.”

CHAPTER THIRTY

Adele channeled John Renee now, squealing up the highway and doing her best to try and break the sound barrier. Paige sat next to her, white-faced, gripping the arm rests.

For one, they had to move *fast* to get there in time. But also, Adele wanted to outpace the horrible memory of climbing down from that stage surrounded by scowling people. At least Paige hadn't abandoned her. Now, though, it seemed like the older agent regretted this choice.

"Slow down!" Paige barked for the second time in as many minutes.

"Can't," Adele said, her eyes glued to the road but occasionally glancing at the GPS on her windshield. "We might be too late already." She was panting, even though the exertion was mostly one of mental focus. The slickness of her brow now prickled to sweat as the anxiety only mounted subsequent to dismounting the stage.

Paige, between sharp breaths, and hyperventilating at their speed, muttered, "Next exit, Adele... Adele... NEXT EXIT!"

The vehicle screeched as Adele, waiting for a truck to pass, was forced to merge just in front of another sedan. The vehicle behind her leaned on its horn, a rarity for the German autobahn, but she managed to swerve into the exit lane and take the ramp, circling to the small town of Stade only fifteen minutes outside Hamburg.

"You better be damn sure about this," Paige was saying. "*Damn* sure."

Adele winced, checking the GPS again. The early purchaser of the chest had lived nearby, according to the auctioneer. And now, the address she'd given was quickly approaching.

"There it is...," Adele said, breathing rapidly as she turned down a main route, then onto a side street. "There—see it!"

A large home sat behind a row of hedges. But the top of the slanted, perfectly shingled roof was visible from the curb as Adele followed the GPS instructions and was rewarded with *Arriving at destination, on left.*

She yanked the car to a stop, indifferent that they were facing the wrong way down the street. Threw it in park then shoved out of the vehicle, slamming the door behind her and hearing Agent Paige do the same.

Evening had long since given to night. Now, under the shadow of a darkened sky, Adele picked up the pace, hastening towards the gate in the large hedges that led to the German manor.

As she hurried forward, she spotted a neighbor, further down the street, walking a poodle. And also, just around the edge of the road, she spotted something that made her pause. Paige was also breathing heavily as she caught up, finally free of the speeding vehicle.

Adele hesitated, one hand on the metal gate latch, but her eyes fixated now on what she'd seen.

A single, solitary car, abandoned on the side of the road.

The old man with the poodle strolled right on past, shooting a curious glance towards the empty vehicle.

What had caught Adele's attention was the front door.

Someone had left it open, a bright, yellow light glowing out into the street. The vehicle itself was an absolute mess. An old, ugly piece of junk, rusted with heavily tinted windows. Adele stared at the abandoned car, frowning. The drive from Spain to Hamburg was a full day affair.

She blinked, but the heard the creak of hinges and turned, distracted to find Paige pulling the gate open.

"Well?" the older woman demanded. "This is it, isn't it?"

Adele nodded, shooting another furtive glance towards the parked vehicle and the open door. No one was around it. No one at all.

Frowning to herself, Adele led Agent Paige through the unlocked gate in the hedge, towards a freshly painted manor house settled in a modest garden. The home was large but not ostentatious. The front doors were plain, wooden with no filigree or decoration. The whole place seemed very clean.

Adele and Paige took the cobblestone path, past the off-set garage and up the stairs to the front door.

Adele knocked first, while Paige pressed the doorbell.

Ding... A predictable chime echoed from within. And then, the two women stood waiting, awkwardly, on the front porch of the house.

Adele was still breathing heavily, and she swallowed, trying to calm herself, to focus. If she'd made a mistake this time, then someone else was already dead. If she'd screwed it up now, then she would deservedly be taken off the case. Maybe even removed from her position at the DGSI.

She shook her head, trying not to let her mind wander down unfriendly corridors.

Paige reached out, trying the doorknob. Locked. She frowned. "What was his name again?"

“Leif Burke,” Adele said, scanning the driveway, and glancing along the side of the house. She didn't see anyone. A truck was sitting in the driveway—had they used this to transport the chest?

“No, not your new suspect,” Paige said, emphasizing the second to last word. “The winning bidder.”

“Oh, umm... Rein Wolf,” Adele said, glancing down at her phone. She knocked again, louder.

“Mr. Wolf!” Paige called. “Hello—Interpol! Is anyone home?”

Adele heard the sound of sirens behind them now. The flash of lights illuminated off the windows of the house across the street. Backup was running behind.

Adele felt a jarring sense of fear. They were late... She knew it. They'd arrived too—

The door swung inwards, presenting a man standing in the threshold, frowning quizzically out at them. He was a slight-framed man, wearing glasses and a curious smile. He had kind eyes which were now creased with worry lines. “Hello?” the man said hesitantly. “Can I help you?”

Adele felt a flash of relief. “Mr. Wolf?” she insisted, pressing forward.

He stepped back, allowing her into his house. “Excuse me,” he protested.

“Interpol,” Adele said quickly, flashing ID. “Mr. Wolf, we have reason to believe you're in danger.”

She stepped further into the house, peering past the small-statured man, and frowning down the nearest long hallway. Tasteful decorative art lined the walls, along with a full-sized marble statute missing both its arms. Adele supposed this was what the more sophisticated sorts called *culture.*

She ignored the statue, frowning off towards another door adjacent to the main atrium. “Where's the chest?” she said.

The man stared at her, mouth wide. “I—I purchased it legally,” he said. “I have the paperwork. Mr. Strobel is a friend of mine!”

“No-no, I'm not saying otherwise, sir. Were you followed home?”

Now, the man went still, the wrinkles around his eyes deepening. “I beg your pardon?”

“Were you followed?” Adele insisted a second time. She stepped past him now, peering into the adjacent room. Empty. “Has anything odd happened with the lights?”

“The light—what are you talking about? I just got home. Are you here because of the auction? Did something happen?”

Adele bit her lip, then glanced towards Paige. "I'll check downstairs if you check upstairs."

Paige nodded, but the homeowner interjected, "Hang on one moment," he said. "I didn't permit—"

Adele cut him off. "Sir—we have reason to believe a serial killer is targeting you." She left out the phrase *might be* and felt a flash of guilt. But now wasn't the time for second-guessing. "For your safety, we need to search the premises."

The man gaped at her, mouth half ajar, caught mid-sentence. He swallowed, looked nervously around, and then puffed a breath. "Fine," he muttered. "Do what you have to. But hang on—a *serial killer*? You can't be ser—"

He went quiet as Adele and Paige were already on the move. Over her shoulder, Adele heard the sound of slamming doors and booted feet. She pointed to Paige. "Can you brief them?"

Paige nodded and Adele now moved down the hall, picking up her pace. The killer was nearby—he had to be. The MO only worked if the victims were stalked, hunted while alone. Somewhere, nearby, maybe even in the house, a killer was hiding. Now she just had to find him.

***

He was used to enclosed spaces. He'd lived in them before. And now there he rested, inside the chest, inside the mansion. Waiting. The rough wood scraped against his shoulders. He inhaled shakily, pressing his eye against the crack he'd made in the lid and the box. He watched shadows move across the hall.

He didn't smile. Not now. Not yet.

Soon, though. He shifted uncomfortably, and the box made a creaking sound. One of the shadows ahead froze. The silhouette began to turn.

He held his breath, waiting. Was this...

The shadow stepped closer.

A woman. Not the man. No. Not his target.

His muscles had tensed. His hand pressed against the lid, preparing to spring forth. But not for her. He wasn't here for her. No. Patience.

What he needed now was patience.

The mouse would wander in for the cheese soon enough.

They always did.

The silhouette scanned the room, listening. But he made no further sounds. Didn't even breathe. The silhouette turned then, moving back out of the study.

***

Adele gripped the edge of the bedframe, bent double and glaring beneath the mattress. Nothing. She straightened, frowning towards the open doors of the dresser behind her. She'd tossed the final room—still nothing. No one.

She frowned towards the man watching her nervously from the doorway. "This is the last room downstairs?" she insisted.

The man winced, shrugging apologetically.

Agent Paige stood behind him, watching with a frown. A German policeman waited in the center of the hall, his silhouette visible from where Adele leaned by the bed. She harrumphed and turned, scanning the large bedroom once more. Her eyes flicked towards the open door of the bathroom again. But she'd already checked this as well. Amidst the tile and glass there was nowhere to hide. She'd even looked under the sink.

Where was he?

Nowhere.

She gritted her teeth against the teasing voice in her mind.

"Now will someone tell me what this is all about?" Mr. Wolf demanded, his voice going high-pitched from frustration.

Adele paused, one hand still gripping the bed. She straightened, glancing out the window at the dark skies beyond, then back towards Mr. Wolf. Paige caught her eye from behind the man, lifting an eyebrow and crossing her arms.

Adele inhaled slowly... Was this a farce? Was she just playacting at this point? It was a guess within a guess within a guess... Then again, if she'd been wrong so far, especially on a case with the executive's own kin, taking things one step further would be the least of her worries.

She felt the determination settle in her gut like a lead weight, and met Mr. Wolf's gaze, giving him a fierce look. "You need to come with us, sir. You can't spend the night here."

"I—you can't be serious. There are like five police outside."

"We can have some cruisers patrol the neighborhood, keep an eye on your place. But you're not safe here."

The man looked frazzled and frightened. He swallowed, shaking his head. "I don't understand."

"Sir," Paige said suddenly, placing a reassuring hand on the man's shoulder.

He jolted and looked sharply towards her, eyes wide.

"It's for your own good," Agent Paige said.

Adele felt a swirl of relief that the woman was backing the play. A night at a hotel under watch wouldn't hurt the man.

"Fine, fine," he said. "I just need to grab my keys. I left them after we dropped the chest off. One moment."

Adele nodded watching as the man slipped between the large police officer and Agent Paige. Paige was murmuring to the cop, "... outside. Keep an eye on the windows and the road."

The officer nodded and then hurried off down the hall as well, heading towards the main door to the street.

Adele's throat felt sore from all the talking, from shouting back at the auction and from the amount of coffee she'd consumed in the last forty-eight hours. Exhaustion hung heavy on her, and she had to practically drag herself back into the hall, rejoining Agent Paige.

The two of them watched as the police officer exited the front door, shutting it behind him with an ominous *thump*. Then, Mr. Wolf veered off towards the adjacent study to the atrium.

"Did you check the study?" Paige asked.

Adele nodded. "I saw the chest—it's still in the box, packaged."

"You didn't find anything down here?"

Adele just winced, shaking her head. "Nothing," she murmured softly.

The two of them waited for Mr. Wolf to reemerge, but time ticked by... He didn't return. Adele frowned. Agent Paige took a step towards the study. The silence weighed heavy all of a sudden in the large home. Adele felt faint prickles up her spine. She swallowed faintly, also beginning to move, as if on instinct. Something was wrong.

Then, all of a sudden, a bloodcurdling scream erupted from inside the room.

Adele cursed and broke into a dead sprint down the hall.

CHAPTER THIRTY ONE

The first thing Adele noticed was that the lights had been turned off in the study. The rest of the house was still illuminated, evident by the trail of light shining from the atrium into the room beyond. The light caught the large package in the center of the room. At least, when Adele had first entered the study, it had only been a package. Now, the chest was no longer shut. The packaging had been half ripped aside. Adele spotted a lid of old, worn wood, etched with iron and silver. But the antique was the least of her concerns.

Two figures were wrestling on the ground in the dark room, struggling desperately for a sharp item in the larger man's hand. Standing in the door, her heart in her throat, Adele stiffened for only a second. It was difficult to make out the figures in the dark. The item they were fighting over, though, was long and thin... A bayonet, like the sort displayed on the historical muskets at the museum auction.

"Get off him!" She yelled, jolting into motion and sprinting forward.

But the two men continued to fight. One of them yelped in pain. In the dark, kicking aside cardboard and Styrofoam, Adele couldn't clearly see Mr. Wolf.

The killer had hidden inside the chest—that much was obvious. He'd been *inside* the house this entire time.

"One eye!" gasped an unfamiliar, shaking voice. "Two eyes. Good boy!"

Another yelp of pain. A hand broke free, gripping the bayonet and trying to drive it into the second figure's chest.

Adele yelled, gun in one hand. She heard Paige shouting behind her, and the sound of rapid footsteps out in the driveway, but they'd arrive far too late.

She grabbed at the larger figure's shoulder, yanking hard. The man lashed out with a snarl, slashing her with the jagged metal piece.

Blood pooled down her wrist. Gasping, Adele tried again, avoiding the slash this time and tackling the man off the smaller Mr. Wolf.

Paige bellowed into the room, her voice booming like someone twice her size. "Get on the ground! Stop fighting or I'll shoot!"

But the man ignored this. In the dark, struggling, Adele could barely see anything. She felt another slash of pain across her upraised hand which she held to defend her face. Another slash as she tried to grab the man's wrist.

He was snarling, trying to get away from her, scrambling across the cardboard and lunging towards Mr. Wolf who was screaming and struggling backwards on his hands and feet, through the cardboard and Styrofoam.

"Mr. Burke!" Adele screamed. "Stop!"

Leif Burke froze, turning to look at her with the same haunted, eerie eyes from his driver's license photo. He was bald, wearing old clothing two sizes too large for him. He also smelled as if he hadn't changed in days. He blinked at her in the dark, his eyes the only part of him truly visible.

Then he cursed, spitting and turning to lunge towards Mr. Wolf again.

But Adele caught his leg, yanking him back, raising her own gun. Burke screamed, kicking upwards and sending Adele clattering into the open chest, nearly falling in.

"Rein—here, here!" Paige was shouting.

Adele, gathering herself, glimpsed Agent Paige dragging Mr. Wolf through the open door, to safety. She raised her gun, pointing towards Burke. But the man snarled and lunged, diving behind the chest, and bringing the line of fire directly across Adele.

Paige cursed.

Adele shoved off the chest, trying to lurch clear, but a hand snaked out from behind the chest, grabbing at her throat and trying to drag her back. She smelled BO, blood. Pain throbbed through her arm now. She let loose a strangled cry, trying to spin around and shove the attacker.

"Adele, get down—get out of the way!" Paige was yelling.

But too late. Adele heard the sound of someone pounding on the front door. Wolf must have locked it again behind the officers.

The grip tightened on her throat, and Adele gasped, trying to reach back, to jab at those haunted eyes. The man howled in her ear, and she felt his teeth near her ear as if he were trying to bite her. She felt a sudden movement near her waist and caught his wrist while trying to twist at the hips.

He was too strong. Paige was still shouting. Someone was now kicking at the door, trying to break it down. Mr. Wolf was screaming for help.

"One eye. Two eyes," the man whispered in Adele's ear. His hand tensed, and she glimpsed the edge of sharp metal extending up towards her ribs. Choking, unable to breath, she twisted at the hips, struggling away from the attacker.

She gouged her fingers into his skin, tearing it. In the darkened room, she couldn't see. Her heart raced a mile a minute. For a horrible moment, she desperately hoped Paige wouldn't shoot. There was no way she could pick out the attacker in the darkness.

Paige growled and suddenly holstered her weapon, picking up a fire poker from the cold fireplace and rushing to Adele's aid, coming in close.

The attacker, spotting this, cursed and suddenly shoved Adele *hard* sending her tumbling back, ricocheting off Paige and rebounding against the wall.

Adele groaned, staggering and trying to reorient. Her head pounded. Suddenly, her heart swelled with horror. The killer had knocked Paige to the ground. He stood over her, his bayonet raised, preparing to plunge it. Adele's eyes widened. She did the only thing she could think of.

While simultaneously reaching for her firearm, her other hand leapt out—where she'd been flung against the wall—caught the light switch and flipped it.

The blade descended, her gun raised, the lights suddenly blazed.

Instantly, as if scalded, the killer yelped and stood blinking, frozen above Paige. Adele's weapon was now in her hand, but Paige was rising to her feet, struggling to escape, and blocking the line of fire.

But for the moment, the urgency seemed to have faded.

Leif Burke stood beneath the lights, blinking and taking in his surroundings. The study was filled with old antiques and items. Rows of paintings on the walls, display cases with ceramics and armors. An old-fashioned weapons rack sat over the fireplace displaying swords and spears.

The man's eyes bugged now as he spun around and around. "No... no...," he murmured.

"Drop the weapon!" Adele was shouting. Paige had now retreated, pulling her own firearm.

The two women were gasping, both bleeding from scrapes and scratches. They stared at the man in the center of the room who still held his bayonet.

He looked from the chest to the ceramics, to the display cases. "No," he whimpered, shaking his head rapidly. "No, no, no..."

"Get on the ground!" Paige barked. "Get down! Now!"

"Not again," the killer murmured, tears now bleeding down his face.

Adele just stared, stunned. She remembered the article of the man's father—he'd been killed in his own auction house, hidden in a chest. Likely surrounded by similar items, a similar set of antiques and displays.

She wondered, in the light, what the man was thinking.

He held an arm up to his eyes, whimpering now. The bayonet fell from his hand, clattering to the floor. He slowly slumped to his knees, sobbing like a child. His shoulders shook, tears streamed. "Please, Daddy," he whispered. "Please don't lock me in here. Not again. Please... Please..."

Adele and Paige just stared, both of them gob smacked.

"I'll be good!" the man was screaming, still kneeling. He'd closed his eyes now as if to block out the light. "Please don't lock me in here...Please! It's too scary! I hate it! I hate it!"

Then, kneeling amidst the antique collection in the study, the killer broke down like a child, still sobbing, still shaking at the shoulders. He collapsed on the ground, heaving gasping sobs against the carpet. "I don't want to... I don't... Don't lock me with the old things, Daddy. Don't lock me in..." He continued to sob, to weep. But then he suddenly grew louder, angrier. "Stop putting me in here! I'll kill you! I'll kill you, you bastard! Stop it! Stop it! I'm not blind, you're blind! Turn off the lights, damn it! Turn them off!"

He suddenly looked up, his face streaked with blood and tears. His eyes zeroed on Mr. Wolf who was standing behind the agents, gaping.

"Never again!" Leif Burke howled, his wide, ghoulish eyes bulging. "I said I'd kill you if you did it again! You bastard!"

And he surged forward, lunging towards Mr. Wolf as if the agents weren't even there. Adele had a brief moment where she could have pulled the trigger.

But then, snarling, she lowered her gun and her shoulder, stepping in front of Paige to prevent the older woman from firing either. Paige yelled in frustration. But Adele didn't hesitate. As the howling Mr. Burke tried to careen past her, she caught him in the ribs with her shoulder, and hooked a leg.

The two of them hit the ground. Burke thrashed and wailed like a cat in water. But Adele landed on top, holding him down, yelling, "Stop struggling! This isn't your father! He's not your father! This isn't your auction house! It's a home... Stop it!"

The man was still fighting, but Paige joined in now. There was the sound of a splintering wood, then the rush of booted feet as the German police finally broke down the door. Large men surged into the study, shouting desperately in a swarm of blue and bluster.

And finally, still weeping, Mr. Burke went still.

CHAPTER THIRTY TWO

The night didn't feel as dark as it once had, now that Adele stood outside Mr. Wolf's manor, on the driveway, listening to the sound of police moving through the house.

Agent Paige was on the phone across from her, her features illuminated by the glow of the screen as well as the blue glower of the moon above. "Yes sir," Paige was saying, bobbing her head—the silver strands of hair standing out in the moonlight. "Yes, we're sure. He admitted to the murders."

Adele watched Paige, wincing as an EMT dabbed a pungent smelling sterilizing fluid to her skin, then applied a bandage to her forearm.

"Thank you, Foucault," Paige said, pausing again. She nodded, adjusting the phone. "Trauma from his past, it looks like." She swallowed, glancing off through the gate in the hedge towards the police car where the suspect was currently cuffed. "His father would lock him in his auction house," Paige said, her tone grave. "Would leave him in the dark for hours... He seemed to think he was killing his father. Again and again." Paige trailed off again, listening. She winced but nodded. "I'll tell her. Yes—have a good night."

She hung up, glancing towards Adele who had finally won her arm back from the EMT. Paige studied Adele a moment, the two women standing outside their latest would-be crime scene, beneath the moon. "Foucault says well done."

Adele nodded. "Thank you."

"I'm surprised...," Paige said, shaking her head. "To an outside observer, what you did tonight might just look like guess work."

Adele was too tired to react. She just nodded once.

Paige trailed off, glancing back towards the house where Mr. Wolf was also being treated by a medic. "Good job, Agent Sharp," Paige said simply. "Foucault can have some amount of peace now."

"You care for your friend."

"Yes," Paige studied Adele. "The nature of my friendship with Foucault is a private matter... I've been thinking. Perhaps that's enough. Whatever happened in that garden... I imagine it was a private affair." The older woman tilted her head as if considering her own words, but then she nodded again. “Yes,” she said. “Yes, I think that fits.”

Adele, again, didn't say anything. She was too tired, too emotionally drained. She needed sleep. But she also felt, briefly, a flash of gratitude. She nodded at Paige, who returned the gesture and then began to move back towards the house.

Adele remained outside in the driveway, under the cover of night. She hadn't pulled the trigger. She could have. He'd been charging towards Mr. Wolf. But she'd saved the killer's life. No matter how many lives she saved, it wouldn't take back what had happened in the garden.

But... She sighed... It helped.

At least a little.

But the guilt was still there... It would still eat at her. It would always be there... at least, until she told someone. She glanced back towards Paige's retreating form, but then looked away again. No—not Paige. Someone else. Someone she could trust. She felt a pang of loneliness at this thought. Robert had been her confidant in the past. She missed him deeply.

One way or another, though, she needed to tell someone.

She was exhausted; night was still on the move. But she didn't want to sleep. Not until she'd confided in someone. The nightmares wouldn't leave her alone otherwise.

So, with a grim resolve, she reached into her pocket, slowly pulling out her phone. And that's when she saw it. The response to her previous message. She'd missed it in all the mayhem and confusion. She'd texted *I miss you.* And his response was, though predictable, enough to bring a lump to her throat. *Miss you too.* Then a little heart emoji. And a video.

Adele frowned, clicking on the video link. She remained motionless, her throat tight, her mind a mess. The video began to play, a short, looping video. The handsome, scarred Frenchman was laying on his bed, without a shirt, grinning up at her. He wiggled his eyebrows and then reached onto his nightstand, pulling a piece of paper and holding it up to the video.

It took Adele a moment but as the paper came into frame, she realized it was a child's drawing. It showed a very tall stick figure, standing next to a much smaller stick figure in a dress. A red house was behind them, and a sun over the house. There was another figure holding the girl's hand on the other side. This one, Adele supposed, was the mother.

But then, she spotted a fourth and final sketch. A woman, judging by the hair and size. And four letters above the figure's head. DGSI. In the image, the tall man was holding this fourth figure's hand. And a heart was drawn between the two of them.

The lump in Adele's throat faded. She stared at the image. John, Claudia, Claudia's mother, and Adele. Perhaps there was still room for her in Renee's life after all.

If anyone deserved to know first, it was John.

She dialed and waited, listening to the phone connect. And then after the third ring, he answered.

“John,” Adele said, swallowing. “We need to talk. Yes, yes tonight. I'll be home in a few hours.”

EPILOGUE

He sat on the edge of the cliff, overlooking the forest below. He watched the way the moonlight reflected off the trailing river meandering through the woodsy grounds. He inhaled deeply, filling his chest and held the breath.

It felt good to be alive.

For years he hadn't been. Not really. But now here he sat, a resurrected man.

His legs dangled over the edge of the canyon, his heels tapping against sharp rock. No humans around for a hundred miles... just as he liked it.

He smiled to himself, adjusting the backpack, and securing the straps. He remembered the man who'd shown him how, all those years ago.

A man he'd come home to visit, in fact.

Slowly, he pushed off the chasm edge, rising on the stone beneath the moon and facing the steep fall below.

The man had shown him many things during their time at war. But wars ended, soldiers came home—some didn't.

The survivor, for that's what he was, tested his backpack once more, then nodded to himself. He winced as he did, the scars along his face and chest and stomach twisting with the motion. Years of surgeries, operations, hundreds of hours in hospitals... Finally, after nearly a decade, the surgeries were over. He was a new man, pieced back together with needle and thread.

He'd endured more pain than any human could imagine. A decade of hellfire.

And there was only one man to blame for it. The same man who'd shown him how to adjust his parachute.

Captain John Renee.

Even at the memory of the name, his face twisted in fury. He'd returned to speak with John... And do other things, too. Not death. No. Death would be too easy.

He'd spent a decade considering his options. A decade.

He knew *exactly,* in meticulous, painful detail what he would do to Captain Renee.

The survivor smiled again.

And then he jumped off the edge of the cliff.

The air embraced him; the wind tugged at his flapping clothing. And then he yanked the parachute cord.

A jolt, the cool breeze gusting over him, and he began to glide... The fabric spread above him like wings.

He glided on the night, above the forest in the preserve, only fifty miles outside Paris. Beneath the moon, above the river, flitting on the breeze, he felt truly free.

He was an avenging angel, after all.

The angel of death.

And his target wouldn't even see him coming.

NOW AVAILABLE!

LEFT TO LOATHE
(An Adele Sharp Mystery—Book 14)

The #1 bestselling series! When FBI special agent Adele Sharp—a German-and-French raised American with triple citizenship—is summoned to hunt a serial killer stalking Amsterdam's red-light district, Adele's skills are put to the ultimate test. She quickly realizes that this is no ordinary killer. And these are no ordinary victims.

"When you think that life cannot get better, Blake Pierce comes up with another masterpiece of thriller and mystery! This book is full of twists and the end brings a surprising revelation. I strongly recommend this book to the permanent library of any reader that enjoys a very well written thriller."
--Books and Movie Reviews, Roberto Mattos (re Almost Gone)

LEFT TO LOATHE is book #14 in the #1 bestselling FBI thriller series featuring Adele Sharp (the series begins with LEFT TO DIE, book #1) by USA Today bestselling author Blake Pierce, whose #1 bestseller Once Gone (a free download) has received over 1,000 five-star reviews.

FBI Agent Adele Sharp is an invaluable asset in bringing criminals to justice as they cross American and European borders, and when bodies begin turning up at brothels around Amsterdam's red-light district, Adele is called in to investigate. But the seemingly straightforward case soon spirals out of control, and Adele must use every trick at her disposal to piece together the mystery.

Who is this killer? Why these victims?

And where will he strike next?

An action-packed mystery series of international intrigue and riveting suspense, LEFT TO LOATHE will leave you turning pages late into the night.

Book #15 in the series—LEFT TO HARM—is now also available!

Blake Pierce

Blake Pierce is the USA Today bestselling author of the RILEY PAGE mystery series, which includes seventeen books. Blake Pierce is also the author of the MACKENZIE WHITE mystery series, comprising fourteen books; of the AVERY BLACK mystery series, comprising six books; of the KERI LOCKE mystery series, comprising five books; of the MAKING OF RILEY PAIGE mystery series, comprising six books; of the KATE WISE mystery series, comprising seven books; of the CHLOE FINE psychological suspense mystery, comprising six books; of the JESSE HUNT psychological suspense thriller series, comprising twenty one books; of the AU PAIR psychological suspense thriller series, comprising three books; of the ZOE PRIME mystery series, comprising six books; of the ADELE SHARP mystery series, comprising fifteen books, of the EUROPEAN VOYAGE cozy mystery series, comprising four books; of the new LAURA FROST FBI suspense thriller, comprising six books (and counting); of the new ELLA DARK FBI suspense thriller, comprising eleven books (and counting); of the A YEAR IN EUROPE cozy mystery series, comprising nine books, of the AVA GOLD mystery series, comprising six books (and counting); and of the RACHEL GIFT mystery series, comprising six books (and counting).

An avid reader and lifelong fan of the mystery and thriller genres, Blake loves to hear from you, so please feel free to visit www.blakepierceauthor.com to learn more and stay in touch.

BOOKS BY BLAKE PIERCE

RACHEL GIFT MYSTERY SERIES
HER LAST WISH (Book #1)
HER LAST CHANCE (Book #2)
HER LAST HOPE (Book #3)
HER LAST FEAR (Book #4)
HER LAST CHOICE (Book #5)
HER LAST BREATH (Book #6)

AVA GOLD MYSTERY SERIES
CITY OF PREY (Book #1)
CITY OF FEAR (Book #2)
CITY OF BONES (Book #3)
CITY OF GHOSTS (Book #4)
CITY OF DEATH (Book #5)
CITY OF VICE (Book #6)

A YEAR IN EUROPE
A MURDER IN PARIS (Book #1)
DEATH IN FLORENCE (Book #2)
VENGEANCE IN VIENNA (Book #3)
A FATALITY IN SPAIN (Book #4)

ELLA DARK FBI SUSPENSE THRILLER
GIRL, ALONE (Book #1)
GIRL, TAKEN (Book #2)
GIRL, HUNTED (Book #3)
GIRL, SILENCED (Book #4)
GIRL, VANISHED (Book 5)
GIRL ERASED (Book #6)
GIRL, FORSAKEN (Book #7)
GIRL, TRAPPED (Book #8)
GIRL, EXPENDABLE (Book #9)
GIRL, ESCAPED (Book #10)
GIRL, HIS (Book #11)

LAURA FROST FBI SUSPENSE THRILLER

ALREADY GONE (Book #1)
ALREADY SEEN (Book #2)
ALREADY TRAPPED (Book #3)
ALREADY MISSING (Book #4)
ALREADY DEAD (Book #5)
ALREADY TAKEN (Book #6)

EUROPEAN VOYAGE COZY MYSTERY SERIES

MURDER (AND BAKLAVA) (Book #1)
DEATH (AND APPLE STRUDEL) (Book #2)
CRIME (AND LAGER) (Book #3)
MISFORTUNE (AND GOUDA) (Book #4)
CALAMITY (AND A DANISH) (Book #5)
MAYHEM (AND HERRING) (Book #6)

ADELE SHARP MYSTERY SERIES

LEFT TO DIE (Book #1)
LEFT TO RUN (Book #2)
LEFT TO HIDE (Book #3)
LEFT TO KILL (Book #4)
LEFT TO MURDER (Book #5)
LEFT TO ENVY (Book #6)
LEFT TO LAPSE (Book #7)
LEFT TO VANISH (Book #8)
LEFT TO HUNT (Book #9)
LEFT TO FEAR (Book #10)
LEFT TO PREY (Book #11)
LEFT TO LURE (Book #12)
LEFT TO CRAVE (Book #13)
LEFT TO LOATHE (Book #14)
LEFT TO HARM (Book #15)

THE AU PAIR SERIES

ALMOST GONE (Book#1)
ALMOST LOST (Book #2)
ALMOST DEAD (Book #3)

ZOE PRIME MYSTERY SERIES

FACE OF DEATH (Book#1)

FACE OF MURDER (Book #2)
FACE OF FEAR (Book #3)
FACE OF MADNESS (Book #4)
FACE OF FURY (Book #5)
FACE OF DARKNESS (Book #6)

A JESSIE HUNT PSYCHOLOGICAL SUSPENSE SERIES
THE PERFECT WIFE (Book #1)
THE PERFECT BLOCK (Book #2)
THE PERFECT HOUSE (Book #3)
THE PERFECT SMILE (Book #4)
THE PERFECT LIE (Book #5)
THE PERFECT LOOK (Book #6)
THE PERFECT AFFAIR (Book #7)
THE PERFECT ALIBI (Book #8)
THE PERFECT NEIGHBOR (Book #9)
THE PERFECT DISGUISE (Book #10)
THE PERFECT SECRET (Book #11)
THE PERFECT FAÇADE (Book #12)
THE PERFECT IMPRESSION (Book #13)
THE PERFECT DECEIT (Book #14)
THE PERFECT MISTRESS (Book #15)
THE PERFECT IMAGE (Book #16)
THE PERFECT VEIL (Book #17)
THE PERFECT INDISCRETION (Book #18)
THE PERFECT RUMOR (Book #19)
THE PERFECT COUPLE (Book #20)
THE PERFECT MURDER (Book #21)

CHLOE FINE PSYCHOLOGICAL SUSPENSE SERIES
NEXT DOOR (Book #1)
A NEIGHBOR'S LIE (Book #2)
CUL DE SAC (Book #3)
SILENT NEIGHBOR (Book #4)
HOMECOMING (Book #5)
TINTED WINDOWS (Book #6)

KATE WISE MYSTERY SERIES
IF SHE KNEW (Book #1)
IF SHE SAW (Book #2)

IF SHE RAN (Book #3)
IF SHE HID (Book #4)
IF SHE FLED (Book #5)
IF SHE FEARED (Book #6)
IF SHE HEARD (Book #7)

THE MAKING OF RILEY PAIGE SERIES
WATCHING (Book #1)
WAITING (Book #2)
LURING (Book #3)
TAKING (Book #4)
STALKING (Book #5)
KILLING (Book #6)

RILEY PAIGE MYSTERY SERIES
ONCE GONE (Book #1)
ONCE TAKEN (Book #2)
ONCE CRAVED (Book #3)
ONCE LURED (Book #4)
ONCE HUNTED (Book #5)
ONCE PINED (Book #6)
ONCE FORSAKEN (Book #7)
ONCE COLD (Book #8)
ONCE STALKED (Book #9)
ONCE LOST (Book #10)
ONCE BURIED (Book #11)
ONCE BOUND (Book #12)
ONCE TRAPPED (Book #13)
ONCE DORMANT (Book #14)
ONCE SHUNNED (Book #15)
ONCE MISSED (Book #16)
ONCE CHOSEN (Book #17)

MACKENZIE WHITE MYSTERY SERIES
BEFORE HE KILLS (Book #1)
BEFORE HE SEES (Book #2)
BEFORE HE COVETS (Book #3)
BEFORE HE TAKES (Book #4)
BEFORE HE NEEDS (Book #5)
BEFORE HE FEELS (Book #6)

BEFORE HE SINS (Book #7)
BEFORE HE HUNTS (Book #8)
BEFORE HE PREYS (Book #9)
BEFORE HE LONGS (Book #10)
BEFORE HE LAPSES (Book #11)
BEFORE HE ENVIES (Book #12)
BEFORE HE STALKS (Book #13)
BEFORE HE HARMS (Book #14)

AVERY BLACK MYSTERY SERIES
CAUSE TO KILL (Book #1)
CAUSE TO RUN (Book #2)
CAUSE TO HIDE (Book #3)
CAUSE TO FEAR (Book #4)
CAUSE TO SAVE (Book #5)
CAUSE TO DREAD (Book #6)

KERI LOCKE MYSTERY SERIES
A TRACE OF DEATH (Book #1)
A TRACE OF MURDER (Book #2)
A TRACE OF VICE (Book #3)
A TRACE OF CRIME (Book #4)
A TRACE OF HOPE (Book #5)

www.ingramcontent.com/pod-product-compliance
Lightning Source LLC
Chambersburg PA
CBHW030616310726
48979CB00003B/746

* 9 7 8 1 0 9 4 3 7 6 1 0 3 *